Patricia

Slow
Hands

Slow
Hands

LAUREN BACH

WARNER BOOKS

An AOL Time Warner Company

Cover design by Diane Luger
Cover illustration by Franco Accornero

ISBN 0-7394-2788-1

Warner Books, Inc.
1271 Avenue of the Americas
New York, NY 10020

 An AOL Time Warner Company

Printed in the United States of America

First Printing: August 2002

To **Mindy Jackson Desmond**
Brilliant, gorgeous, talented . . .

And **Hannah Luanne Desmond**
My beloved, adorable, precious angel . . .

*I will never be good enough to
deserve having you two in my life.*

Slow
Hands

Prologue

Alec Dempsey preferred to stay north of the Mason-Dixon Line. Way north. Like Seattle.

He wasn't happy to be in Tennessee, in a suit and tie, in the stuffy conference room of the Memphis FBI field office.

He also preferred to work with his own kind. ATF. Alcohol, Tobacco and Firearms.

FBI agents hogged the spotlight in joint ventures. They had huge egos, big superiority complexes. *Little dicks.*

The two FBI agents sequestered with him were prime examples. Condescending, but polite. After all, they wanted something from him.

His boss said he'd been specifically requested for this assignment, had urged him to consider it. Alec's gut told him that wasn't a good sign. He'd just been cleared for active duty after two months warming a desk. He wasn't in the mood to play second string.

Special Agent Horace Phelps, balding and overweight, sat directly across the table. He bared his teeth in what Alec presumed was a smile.

"I'll cut to the chase, Dempsey. We want you for an undercover job in Freedom, Arkansas."

The tightness in Alec's middle increased. "You're

joking." He looked from Phelps to the second agent, leaning silently against the wall. Neither man laughed. "Undercover? In my hometown?"

"Yeah. You'll go in as yourself," Phelps went on. "The prodigal son."

From what Alec recalled, the prodigal son was welcomed home with open, loving arms. Few arms would be open in Freedom. He doubted anyone even remembered him.

And the one person who knew him best would probably prefer to see him crucified.

Though he already knew he'd refuse the assignment, he feigned interest, more than a little curious. "What does the FBI want in Freedom?"

Phelps slid a mug shot across the table. "This guy look familiar? Ian Griggs. AKA inmate number 84736. You went to school with one of his younger brothers."

Alec looked at the photo, eyes narrowed. He remembered the brothers Griggs. They'd been the town scourge. Bad seeds, all three of them. And they'd come to an even worse end.

"I think half the country remembers those boys," Alec drawled.

Five years ago, Ian Griggs and his two brothers had hijacked an armored truck outside Little Rock and made off with two million in cash. The money was never recovered.

Alec recalled the story. Or at least the sensational headlines the media frenzy generated. As rumor spread that the pilfered cash was stashed in the Ozarks, treasure hunters descended in droves, clashing frequently with private landowners, and even forcing the closure of several state parks.

The news coverage had also brought to light another, lesser-known story that Alec had followed with far more interest. His unease grew.

"Two of the brothers died in a fire after a shoot-out with police," Phelps continued. "Ian Griggs went to prison, refusing to plea-bargain the location of the money in exchange for a reduced sentence."

Alec's frown deepened. "I thought he claimed one of his brothers hid the money. That the secret died with him."

"Yeah, right." Phelps made a jerking-off motion with his hand. "Everybody believed that one."

"Then what's the deal? Has the FBI decided to search for the money again?" If they thought Alec would make a good tour guide, they could think again.

Phelps shook his head. "Griggs's sentence just got commuted. Which means he qualifies for parole at the end of this month. He's been a model prisoner, and we believe the request will be granted."

"Commuted?" Alec stiffened. "And you're not opposing it?"

"We're pressing for supervised probation in a halfway house in Freedom." Phelps leaned forward. "He's got two million reasons to return, and we want someone there to watch him."

Alec glanced at the mug shot. While the news of Griggs's likely parole surprised him, it wasn't shocking. He'd been with ATF five years. Army Special Forces before that. He knew justice wasn't always served, accepted it.

Except in this instance.

Ian Griggs had never even been tried for the worst of his crimes. *Assault and battery. Attempted rape.*

"You're perfect for this job," Phelps pressed.

No, he wasn't.

Alec shoved the photo away. He'd heard enough. He'd left Freedom ten years ago, sworn he'd never return. It had been the right choice then. It was the right choice now.

Pushing his chair back, Alec stood. "Find someone else."

Phelps's fake smile evaporated as he scrambled to his feet. "There is no one else, and time is short. You know yourself how tight-knit those people are. Fucking clannish. And they can spot a Fed a mile away."

Meaning the FBI had already tried and failed.

Alec could imagine the problems they'd encountered trying to plant an agent in town. Ignorant people, like Phelps, thought of Freedom in terms of Dogpatch. Thought everyone there was a hillbilly relative of Snuffy Smith. A little condescension went a long way in Freedom.

Of course, from what he remembered, the town could give as good as it got.

Alec snorted. "An ATF agent would be particularly unwelcome there."

Besides being the hometown of the state's most notorious criminals, Freedom, Arkansas, had a pre–Civil War history of producing the finest moonshine in the South.

Thanks largely to ATF anticrime initiatives, few people actually made a living making 'shine anymore, though lots of old-timers kept stills. *And believed the only good revenue agent was a dead one.*

"Obviously we'll fudge that part." Phelps had an answer for everything. "You've been undercover since joining ATF, which is another reason you're perfect for this. Outside of your immediate supervisor, who knows your real employer?"

"My mortgage company. American Express."

Phelps didn't blink. "I'm serious."

"So am I." Finished, Alec took a step toward the door. "I'm not interested in this job."

"Keira Morgan is in danger." The second agent, Miles Ostman, who'd been quiet up to then, moved forward. *Mr. Nice Guy.*

Alec turned. He recognized the ploy. Good cop, asshole cop. Agent Phelps cleared his throat and sat back down, grinning, arms tucked behind his neck, his part of the job complete.

Alec closed the door and leaned against it, legs spread slightly, eyes hooded. "What about Keira?"

"Ian Griggs blames her for the death of his brothers," Ostman said. "Word is he's going back to Freedom to claim his cash *and* to settle the score with Miss Morgan."

"Take her into protective custody. Now."

"The request got denied."

"By whom? Did they know what Griggs did to her before the robbery?"

"Officially, those charges were dropped." Ostman shrugged, noncommittal. "But maybe it's just jailhouse talk. Griggs would be a fool to jeopardize his parole for the sake of vengeance. My professional judgment says he'll grab the loot and run. Be in and out of Freedom within a week."

Alec's jaw tensed. Ostman wouldn't know professional judgment if it bit him on the ass.

Alec was being manipulated, didn't like it. He knew
Griggs's history, knew the man posed a very real danger
to Keira. And they knew he knew.

The FBI had obviously snooped into Alec's background before approaching him. Oily bastards. He didn't
like it, but he understood the rules of the game, had bent
them himself a time or two.

He cut straight to the real problem. "If you know
about my past with Keira Morgan, then you know I'm
the last person she'd want to see."

"We'll handle that," Ostman countered smoothly.
"Before you go in."

"Using what cover?" *Prodigal SOB?*

"We'll play it like you've just been discharged from
the army, following an injury from an explosion. You've
completed physical therapy and are looking for a quieter,
safer line of work."

Alec had just completed physical therapy for an injury received during an ATF raid. "And why would I
look in Freedom?"

"You used to be fairly close to Keira Morgan."

Fairly close was the mother of all understatements.
At one time, Alec couldn't envision life without her.

"She's still attractive as hell, currently unattached . . ."
Ostman let the sentence hang. "In fact, you used to work
construction with her, didn't you? Electrical contracting?
She owns her own business now, and we hear she's hiring."

Ostman's innuendo didn't faze Alec. Exploitation—
or sexploitation—was the chief weapon in an undercover

arsenal. The FBI wouldn't think twice about asking him to seduce his way back into town.

What bothered Alec was the underlying note of desperation in the other man's voice. What was he hiding? "Quit blowing smoke." Alec called his bluff. "What are you really after?"

The two agents glanced at each other. Phelps shrugged. Ostman shook his head once, slightly.

Alec turned away, uninterested in playing games. "I'm out of here."

"Wait. Shit, you win. But this doesn't leave the room." Ostman pulled out a crushed box of Marlboros. "The truck Griggs knocked off that night was one of old man Ciccone's. Used to transport his freshly laundered money."

Alec recognized the name. Joseph Ciccone headed up the south-central mob. Had his fingers in everything illegal from Memphis to New Orleans, then ran legitimate businesses, like the armored truck service, to cover. He had a nasty reputation for eating his own kind. Few federal authorities cried over the news that one of Ciccone's trucks had been hit. In fact, Ciccone had probably been a suspect himself until Griggs was arrested.

"Don't tell me you want to protect Griggs from Ciccone?"

Ostman shook his head. "Don't need to. They're practically in bed together."

That surprised Alec. Most people who crossed Ciccone ended up dead. Hell, Ciccone could have had Griggs executed in prison. Easy.

"Griggs has something Ciccone wants. Bad," Ostman continued.

"The two million?" Alec raised an eyebrow. "I guess that's a lot of dough to lose even for Joseph Ciccone."

Ignoring the NO SMOKING placard, Ostman lit a cigarette. "Believe it or not, Ciccone's not out a dime. Insurance ate the loss. Ciccone's real good at covering his tracks, so on paper it all looks legit."

Which was why Ciccone was so damn hard to nail. Alec knew ATF tried to tie him to gunrunning a few years ago. Their key witnesses *disappeared.* "And now the greedy bastard wants the stolen money back, too, right?"

"Exactly. We believe Ciccone offered Griggs a deal. Ciccone bribes a judge or two, calls in a favor from someone on the parole board. Griggs gets out, recovers the money, and gives it back to Ciccone, who makes out like a bandit." Ostman paused, exhaled. "Until we bust him with stolen property."

Bingo, Alec thought. The FBI didn't care about Ian Griggs or the money. *Or Keira.* They wanted a mob bust. They wanted Joseph Ciccone. He'd be a huge star on someone's record.

Which meant this case had a wider scope than these two clowns let on. He made a mental note to check on a few things.

"Have you considered that my sudden reappearance in Freedom, right on the heels of Griggs's return, will raise questions?" Coincidence only stretched so far.

"Not with the right romantic spin, it wouldn't," Ostman said. "We've done our homework. You'll go in right away, *before* news of Griggs's release is even made public. We'll let it slip you and Miss Morgan have been corresponding on-line for a while. Worked out your differences. Then we'll cement it with rumors of an impending engagement."

Alec almost laughed. No wonder the FBI had been so unsuccessful in planting their own agent in Freedom. *Homework?* They didn't know jack.

"I can tell you right now Keira Morgan won't buy into that one."

Phelps guffawed, then tried to cover with a cough. Ostman shot him a quelling look.

Alec didn't miss the exchange. "You've already talked to her, haven't you? And she turned you down. Probably told you where to stick it."

Ostman sighed. "We figure she'll come around when we mention your name."

Now Alec did laugh. Ostman had no idea who he was up against. Keira would not *come around.* Not where Alec was concerned. And with good reason.

Though they didn't realize it, he was off the hook. "I'll tell you what. You get Keira Morgan to agree up front to hire me on *those* terms, I'll do it." Alec opened the door, confident he'd heard the last of the subject. "Good-bye, gentlemen."

As soon as Alec left, Ostman turned to the other man and started swearing. "You almost blew it!"

"Sorry." Phelps didn't look apologetic.

"Have you talked with the Morgan woman again?"

Phelps shook his head. "She won't return my calls. And her secretary's a real snot. Want me to fly over and see her in person?"

"No. It'll raise more flags. I'll try her at her home tonight myself," Ostman said.

"So what's this big fucking secret you promised to let me in on?"

For a moment Ostman remained quiet, debating the wisdom of showing his hand.

Thus far, Phelps had followed his lead blindly. But Ostman knew his partner was growing nervous. Uncertain. Ostman needed to throw him a bone if he wanted continued loyalty.

And Ostman definitely needed help to pull this off quietly, help from someone who'd follow orders with a minimum of questions.

He picked up his cigarette, inhaled, blew out a stream of smoke. "You know all that crap about angels looking out for fools? It's true. Besides the cash, that armored truck was transporting a cache of stolen, rare gold coins, scheduled to be fenced in Miami."

"Where the hell did you hear that one? Two million plus a bonus in gold. Right! Bullshit stories always pop up after sensational crimes." Phelps hee-hawed. "This sounds even better than that hokey story the Freedom Chamber of Commerce prints in their tourist brochures about the Lost Confederate Gold. Supposed to be a cache of it hidden in the Ozarks."

"That's an unproved legend. This isn't."

Phelps quieted at the other man's tone. "What makes you so sure?"

"I recently busted a guy in New Orleans for running crooked slot machines on the riverboats. He started talking in hopes of cutting a deal. This guy gave the gold to Ciccone to have it fenced in lieu of protection money. But get this: He didn't trust Ciccone to give him credit for the gold's full value, so he had the coins privately appraised and photographed. Gave me a copy of the report."

Phelps nearly fell out of his chair. "Jesus H. Christ! We recover those coins, we can tie Ciccone to money laundering, racketeering. It will be the bust of the century."

Ostman nodded. Possession of stolen property was an easy rap to beat. RICO violations were a different ball game.

"No wonder Ciccone's playing nice to Griggs." Phelps lowered his voice. "So what did the boys upstairs say?"

"They don't know the full story. *Yet.* I figure we'll hand them Ciccone's head on a platter." That way no one else in the Bureau could claim the credit.

Nailing Ciccone meant a guaranteed promotion. And tremendous stature. Ostman had been beaten out of both before. It wouldn't happen again.

"One thing: We have to make certain Ciccone gets his hands on the gold first."

"I don't follow," Phelps said.

"We have to let Griggs recover the loot and actually turn it over to Ciccone. When it's in Ciccone's possession, we move in." Ostman stubbed out his cigarette. "This is so big, I figure Ciccone will keep a finger on it personally. So while Alec Dempsey does the grunt work on the inside and follows Griggs, you and I will keep an eye on Ciccone."

"What if Dempsey makes the bust too soon and blows it?"

"Won't happen." Ostman shook his head. "I plan to pull him off the case at the last moment. It should be a cakewalk."

"Cakewalk my ass." Phelps winced. "You haven't talked to the Morgan woman yet."

*   *   *

The inside of Ian Griggs's prison cell was dank. Dark. *Lights out* was an hour ago, but sweet dreams eluded him.

He heard the inmate in the next cell urinating. Muffled voices drifted as the guard stopped to talk to another inmate, a planned distraction. Behind the guard's back drugs were passed from cell to cell.

Griggs paced the short distance to the calendar he had scratched in the wall. Lighting a single contraband match, he marked an X through another day, then closed two fingers over the flame, relishing the slight burn.

The line from an old Janis Joplin tune rolled through his mind. *Freedom's just another word for nothing left to lose.*

Griggs had nothing left to lose in Freedom. And everything to gain.

He contemplated his plan, reviewed the steps. One, two, three.

Money.

Revenge.

Whiskey.

Not necessarily in that order.

Five years behind bars had taught him the virtue of patience. Of restraint. Of moderation. And of keeping a few cards up his sleeve.

"Soon, Keira," he rasped to his empty cell. "Soon your nightmare will begin."

Chapter One

Keira Morgan ignored the posted speed limit, her gaze flicking between the clear road and the speedometer. Sixty in a forty-mile zone and still running late. She punched it. Sheriff Cowart's men knew her truck. They wouldn't stop her unless she exceeded eighty.

It was the middle of June, and the Ozarks baked in an early-summer heat wave. The surface of the asphalt roadbed melted beneath the sun. Even the trees looked wilted.

She eased off the gas as she crossed the railroad tracks near the new Chevy dealership they were building, yet another sign of Freedom's growth.

And another reminder of things gone awry. Like the fact the Barry brothers undercut her bid for that job. *Jerks*. And the fact her truck's air conditioner had picked a ninety-six-degree day to conk out. *Damn thing*.

All she needed was a flat tire or two, and the day would be perfect.

"Just perfect," she grumbled.

Sweat trickled down her neck. She thought longingly of her apartment. It had been a grueling week, and the only thing she wanted was to go home. The AC there would put frost on these windows. And the long-neck bottles of beer in her 'fridge would be exactly two degrees above freezing.

Unfortunately, she had an appointment at Franny's Style Salon.

She glanced at the dashboard clock. Luckily, Franny was her best friend. She was also the only reason Keira broke her neck to get back from Hot Springs.

Tonight was the big kickoff dance for their ten-year high school reunion. Personally, Keira wanted to skip the entire weekend. A trip down Memory Lane to her senior year held as much appeal as elective brain surgery.

Especially now. It had been a week of rotten news followed by even worse news.

On Monday, she'd received a call from the FBI, informing her that Ian Griggs, the man who'd put her in a hospital five years ago, had had his sentence for armed robbery commuted—*for good behavior!*—and was expected to make parole in a few weeks.

His postparole destination: A halfway house in Freedom.

With that little bombshell, she'd learned the real reason the FBI was calling. They wanted to plant an undercover agent in Freedom, to keep tabs on Griggs.

The agent's sympathetic noises and reassurances fell on deaf ears. Keira was livid. She had been told—promised—Ian Griggs would serve his full sentence of life in prison without chance of parole. Now some stupid judge commuted his sentence? Just like that?

"Can't you stop it?" she had asked. "Or can I protest it?"

"We understand your concern. But it's not that simple." The agent launched into a laundry list of excuses. Prison overcrowding. Rehabilitation.

The pieces fell into place as soon as Keira remembered

that *the money from the robbery had never been recovered.*

The FBI was after the two million. Their regard for Keira was window dressing.

She'd told Agent Phelps exactly what he could do with his little request. Wanting to scream, she'd hung up and tried to digest the news. It felt like she'd been kicked. Betrayed.

After the shock wore off, Keira started formulating her own plan. While the news of Griggs's pending release still infuriated her, she was determined not to let it frighten her.

Agent Phelps said they expected Griggs to retrieve his money and run. Maybe within days of being released. Well, forewarned was forearmed. If Griggs came near her, she would use whatever means necessary to protect herself.

Then two days ago a different agent called. Miles Ostman.

He'd explained new information had been received indicating Griggs plotted revenge against her grandfather for the part Keira had unwittingly played in his arrest. An eye for an eye. *A family member for a family member.*

Ian Griggs blamed her for the deaths of his brothers.

If Griggs had wanted to go for her weakest spot, he'd found it. Willis was the only family Keira had.

Her first instinct was to ship Willis off, get him out of town. Except her grandfather would never leave Freedom. Willis had never set foot outside of Arkansas and was proud of it.

And while news of Griggs's release would be made public after his parole hearing, she didn't dare tell her grandfather the truth about Griggs's threat of revenge. Willis was old school and stubborn as bedrock. He'd force a showdown.

Mano a mano.

Even though she'd place even money on her grandfather, it was a lose-lose situation. If Willis harmed Griggs, he'd go to jail. Worse was the thought on the other hand.

As much as she hated to, Keira had been forced to reconsider the FBI's request—to protect her grandfather. Which might actually mean shielding Ian Griggs, the bastard. Once Willis learned Griggs was returning to Freedom, he might pick a fight anyway, to balance the scales.

She had swallowed her pride and relented. And nearly choked when she learned *who* they wanted to send in.

Alec Dempsey.

Satan himself would have been more welcome. Or so she told Miles Ostman.

If Ostman knew what Alec had done to her, he didn't let on. Instead the agent rambled on about how Alec was a rational choice. He'd been born and raised in Freedom. He knew the area—or had once upon a time.

"It would be easy to concoct a plausible story to explain Alec's return," Ostman said. "Has anyone in town even heard from him since he left?"

"No," Keira admitted. Last she'd heard, he'd joined the army. That was ten years ago. It was strange to think he was with the FBI now.

"Then anything we choose to say about his homecoming can't be disproved," Ostman said.

As much as she didn't want to see Alec again, she had to admit, grudgingly, that Agent Ostman had a point.

Once Griggs returned, the town would be inundated with press and treasure hunters. Just like before. Freedom would close ranks, and all strangers, newcomers, would be looked at with suspicion. As a native son, Alec had a better chance at blending in.

And if Alec kept Griggs under surveillance, then Gramps would be safe.

Feeling stuck between a rock and a hard place, Keira agreed.

Ostman said Alec would contact her a few days before Griggs showed up to discuss the particulars of his cover. Which gave her at least two weeks to get used to the idea. She sighed, already wishing she had more time.

She hadn't thought of Alec Dempsey in years. Well, maybe with all the talk of the high school reunion, he'd skittered in and out of her thoughts lately—like a cockroach avoiding light.

Keira had just turned twenty-eight, which meant Alec would turn thirty soon. He'd graduated two years ahead of her, so there hadn't been any danger of his being invited to the reunion. It was just the recollection of her senior year . . .

Her truck bounced as she hit a deep pothole, jolting her. Slowing, she forced her mind back to driving. There'd be time to think about Alec and Griggs later.

Within minutes, she pulled onto Main Street.

Grand old Victorian houses graced this end of Main. A few years ago, her friend Franny had bought one at auction, turning the ground floor into a glitzy, full-service salon, while converting the second floor into living quarters. After Franny's success, others followed suit and helped breathe new life into the historic downtown district.

These days, Freedom was known as a chic, antique Mecca. *One of the South's hidden jewels,* to quote the guidebooks. Many of the people returning for the reunion would be shocked by the town's metamorphosis. Freedom had changed.

Keira slid into the single empty parking spot on the street. One of the salon's doors opened, and a blond head popped out. *Franny.*

From this far away, Keira couldn't hear her words, but judging by the way she waved her arms, she wasn't happy that Keira was running late.

Slamming the truck into PARK, Keira jumped out of the cab and headed up the sidewalk.

A man and a woman stood in the middle of the concrete walkway, blocking it. The woman made eye contact with Keira and sneered, dismissing her.

Great. Just who Keira wanted to see. Her nemesis, Scarlet Chambeau, class bitch and cochair of the reunion.

Scarlet was yammering excitedly about tonight's dance. It was obvious by her perfectly coifed brown pageboy that she had just left Franny's.

Keira raced by, eyes averted. Ignoring Scarlet wasn't a problem and the man had his back to her. Keira spared a glance for his denim-clad rear. Nice ass, but not one she recognized. Probably someone in town for the reunion.

As she sidestepped the pair, a hand reached out and grabbed her upper arm, wheeling her back around in a tight semicircle.

"Hello, babe."

Keira's pulse skittered. *"Alec?"*

Time ground to a painful halt as she stared at the long, strong fingers. She looked up, past his broad shoulders, her breath catching as he peeled off a pair of Serengeti sunglasses.

Alec Dempsey.

The past decade had only improved his tall, dark perfection. His coal black hair, inherited from his Italian mother, was a little longer now, brushing his collar, but still thick and straight, without the first hint of gray.

His black-brown eyes glittered in some secret amusement as his mouth played into a raw, sexy smile, exposing a single killer dimple.

Her heart swelled, then constricted with an intimate memory of that mouth. Of being loved. Of being left.

What the hell is he doing here now?

Rattled, she tried to play dumb. "Ahhh, Darry, Darwin? I'm sorry, I forgot your last name."

The smile grew and included a wink. "Dempsey. You remember."

"Vaguely." It gave her hives to remember. She'd dreamed of sharing that name. And more . . .

Long-buried hurt scratched at her lungs. What in the world had made her agree to the FBI's request? Had she honestly believed she could do this and feel nothing?

She blinked. "Well, it was nice seeing you again. You, too, Scarlet."

She yanked her arm, to break his hold, felt it yanked in return, only harder. The move caught her off guard, pitching her almost flat against his chest.

His little show of strength pissed her off. The hurt

disappeared, reminding her *she* had been the injured party. Technically, this man had no right to breathe the same air she did. How dare he touch her?

She met his gaze, willing him to back down. His eyes held, the challenge plain. *Make me.*

"In a hurry?" he taunted.

For a moment, she debated giving him a knee in the groin. Lord, he deserved it. Instead, she shot him a dirty look and stepped on his foot, hard, twisting free. "I'm late."

"Better let her go. She looks like she'll need extra time as it is." Scarlet wrinkled her nose and gave Keira a toothy, badgerlike smile before placing her hand on Alec's arm and moving closer, shoving Keira off the narrow sidewalk and into the neat flower bed.

Keira's arms windmilled as she tried to avoid crushing the newly planted pansies with her heavy work boots.

"Oops." Uncontrite, Scarlet batted her eyes at Alec. "The dance starts at eight, and I won't take no for an answer."

Alec reached for Keira's elbow as she struggled for footing in the soft dirt. "Scarlet invited me to the reunion dance tonight. See you there?"

Keira dodged his hand, stepping into the grass. "Maybe. Gotta go."

It was all she could do not to run the remaining distance to the salon.

Franny held open the door, her voice a whisper as she squeezed Keira's hand. "He stopped by earlier. I tried to reach you on your cell phone to warn you. I was hoping he'd be gone before you got here, but ole' Scarlet-the-Harlot sank her claws into him."

Keira trembled, and for a moment she couldn't catch her breath. Her mind reeled. "I wasn't even expecting to hear from him till after next week!"

Franny knew everything that happened in Keira's life, so in spite of the FBI's warning for Keira not to tell anyone, she'd told Franny. Franny had been furious, but promised to take the secret to her grave.

"No one could get a word in once Scarlet opened her mouth." Franny tugged Keira off to one side. "And believe me, I tried."

"Did he say why he's here now?"

"Shhh. No, he didn't. We'll talk later." Franny pressed a finger to her lips, then cocked her head toward the salon's main room. "Cissy's here."

Keira glanced around the salon's bright silver-and-pink interior. Two of Franny's employees were still there, but Cissy was the only customer.

"Great," Keira muttered. "Bad luck does travel in threes."

"Well, well. Look what the cat dragged in." Malice permeated the air as Cissy Odum, Scarlet's best friend and cobitch of the reunion, spotted Keira. Cissy's eyes glittered as she lifted the dryer hood. "You just missed the love reunion of the century."

"Love reunion?" Keira repeated.

Cissy sashayed over to one of the styling cubicles, where she started taking out her own rollers. "Why, Alec Dempsey and Scarlet! Guess he heard she and Jake are divorcing and knew the ten-year reunion would be a great place for him to pick up with Scarlet."

"Pick up?" Keira felt heat rising in her cheeks. Was *that* the cover he planned to use? Chasing Scarlet?

"Why else would he come back?" Cissy asked. "Scarlet was one of the few people willing to overlook his past."

By *his past*, Cissy could mean several things. In high school, Alec had a bad reputation for a short temper. He smoked, he drank, he cussed. He fought, usually in defense of his illegitimate lineage. Guys avoided him, girls swooned—much to their parents' chagrin.

"Some people were never bothered by his past to begin with," Keira shot back.

Cissy shrugged. "Personally, I always suspected he had a secret thing for Scarlet."

Franny turned on Cissy. "Alec never had a *thing* for anyone but Keira."

Cissy plunked down in the stylist chair, clearly enjoying herself. "Right. Look at her."

Keira looked down at her clothes. She was wearing canvas overalls that looked as if they hadn't been washed in a week. Her T-shirt was soaked with perspiration and smeared with dirt.

She caught her reflection in the mirror behind Cissy. Frizzy tufts of bangs stuck out from her grubby baseball cap, her red hair streaked white with plaster dust. But the worst was the thick black smear of grease across her cheek.

Keira caught Franny's gaze in the mirror and groaned. "Have I ever looked more terrible in my life?"

"Yes," Franny defended.

"No," Cissy attacked simultaneously. Then she stood and started singing. "*Here she comes, Miss America.*"

That was the final straw. Keira opened her mouth, then closed it. She wanted to lambaste Cissy, but couldn't.

A week's worth of frustration simmered just below

the surface. Hot, angry tears prickled at her eyelids. Dammit! She hadn't cried over anything in ages. And the last thing she wanted Cissy to think was that she was crying over Alec.

Franny sailed over to Cissy's side. "Too bad you have to leave. We just closed."

The other women in the shop moved up behind Keira in a show of solidarity.

Cissy pointed to her now-rollerless head in outrage. "Mabel's got to comb me out."

Franny exchanged glances with Mabel, one of the salon's other stylists.

Mabel nodded, then wrapped her arm around Keira's shoulder. Sixty-three and childless, Mabel considered Keira and Franny surrogate daughters. Her loyalties were unquestionable.

"There now," Mabel whispered. "Don't pay any attention to Cissy. You know she's just out to get your goat."

"Poor goat," Sally, the nail technician, muttered.

Mabel hugged Keira. "I'm sure there's a reason Alec's back in town."

Her sympathy upset Keira even more. While Franny knew the truth of Alec's return, no one else did, and Mabel had assumed his reappearance would devastate Keira. So much for giving her credit for being over the man.

Grabbing a comb, Franny shoved Cissy back into the chair. Keira watched as her friend ratted Cissy's hair with lightning speed, then smoothed it into a massive helmet and shellacked it with hairspray. The whole thing took less than two minutes.

Franny handed Cissy her purse and escorted her to the front door.

"I ain't paying full price for this," Cissy complained. "I took my own rollers out!"

"It's on the house." Franny slammed the door.

Mabel and Sally applauded. Franny curtsied, then immediately rushed to Keira.

"She's gone. Go ahead and bawl," Franny said, grabbing a tissue. Licking it first, she started rubbing at the grease spot.

A tear rolled down Keira's cheek, followed by another.

"Cry a little harder," Franny encouraged. "Then I won't have to spit on the tissue again."

"I'm not crying," Keira sniffed.

Mabel started clucking. "Of course you're not. There's not a man on this earth who's worth getting upset over."

"Stan is," Sally chirped.

They all gave her a look, but not too harsh. Sally and Stan were getting married soon, and Sally's only dilemma in life was deciding what mints to have at her reception.

"All men suck except Stan," Mabel corrected. "And of course, my Fred."

"Darryl's pretty sweet, too," Franny chimed in.

Keira scowled, snatching a tissue to blow her nose. "Thanks! Next you'll tell me how good you thought he looked."

Everyone grew quiet. *Guilty.*

"Okay, I admit it. My eyes weren't complaining." Mabel patted her arm. " 'Course I know you'd feel better if he'd gone to seed. Was missing a few teeth and most of his hair."

Sally nodded. "Yeah. And remember—looks aren't everything. He could be gorgeous but impotent."

Keira rolled her eyes, then looked at Franny, knew her friend would tell her everything later. But she couldn't wait. "Did he say anything?"

"Not much. Said he got discharged from the army a few months ago. Been in some kind of accident," Franny said.

"Grenade exploded," Mabel confirmed.

An explosion? Keira shivered, closing her eyes. How many times had she wished him dead? The grenade could have killed him, and she'd have never known.

Remorse swamped her—until she reminded herself the story probably wasn't true.

Alec worked for the FBI. She knew he had to concoct some sort of cover story—Agent Ostman had told her as much. Of course, he'd also told her she'd be fully briefed before Alec arrived. *Lying bastard.*

"Guess Alec wants a quiet place to recuperate," Sally offered. "Said he's had enough of big-city life."

Franny squeezed her shoulder. "You okay?"

Keira shook her head, motioned at her filthy overalls. "On top of everything else, he would have to catch me looking like this."

"Then after the dance we'll make a point of looking him up," Franny said. "We'll check all the motels, find out where he's staying—"

"I'm not going to the dance," Keira interrupted.

"*He'll* be there. Scarlet invited him."

"That's perfect!"

"No. It's not."

"Do you want him to think you're hiding from him? Ha!" Franny frowned, eyes narrowed. She reached around and grabbed the thick braid of hair trailing down Keira's back. "I've got a better idea."

Franny snapped her fingers, pointing at Mabel. "Nine-one-one. Lock the doors and pull the shades. It's fairy godmother time."

Mabel grinned, then saluted. "I'll heat the wax."

Sally started shaking bottles of nail polish while she called her fiancé to let him know she was working late.

Franny pushed Keira toward the staircase to her apartment. "Hit the shower, girlfriend. Then throw on a robe and get back down here, fast. Mark my words, we will rule at the dance tonight."

"Sock hop," Mabel scolded. "It's a fifties theme. Remember?"

Keira's frown deepened. "I don't know—"

"What's not to know?" Franny stuck her fist on her hip, shook her platinum blond head. "He caught you off guard. Tonight you'll be prepared. In control."

In control. Keira's motto.

She looked down at her clothes. If she could turn back time, Alec wouldn't have caught her off guard this afternoon.

If she could turn back time, Alec wouldn't have done a lot of things.

Her choices were simple. Run and hide. Or face the enemy.

She straightened. She'd never run a day in her life.

"But my poodle skirt." Keira glanced at her watch. "It's at my apartment."

"Fuck the poodle skirts." Franny started plugging in banks of hot curlers. "This is war."

Chapter Two

Alec stood inside the high school gymnasium.

It looked like a crepe paper factory had exploded. Blue and gold, the school colors, covered everything. Chairs, tables, walls. Little had escaped. Aside from that—and all the goddamned balloons—the place hadn't changed since he had graduated twelve years prior.

It was still a backwoods school in a Podunk town. A place to hurry up and leave before it grabbed you by the throat and slowly strangled the life from you. *What the hell am I doing back here?*

A banner sagged overhead. *Welcome home, Senior Class.* He ignored it. This wasn't his class. This wasn't his home. He didn't feel welcome.

In fact, being there gave him the creeps. *Déjà fucking vu.* He frowned, recalling his wild high school years. His less-than-sterling reputation. His longing to get away from the oppressive atmosphere of small-town life, of people who looked down on him.

Freedom was the butt end of the world. If you stayed there, you either faced a career as an assembly line worker at the bait factory or you commuted a long drive to Hot Springs for construction work. He did the latter for two years. Hated it. He'd wanted to see the world. He'd wanted to forge his own path.

Had he?

He'd seen the world and had forged several different paths. First, there had been the army. And a hard-earned college degree. Then he'd joined ATF. But only now did he realize he still hadn't found what he was looking for. Realized he'd given up looking.

Uneasy with his retrospection, he checked his watch. The dance had started thirty minutes ago.

Where was Keira?

He frowned at the gym's entrance and reminded himself, again, that this wasn't about her. It was about his assignment. He'd come to Freedom for one reason, and when that was over, he'd leave.

The lie stuck in his craw. It had been about her since Agent Phelps first mentioned Freedom.

Keira.

He thought back to their meeting earlier that afternoon. She clearly hadn't expected to see him this soon. Hell, he was supposed to be on vacation another week.

But he knew he needed to talk to her up front and off the record. Settle the unsettled business between them. *Pay the piper.* God knows he owed her that much.

If Scarlet hadn't stopped him outside of Franny's, he'd have missed Keira. He'd spotted her first, had expected her surprise. Hell, he'd even expected her anger.

What he hadn't expected was the fierce body rush at seeing her again. In those first moments, he realized that while he'd dated a lot of women—hell, he'd even been married—no female had ever affected him like she had. Had ever left him feeling weak in his knees and groin.

The memory of loving her came back just as sharply

as if he'd left her bed yesterday. So, too, the memory of having hurt her.

Seeing her again brought it all back—the joy, the pain. The regret. Jesus, he'd screwed up. Should have resolved this a long time ago.

The disc jockey announced a slow song by the Platters. Alec searched the gym one last time. Scarlet would be wrapping up her hostess duties shortly and would come looking for him.

He reminded himself he had to play nice with Scarlet. After all, she had invited him to the dance. But he'd also caught the predatory gleam in Scarlet's eyes, noticed it heightened in Keira's presence.

Scarlet hadn't changed. She and Keira had been fierce rivals in high school.

He knew her friend, Cissy, had started the rumor that Alec had returned to see Scarlet, a lie he let stand for the moment because it gave him a fallback position. And with it, no one questioned his presence at the dance.

But there was only one person Alec wanted to see. And she foolishly thought she could avoid him. Damn it, he'd go looking for her. The town wasn't so big she could hide for long.

Impatient, he headed for the exit. Halfway there he caught sight of Franny and her boyfriend, Darryl. Franny was Keira's best friend. She'd know where Keira was.

At that moment, one of the front doors opened.

Alec turned back, looking up just as Keira slipped in. Alone.

His heart flat-lined. His field of vision narrowed as his eyes played over her, starting at her toes and working their way up.

Her feet were encased in come-on shoes: black with stiletto heels, buckled at the ankle. She wore sheer, sparkling nylons that disappeared beneath a short hemline. The short hemline of a black, body-hugging dress that was probably illegal in some states.

Her shoulders were bare, exposing creamy skin and a generous bosom. He wondered what she wore underneath. Nothing? *In his dreams.* More than likely a strapless black lace teddy.

Sexy underwear had always been Keira's paean to her femininity. Years ago, when they'd both worked construction in high school, it had driven Alec crazy to see her at a job site, knowing she wore something utterly naughty beneath her flannel shirt and jeans. Vixen that she was, she'd sometimes whisper hints at break, or worse, flash her pointed nipples, leaving him to fight a hard-on till quitting time. Then he'd make her pay . . .

He stared, caught himself drooling. Her hair, free of the braid and clean, hung down one side to her waist in a shimmery mass of red curls. God, he loved her hair, remembered the feel of it in his hands, trailing across his body.

For a moment time reversed. They were at Keira's senior prom. Graduation was six weeks away, and he couldn't wait any longer. He'd heard about a job in St. Louis, was sick to death of the dingy boardinghouse in Hot Springs he called home.

He'd been on his knees, begging. Scared to death she'd refuse. *Come on, babe. Say yes. We'll move to St. Louis. We'll get married. Hell, I love you, Keira.*

He'd lied. He'd left town, promised to come back the next morning . . . and never returned. Prodigal bastard.

He watched as she turned, realized she was getting

ready to bolt. Moving swiftly, he took the stairs two at a time, startling her when he reached for her hand.

"Hello, Keira." His eyes caught, held hers.

What he saw threw him. Cool, clear, confidence radiated from her deep green eyes. Nothing else.

He'd expected contempt. Accusation. Had deserved no less. He'd been prepared to fight with her, been prepared to make excuses. Now he simply wanted to beg. For forgiveness . . . or for mercy?

That afternoon she'd reminded him of the girl he'd left behind. Feisty. Determined. A starry-eyed eighteen-year-old who needed him.

Tonight she reminded him she was tough. And smart. And capable. Major turn-ons. She was pure woman, more potent than ever. Moreover, she needed no one.

Least of all him. The thought jarred.

He pulled her hand to his mouth, brushed a kiss across her knuckles, then turned it over, and uncurled her tight fist to press yet another kiss to the center of her palm.

"You look stunning," he said finally.

For a moment Keira felt glad she'd come to the dance. She and Franny had pulled out all the stops, dusted off every trick in the vamp book. Damage Control 101.

Franny had been right. The look of sheer male appreciation on Alec's face was worth the effort. Vindication was sweet. Maybe not quite as satisfying as full-blown revenge, but a great first course.

Then Alec kissed her hand, and she remembered how hazardous electricity was, remembered how she'd almost perished all those years ago. She had planned to play up to him tonight. Flirt. String him along, then crush him. Tell him exactly what she thought of him for leaving all those years ago.

Except . . . well, now, this whole charade seemed like a bad idea.

The last thing she wanted was for Alec to think she carried a torch for him. That she hadn't gotten over him. She had. He was nothing to her.

She took a step away and started down the steps. "Good evening, Alec."

Alec knew he'd rattled her icy poise by kissing her hand, wondered what she would have done had he kissed her lips. Wondered if *he* could have handled that.

He took her arm. "Allow me."

Once again, she struggled to free herself. Once again, she lost. "Let me go!" she hissed.

"I was afraid you'd chickened out."

"Chickened out of what?"

"Coming here. Tonight. Knowing I'd be here."

It irked her he assumed his presence mattered. Granted, she hadn't expected him early, but she'd known since talking with the FBI that Alec would be returning.

"You think your being here bothers me?" She tried once more to disentangle her arm.

"I think it scares you."

"I'm not afraid of anything. Least of all you." She lightly kicked at his shin, then jerked free.

Alec chuckled, dropping down a step in front of her, blocking her flight. She was still tiny as hell, scarcely five-foot-four. And he'd baited her on purpose, just to ruffle her feathers. See if she was still beautiful when mad. "You haven't changed."

Keira locked eyes with him, annoyed she still had to

peer up to meet his dark gaze, annoyed he was still so fine-looking it hurt to see him. *Annoyed her heart felt like it could break in all the same places.* "We've both changed."

Scarlet Chambeau moved in, hooking her arm in Alec's. Keira eyed the woman's poodle skirt. Not to be outdone, Scarlet had three poodles decorating her felt skirt.

"I'm here to claim my dance." Scarlet pouted, tugging his forearm. She looked at Keira. "He promised."

Keira smiled coldly. "You're welcome to him. Not sure he's got a grasp on keeping promises, though."

Spinning on her heels, Keira turned and headed for where Franny and Darryl sat. Franny high-fived Darryl and pushed to her feet.

"You looked like Cinderella arriving at the ball," Franny gushed. "Everyone stared. Scarlet turned pea green. The DJ even missed his cue and let the music stop. Am I a freaking genius, or what?"

Ever the gentleman, Darryl stood, holding Keira's chair. She brushed a kiss to his cheek.

Darryl and Franny had dated since high school. Darryl, a lanky, blond fireman, worshiped the ground Franny walked above. They'd marry eventually, Keira knew, though Franny claimed the sex was too good to bother with making it legal. For a moment, Keira envied them.

When Darryl left in search of drinks, Franny huddled closer. "Everything okay?"

"Sure. My stomach is rolling around on the floor somewhere, but other than that, I'm fine."

Franny patted her arm. "You sure you're up to this?"

Keira took a breath, held it, reminding herself of why she had agreed to go along with the FBI's plan. *To protect her grandfather.* She knew too well what monstrosities Ian Griggs was capable of.

She exhaled. "No, I'm not sure I'm up to it. Which doesn't matter." This wasn't about hearts that were broken long ago. It was about the very real threat her grandfather faced here and now.

"Did he say why he showed up early?"

Keira shook her head. *The million-dollar question.* "He didn't say and I didn't ask."

"Bet he's singing the blues now, after seeing you in that getup."

Keira doubted it. He was center court, with Scarlet, on the dance floor.

She frowned, reminded herself she could care less.

Darryl returned and handed each woman a tall Dixie cup. Keira took a sip and erupted into a coughing fit.

He grinned. "Three people have spiked the punch so far."

Franny tried it, then smacked her lips in approval. "Whoa! A girl could get a little crazy on this."

"I'm designated driver," Darryl murmured, sweeping his lips across Franny's. "Knock yourself out."

Keira's gaze drifted to the dance floor. A slow song played, and Scarlet was plastered against Alec's chest, whispering in his ear. As luck would have it, Keira's eyes met his. He winked. She quickly looked away, peeved he'd caught her staring.

Now that she'd gotten over the initial shock of seeing him, she was more than a little curious as to why he'd shown up early.

Not for a second would Keira entertain the thought it

had anything to do with her. She and Alec were ancient history. A bad end. Period.

Which meant it had to be something related to the case.

She chewed her lip. Was there a new twist to the nightmare? Had Griggs made yet another threat? She thought of her grandfather, had an urge to go call him. Except it was late. Willis would be asleep already.

Several classmates drifted over, and for a while she was lost in the numbing jumble of small talk. Photos of kids were exchanged and bragged over. E-mail addresses swapped. Careers discussed, husbands trumped.

Finally, Franny tugged her toward the bathroom. "Damn, how much of that punch have I had?"

"Are you seeing double yet?"

"No."

Keira held up three fingers. "Darryl's been keeping us primed. I've got a nice buzz going." Not to mention the fact she hadn't eaten since noon. And had had a margarita or two at Franny's shop.

Four women were leaving the ladies' room, all dressed in identical poodle skirts and saddle shoes. Cissy was with them, all smiles.

"God, I'm glad we didn't wear ours." Franny smoothed her own red-sequined mini. "You know how I hate looking like everyone else."

Keira ducked into the closest stall. *Alec loves Scarlet* was scribbled on the wall in black marker outlined with a lopsided heart. She touched the ink, found it still wet enough to smear.

"Cissy strikes again." Keira sighed. Obviously, she wasn't the only one who had noticed Alec and Scarlet on the dance floor.

"That little witch," Franny called from the next stall. "I bet she wrote this on every door. No wonder she smiled when we came in."

"And she's probably dying to see the look on my face when we come out."

"Then we'll stay in extra long. Make her wonder what we're planning to get even."

A few minutes later, Franny primped in the mirror. "Here." She handed Keira a tube of lipstick. "Try this one."

Keira swiveled the tube, frowned at the deep cinnamon color before looking at the label. "Passion Igniter? Wasted on me."

Franny spritzed cologne first on herself, then on Keira. "You know, I've been thinking about that. You haven't dated anyone seriously since Steve Perry left town last year. It's time to find you a new man. What about that hunky blond you hired?" She whipped out her cell phone. "We could call him right now. Invite him to the dance."

Keira dabbed on lipstick. "Reggie? We're just friends."

"You go rock climbing with the man every weekend. There has to be something there."

"Nothing romantic. He's teaching me some advanced techniques in exchange for the chance to tackle some uncharted territory on Fire Mountain."

Reggie was a rock jock and had done a lot of climbing out west on the sheer verticals in Yosemite. While the Ozark climbs couldn't begin to compare, some of the cliffs in Culverleaf Park had proved more challenging than he'd initially believed.

And recently they started tackling the virgin back side of Fire Mountain. The tallest peak in the area, Fire

Mountain had been owned by Keira's ancestors for over two hundred years. Her grandfather lived on the mountain, and few outsiders had ever set foot on it.

"I bet he could teach you some other *advanced* techniques."

Keira shook her head. "I don't date employees."

"*Date-schmate.* We'll call it something else. Isn't he also helping you build your cabin? That sounds a little cozy to me."

"Sounds like *hired help*, to me. I pay him for that, too."

"Yeah, but he's not really an employee."

"He's from a temp agency. Same thing."

"Nah. Even if it was, I'd make an exception for him," Franny scolded. "Guy's got a hot bod and a nice bulge under the button fly."

"I'm not interested in dating Reggie. And sex isn't a magic cure-all," Keira huffed, annoyed at her friend's line of thinking.

"How would you know?" Franny started fluffing Keira's hair with a comb. If Franny liked you, she groomed you like a mama chimpanzee fussing over her furry little baby. "What about Alec then? He's been staring at you all night."

"Uh-uh. Don't go there." Keira dropped her voice. "You know why he's here."

"So? Hold still." Franny tugged Keira's neckline lower, then stepped back, admiring her handiwork. "There."

"I know what you're up to." Keira readjusted her dress. "And it won't work. Neither one of us cares."

"Neither one of you wants to admit it, you mean. I saw the look on his face when you walked in. Pure longing."

"There's a difference between lust and true caring."

"Yep. Lust is infinitely more fun." Checking her own cleavage one last time, Franny rifled through her purse, pulled out a compact disc case. "Come on. We're gonna liven up this party."

The DJ had his stand set up a short distance from the ladies' room. Franny slid him the CD case and a twenty, then bent low, whispering in his ear. The man nodded, ogling Franny's chest.

Keira stood idly by, avoided looking at the dance floor. Another slow, moony tune was playing. No matter how much she didn't care, she still didn't want to see Alec cheek to cheek with Scarlet. Maybe it was time to leave.

Franny returned, all happy, and tugged Keira toward the dance floor just as the slow song ended and Aerosmith screamed from the speakers. Applause rippled through the room as people poured onto the dance floor.

"Let's show them how you do it in high heels," Franny shouted, shaking her hips.

Keira had no choice but to oblige since she and Franny were sandwiched in the middle of the now-crowded dance floor. Besides, she loved Aerosmith.

After three songs, the DJ announced another slow one. Keira started weaving toward her chair as Darryl sidled up and took Franny in his embrace.

Two hands snaked around Keira's waist before she got off the floor. She turned and found herself in Alec's arms.

"Dance with me." His voice was a caress. "I've been trying to catch your attention all night. You were ignoring me."

"I'd have to see you to ignore you."

"Smart mouth." He tugged her close as more people crowded onto the floor.

She resisted, but Alec prevailed, pulling her into a sweep that matched the soft, mellow beat.

He was wearing dress khakis and a white oxford button-down. His tie had disappeared, his shirt open at the neck exposing a smooth vee of tanned skin and a tantalizing hint of dark chest hair. His arms were solid, his thighs firm as they brushed against hers.

She shivered against an unwelcome memory of how he'd looked ten years ago. *Naked.* All muscle. Sinew. And well-hung testosterone. Alec had always been in peak physical shape. He could peel off his shirt at a construction site and make her want him on the spot.

She caught an intriguing scent of aftershave, felt the rasp of his chin as he brushed his lips close to her ear. Her carefully cultivated alcohol buzz suddenly turned tricky, like going from a rambling river to class-five rapids without warning.

Keira struggled to regain some distance. She had told herself she was fine with Alec returning—had even practiced a speech, planned her first words. They had been bitingly clever. But damn if she could remember what they were now.

She battled to shore up her crumbling defenses. Alec was a dangerous temptation. With each touch, each heartbeat, came memory after memory of bliss. And sorrow. The man had wrought both.

And just then it was difficult to remember which had been sharper. The pain? Or the pleasure?

"Do you feel it?" he whispered.

The hushed, sexy timbre of his voice caught her off

guard. Keira misstepped. She lowered her voice to cover her distress. "Do I feel what? Your erection? Since you had it when we started, I assume it's a leftover from Scarlet."

He chuckled. The lady was as bold as ever. That had been just one of the things he'd loved about her. Her sharp wit and tongue. "I was talking about the electricity, babe. Between us."

"There's nothing between us, Alec. If you're feeling something funny, it's the punch." Leaning away, she glared up at him, silently daring him to contradict her.

Instead, he changed the subject. "Meant to ask you earlier how your grandfather's doing. He still on Fire Mountain?"

"He'll die up there. After outliving all of us."

"I figured Willis would be retired now, but I hear he's partners with Lacy Hicks in that new mining attraction outside of town."

Keira shrugged. "Gives him something to do."

She almost said, *"Gives him something to do since he's not doing so much moonshine,"* but she didn't.

Not that Alec didn't know that about her grandfather. Back in high school, before ATF and the state squeezed the flow of illegal whiskey down to a trickle, Alec and his friends used to run moonshine. Now . . . well, in spite of the fact he was born here, Alec was an outsider. And there were strict rules about outsiders and moonshiners.

But his questions about Willis reminded her of why Alec had returned. And the fact he'd arrived unannounced.

"I was told you weren't coming here until next week," she blurted in a worried whisper. "Has something else gone wrong?"

Alec saw the tiny furrow between her brow, knew exactly what prompted her question. She was concerned about Griggs's threat to harm her.

"There's nothing new wrong," he said, hoping that soothed her. "I came early because I figured we needed to talk. Plan a strategy."

For the first time since accepting the job, he actually felt like he could do it. He'd get the money, protect Keira from Griggs. Then he'd get the hell out of town, leave before Freedom got to him.

And this time, he'd leave without hurting someone. Be free of the past once and for all. "I also wanted to make certain you were okay with this."

She shrugged. "It's a means to an end. The hard part will be figuring out what we'll tell my grandfather so he doesn't become suspicious. You know Willis. He'll want to settle things with a load of buckshot."

Alec straightened. He'd known from the beginning that returning to Freedom meant facing Keira *and* her grandfather. If Willis wanted to deck Alec for jilting Keira, he'd take his licks. He deserved them. Guns were another matter.

"Maybe I should meet with Willis alone."

"No. I don't think it's wise to let him know Ian threatened him, Alec."

Her words caught Alec broadside. Keira believed Ian had threatened *her grandfather*? "I don't—"

She cut him off. "I knew you'd disagree. But you've got to trust me on this. Willis will be a lot less trouble if we keep him in the dark."

"What exactly did Ostman tell you?" Alec asked, cautious.

"That Ian has sworn to harm my grandfather in retaliation for his brothers dying. An eye for eye. Or so, Agent Ostman quoted." Keira looked up. "Quite frankly, that's the only reason I agreed to this. You know what Willis means to me."

Alec knew exactly. After all, he'd once been considered a part of their family.

Grim, Alec thought back to his meeting with the two FBI agents. *"You get Keira to agree to those terms . . ."*

He'd been had.

So had Keira, but she didn't know it. Ostman had no doubt twisted the truth to force her cooperation. Told her Griggs threatened Willis Morgan, not her.

No wonder she'd changed her mind and agreed to help the FBI. She'd do anything to protect her grandfather.

Ostman had played Alec for a fool.

"Your grandfather's going to be just fine," Alec reassured. He needed to change the subject again. Yeah, he and Keira had a lot to discuss, but not until he spoke with Ostman.

He dropped a hand to her hip, pulling her closer as he swung left, then right, fast enough to keep her off-balance. But she didn't miss a step.

"You remember the moves?" he said.

Keira pretended not to hear. She remembered more than she wanted to. Like what a great dancer Alec was. And exactly how tall six-foot-two was; how perfectly her body pressed against his. *How it felt to be in his arms.*

She fought to reclaim some space, but he parried, dipping her back on his arm. She watched as his eyes drifted to her breasts.

She knew with his height he could probably see

clear to her navel. Never mind the fact she was wearing a platform bra that thrust her already full breasts unnaturally high. Or that she'd dusted her cleavage with body glitter. Or that she'd remembered Alec was a breast man.

At the time, she'd wanted to go straight for his jugular. The one between his legs. She had hoped to entice him, tease him, tempt him. Build up his hopes and dash them.

Except . . . now it suddenly lost appeal. It had never been about the sex.

"Quit staring, Alec," she snapped, straightening. "It's tacky."

"So I'm tacky. Can't help it. It's the dress." He shook his head. "Actually, it's the woman in the dress."

Keira met his gaze. In the dim light his eyes were so dark, so dilated, they appeared totally black. Bottomless. They made promises, hinted at secrets.

The memories came out of nowhere, nearly suffocating her.

She recalled the magic. The heat. The fire. The way he kissed, the way he touched. Alec had been a gifted lover. Wild, daring, demanding. He'd branded her with possessiveness. Spoiled her with tenderness. And so much more.

Damn him for making her remember.

She looked away, torn but resolute.

Oh, she was tempted.

The devil almost had her soul.

Except what had passed between them was beyond talk. It required yelling, screaming, glass breaking.

Once upon a time, she'd been young and stupid and foolish at love. Alec had been a trusted friend. Closer than Franny even. Keira had thought the earth revolved around him. She had entrusted him with her body, mind, and soul. Which made his betrayal all the worse.

She learned the hard way you didn't actually die from a broken heart. It just felt like you would.

And when it was all said and done, nothing changed. It ended ten years ago. She'd chalked it up to experience, got on with her life.

So had he.

Yes, she'd been the injured party, but dissecting it at this point felt . . . futile.

Acknowledging that left her feeling a little freer. And a little sadder.

Alec was here doing a job. Period. When it was done, he'd leave. Again. *But this time without her heart.*

"About us," he began. "We need to talk."

"It's too late to talk, Alec. Just let it go."

The song ended, and Scarlet Chambeau materialized at Alec's side. Wearing his tie. She cast an evil look at Keira.

"Dibs on last dance." As if on cue, Scarlet tilted forward, fell into Alec's arms, forcing Keira back. "Wow. What's in the punch?"

Alec held Scarlet upright. "How much have you had?"

"Four or five. You'll have to drive me home, Alec. After breakfast?" Scarlet turned to Keira. "You'll excuse us, won't you? We want to be alone."

Alone? Keira started to tell Scarlet to take a flying leap. Without Alec. With Alec.

Shit, she'd had too much to drink herself.

Not enough.

Keira backed away, hands up, palms out. "Have at it, Scarlet. Good-bye, Alec."

Keira left the dance floor, stopping by Franny's table to tell her friend good night. Then she walked out of the gym alone and didn't look back.

Something she should have done ten years ago.

Once outside the gym, Keira realized she'd given her car keys to Darryl for safekeeping. *Friends don't let friends drive drunk.* Damn it! So much for her grand exit.

The last thing she wanted to do was go back into the gym and see Alec again. With Scarlet.

Or worse, be standing outside when they came out. And she had no doubt they would leave together. It was clear Scarlet had set her cap for Alec.

Sheesh! She was pathetic. Why in the hell did she care what either of them thought? Scarlet was a bitch. Alec was a rat bastard. A match made in heaven.

She looked down the street, hiccuping. Wonderful. She hated hiccups.

With a sigh, she took off walking, reminding herself it really wasn't far. And her pride was at stake. If pride goeth before a fall, she wanted to be home before hers hit the ground.

But what should have been a twenty-minute stroll turned into a thirty-minute hike.

By the time she reached her apartment building downtown, she was miserable. The four-inch heels had her arches stretched to the verge of collapse. Not to mention that in the sticky, eighty-plus-degree weather, the glittery fabric of the tight dress rubbed her raw.

Her apartment building was actually an old, recently renovated hotel. The rooms were spacious, with high ceilings and gobs of ornate molding. Keira's apartment was on the third floor, in the back. Very private.

Limping, but pride intact, she retrieved the hidden key from the plant stand on the landing and let herself in.

She stood in the dark doorway, listening to the faint, welcoming hum of the air-conditioning. The blessedly cold air revived her alcohol buzz.

First things first.

Kicking her front door shut behind her, she reached around and unzipped the dress while still in her foyer. She shimmied, letting the damp dress fall to the floor on a blissful sigh.

Stepping free of the fabric puddle, she closed her eyes and reveled in the feel of cool air against her chafed skin.

She quickly opened her eyes, nearly losing her balance as the room spun.

Ah, the price for liquid courage. She'd had way too much to drink and would pay for it tomorrow.

Not bothering to turn on a light, she carefully snagged the dress with one hand and tossed it toward a dining room chair so she'd remember to drop it off at the dry cleaners in the morning.

Reaching around to wrestle with the clasp on the strapless bra, she headed unsteadily toward the bedroom. Her feet throbbed. As soon as she sat down the shoes were coming off, then—

She stopped, stumbling as her eyes adjusted to the dark. A slight movement through the open bedroom door caught her eye.

Then she heard a soft noise. A different sort of chill ran up her spine, paralyzing her.

Someone was in her apartment.

Chapter Three

Keira saw a second glimmer of movement in the darkness beyond her bedroom door. She took a careful step backward, then another, retreating.

A glance at the phone on the kitchen wall sent her courage south. The cradle was empty. God only knew where she'd left the cordless. In the bedroom? Bathroom? And her cell phone was in her truck at Franny's.

Only a sliver of ambient light filtered in the living room windows, leaving most of the apartment steeped in shadow.

She grabbed the heavy, lead crystal vase from the kitchen counter, holding it aloft in one hand as she continued backing away. Without a phone to call for help, she'd have to run to a neighbor's apartment.

She glanced down at her scanty underwear, then looked helplessly at where she'd tossed the dress: on the far side of the dining room table, close to the bedroom door.

Another slip of sound, all the spookier for being *hushed*, drifted across the silence, electrifying the fine hairs at her nape. She quickened her retreat. No friggin' way she'd go back after the dress now.

When she reached the front door, she eased it open and backed halfway out into the hall.

Feeling braver with an escape route, she yelled, "Come on out! I know you're in there!"

"Who's in there?"

Keira shrieked.

Alec caught the vase with one hand as he pulled her the rest of the way out into the hall and thrust her against the wall.

His eyes dropped, following his jaw to the floor.

Holy shit.

He'd been wrong about the teddy. She wore a strapless bra, a microscopic bikini, thigh-high nylons, and the sex-goddess heels. All in black. With tiny, strategically located satin bows. And a mile of wild red curls.

"What in the hell are you doing out here dressed like that?" he growled.

"You pulled me out here!" She lifted her chin, indignant. "And someone's in my apartment."

Alec straightened, reflexes alert. A gun appeared in his hand as he pressed a finger to his lips.

"Stay here." Then he disappeared inside.

Keira listened intently, heart pounding. Not a sound came from her apartment. Had Alec walked into danger? Should she go for help?

She crept closer to the open doorway, careful to stay against the wall.

She screamed as Alec suddenly rounded the opening, nearly knocking her down. His hand clapped over her mouth, silencing her as he dragged her against him.

"Shhh. It's okay. They're gone."

As soon as he dropped his hand, she glared at him. "You scared the hell out of me!"

"Why were you right next to the door? I told you to stay back."

"I was worried— Oh no!" A neighbor's door creaked open behind Alec.

Hugging her close, Alec totally concealed her body with his. The cold metal buckle of his belt bit into her abdomen.

Keira felt his fingers splay across the small of her back. *Across bare skin.* His nails grazed her flesh as he pressed her flat, to his chest. She looked up, whispered a swear word.

Alec raised an eyebrow. "Stay close against me, and he won't see you," he whispered back.

Careful to remain shielded, Keira peeked only her head around Alec. "Hi, Mr. Marks. Sorry if I bothered you. Just saying good night."

Her neighbor looked at Alec's back disapprovingly and nodded.

As soon as his door closed, Keira dashed inside her apartment.

Alec followed, cell phone in hand. "Don't go too far. I'm calling the sheriff."

"The sheriff?"

"Somebody definitely broke in, but they were gone by the time I got there."

"What?" Keira headed straight for her bedroom.

Alec stopped her at the doorway, preventing her from entering as he flipped the light switch.

She gasped. Her bedroom wasn't exactly vandalized . . . yet someone had rifled through several of her drawers.

Actually, it appeared they'd only made it through the top two drawers. Brightly colored lingerie—panties, cami-soles, nighties—was strewn haphazardly about.

She looked to where the drapes flapped in the night air. The window was wide-open, affording a perfect view of the iron fire escape outside. Obviously, her intruder had left the same way he came.

Keira marched over, slammed the window. When she found out who did this—

Alec's arm looped around her waist as he literally lifted her away from the window. "Don't touch anything. You'll compromise the crime scene."

"Crime scene?" Keira moved back, teetering unsteadily on her feet. "Don't you dare call the sheriff. This is a prank, Alec. It's got *high school* written all over it."

"A prank?"

"Yeah. Tomorrow morning one of my bras will be flying on a flagpole downtown. They'll put out an APB for the owner."

Alec looked unconvinced. "You sure nothing's missing? Jewelry? Cash?"

Keira glanced at the room. Her stereo and VCR were untouched. And the most valuable piece of jewelry she owned—a gold necklace her grandfather had given her—was at Franny's with her work clothes.

"I don't keep cash here." She waved her hand toward the dresser. "And offhand, I probably couldn't even tell you if any underwear was actually missing."

He shook his head. "How often does this happen?"

"Not often. Believe me, Freedom still has the most bored sheriff's department in the state. If it weren't for the high school kids cutting up on Friday nights, *rigor mortis* would set in."

"I still don't like it." Alec knew most people in Freedom still left their houses unlocked. *But most people didn't have to worry about Ian Griggs return-ing.*

He pointed to the window's lever-type lock. "There's part of the problem. Slip a knife between the panes, pop the latch, and you're in. Have those replaced. And keep 'em locked."

The authoritative tone in his voice irritated her. She straightened, riled. "Don't think you can walk in here and tell me what to do, Mr. FBI."

FBI? Alec's jaw tightened at the insult. He was ATF, damn it.

Either Keira had misunderstood Miles Ostman's explanation and thought Alec was FBI . . . or Ostman had purposely misled her and didn't mention this was a joint investigation. Given the fact Keira's grandfather actively produced moonshine, he'd bet on the latter.

He needed to tread carefully until he knew exactly *what* Ostman had told Keira. And perhaps more important—what he *hadn't* told her.

Cementing a solid cover was Alec's first objective. He knew Keira hadn't wanted to cooperate to begin with. The last thing he wanted to do was antagonize her and blow this assignment before it even got started.

Alec took every job seriously, had a reputation for flawless execution. He wouldn't allow personal issues to interfere.

He met her stare, saw the stubborn set of her chin. He hadn't missed the slight wobble of her step earlier. Nor her slurred words. He'd known she'd overimbibed. But he hadn't realized how badly until just now.

She was snockered. Whoever doctored the punch must have used pure grain alcohol. Maybe even some moonshine.

Now what did he do? Keep arguing? Or give up?

His eyes dipped lower, briefly. Painfully.

Crossing the room, he grabbed a black satin robe off the floor and thrust it at her. "Okay, the half-naked lady wins the first round."

For the second time that night, Keira remembered she wasn't dressed. Damn the man for distracting her.

She snatched the robe and stuffed her arms through the openings as she stalked out of the bedroom.

Pausing in the dining room, she looped the sash, rocking lightly. As the adrenaline rush subsided, the alcohol in her bloodstream spiked upward again, reminding her that sobriety gave him the edge.

It was still her apartment, however. She cleared her throat. "You can leave now."

Alec moved closer. "Don't I get a kiss or something for rescuing you?"

She frowned. "Can the *or something* be a sharp stick in the eye?"

He grinned. "No."

"Rats. Besides, you didn't rescue me. I had the situation totally under control."

"Right. Crystal vase. Sexy underwear. I'd have surrendered."

Keira shrugged, nearly toppled. "They were gone, weren't they?"

Alec caught her chin, raised it. "Admit it. You were scared."

She pulled away, her skin tingling from his touch. "There's a world of difference between fear and surprise. You caught me off guard, sneaking up behind me."

"I should have let old man Marks see you. Next time I won't be so neighborly."

Keira shifted from one high heel to the other, unsteady. "What do you mean, neighborly?"

He tapped his forehead like he'd just remembered something. "Didn't I tell you? I rented the apartment next door. We share the fire escape."

Keira's gaze shot back toward her bedroom. The fire escape served as her private balcony. A perfect place to sunbathe, to think, to relax. She had enjoyed not having to share it, had hoped the other apartment would remain vacant.

"If you think that makes me happy, Alec, you're wrong."

"Still holding a grudge, huh?"

"A grudge?"

He ducked as she took a swing.

"Damn you! I want you out!" She took another swing, tipping precariously.

Alec knew she was mad. Knew she had a right to be. Yeah, he'd purposely provoked her. The ice between them had to be shattered, and Keira's temper was the perfect tool for it. At some point, they needed to deal with their past issues in depth. *When she was sober.*

He grasped her wrists, holding her steady as she danced around, struggling to regain her footing. The shoes, sexy as they were, had to go before she broke her neck.

Moving quickly, he swung her up in his arms and carried her to the living room sofa, where he sat down with her.

Outraged, she scooted across the cushions, nearly falling off the edge. He grabbed her legs, and tugged her back in place, thwarting her escape.

Holding her left ankle, he unbuckled her shoe. Snagging her other foot, he removed that one as well.

"Better?" he asked.

Her first instinct was to deny it. Except . . . she grimaced. It did feel better. Keira wore steel-toed boots most days, not four-inch spikes. The soles of her feet were on fire, especially after the long walk home.

Then she remembered the reason she'd walked home and scowled at him. "I thought you were having breakfast with Scarlet."

Alec started to remind her—as part of his cover—the two of them were supposed to be playing long-lost lovers. Except he had a funny feeling Ostman probably hadn't explained that aspect either.

"Scarlet's sleeping off the punch." Actually, Scarlet had passed out in his car, and he'd carried her inside, left her on her couch. "Same thing you should be doing."

Keira squared her shoulders. "Are you insinuating I can't handle my liquor?"

Alec met her gaze. The makeup made her eyes look exotic. Smoky. And they snapped with green fire. His insides quaked. He was the one that couldn't handle it.

"You could handle anything, Keira. I always admired that."

She bit back a denial. He hadn't been around to see how she'd *handled* his leaving ten years ago. The aftermath had been disastrous.

"Why did it have to be you?" she said instead. "Of all the people they could have sent."

"I grew up here. I was a logical choice."

A logical choice. What had she expected him to say? That he'd jumped at the chance to return? He'd had ten years to come back. The fact he hadn't said it all.

"You hated Freedom," she said.

He sighed, wished he had a legitimate rejoinder. "It wasn't Freedom, per se. It was the lack of opportunity." How could he explain something that was more *feeling* than *reason*? "I think 90 percent of the males I graduated with felt the same."

His answer, while disappointing, didn't surprise Keira. Each spring, the male high school seniors flocked out of town, even those not headed to college.

She knew all the reasons: They had to see if the world was round . . . follow their wanderlust . . . prove the girl next door wasn't enough.

Metropolis was a powerful lure. She remembered being tempted herself.

She grabbed for a blasé response, sorry she'd brought the subject up. "Yeah. Well, in spite of the exodus, the town's still grown."

"I was wrong to leave the way I did."

His words caught her off guard. And made her mad.

She didn't want to hear excuses. Not now. *I was wrong to leave the way I did.* What did he mean? That he should have found a better way to leave? Or that he should have stayed?

"I got over it a long time ago, Alec. It doesn't matter anymore."

"It should. Once we couldn't stand to be apart. Now you can't bear to be in the same room."

"And this surprises you?"

His words tore at her reserve of ill will. Every terrible

thought she ever had about Alec Dempsey was stored in one place. And she didn't want to go there. Not now, not when she didn't feel totally in control.

She bit her lip, silently counting, determined not to let him get to her.

But it was too late. Her heart had waited ten years for its chance to tell him off.

"I told everyone in town I was leaving with you, Alec," she blurted. "That we were getting married. I waited forever for you to return."

The moment came screaming back as if it were yesterday. She had agreed to elope with Alec the morning after her senior prom. She had gone home to pack and tell her grandfather.

But Alec didn't return the next day. Or the next. Or the next.

Quite simply, she never saw or heard from him again. Until today.

Oh, she'd heard *about* him. Had sent a message to him through his mother. But then nothing.

Keira closed her eyes, drew on the internal strength that had gotten her through the difficult moments of her life.

"At first I was certain something tragic had happened," she whispered. "That you were comatose in a hospital and couldn't reach me. Then I heard you joined the army. Heard you married. For a long time I hated you. But mostly, I wished I'd never met you." She cleared her throat. "Then I got over it."

"I didn't mean to hurt you—"

Keira rose, cutting him off with a faltering wave of her hand.

She didn't want to hear she'd been a mistake. Or

they'd been too young. She knew all the reasons, could even agree with all the logic. And until that day, she'd believed she had no feelings left for him. Good or bad.

Damn him for proving otherwise. For proving she still hated him.

"Look, I've got to be up early. You need to go."

Alec stood. She'd gone from ordering him to leave to telling him to leave. The difference was monumental. They had a lot of unfinished business between them, but at least it was out in the open.

He turned to say good-bye, but found her robe had parted.

Even in the dim light, the glitter sparkled invitingly along the lush curve of her breasts. The enticingly low cut of her bra skimmed the edge of her aureoles. He could see the sharp indent of hard nipples restrained by black satin.

His eyes dropped, caught the lacy tops of the sexy nylons, wondered how she'd look in a garter belt and G-string. *Perilous thought.*

Keira followed his gaze, found the whole front of her robe gaping open. Cursing, she refastened the tie. The gown was one she never wore for that reason: It wouldn't stay closed. He would pick *this* one.

"What are you staring at now?" she snapped. "Show's over."

"Hell of a show, babe." Already the fabric gaped wide again. He liked this robe. He ran a finger lightly down her sternum, then tugged her lapels closed. "What kind of bra is that anyway?"

A wonder-shelf bra, she almost answered. Or so Franny dubbed it. Strapless black lace over nuclear-powered spandex and satin. With a matching French-cut bikini that left little to the imagination.

She raised her chin, batted his hands away, refusing to fall for his charm or his easy smile that melted a woman's defenses. "It's a none-of-your-bees-wax bra. And I'm not your babe."

He watched as she swayed sideways, off-balance. He grabbed her, wondered if she even realized how drunk she was.

For a moment, she leaned into him and looked up, eyes wide. Guileless. Then she licked her lips. His control crumbled. No way in hell he could resist that kind of temptation.

His hand moved to her nape and drew her in. Caught off guard, she tumbled fully against him. Alec didn't waste time with gentle kisses, afraid they'd be rebuffed.

His fingers splayed against her scalp, pressing her close as his other hand cupped her cheek, holding her immobile, as his tongue swept between her parted lips.

He knew her mouth wasn't open in invitation. It was open in shock. The kiss caught her unaware, and he pressed the advantage, unable to stop himself.

Over the years he'd told himself time had embellished his memory. That the reality of kissing her, holding her, loving her, hadn't been as powerful as he thought.

He'd been dead wrong.

His tongue swept deeper, as he caught her bottom lip lightly between his teeth, his senses overloaded.

Then he felt it.

The single tear.

Good God, he was an idiot.

He pulled back, her head still cradled in his hands. The torment in her eyes tore at him.

He apologized. "I'll leave."

"Damn you, Alec Dempsey! Don't ever do that again."

He caught her just as she passed out.

Alec searched her drawers and found a large T-shirt. He coaxed her into semiconsciousness long enough to slip the shirt over her head. She fussed with the bra, briefly exposing her tits before managing to unsnap it. Then she passed out again.

Shaking his head, Alec tucked her into bed, then sat beside her, watched her sleep. How often had he done that ten years ago? Watch her sleep.

Keira had lived with her grandfather in a cabin near the top of Fire Mountain. How many nights had he taken her home only to sneak back through her bedroom window later?

Even after she'd fallen asleep he'd lie there and find peace in the light rise and fall of her chest. In just being close. It was as if he couldn't bear to be apart from her.

Funny. He and Keira had been lovers in high school, but they'd never *slept* together an entire night, never wakened in each other's arms.

He fingered a long strand of rich hair. The color was deeper, a more vibrant red than he remembered. Just as long though, a tumble of thick curls that fell almost to her trim little butt.

He needed to watch his step with this woman.

That afternoon, when she'd been in dirty work gear, he'd been so turned on he could scarcely think. And she'd been determined to ignore him, which only inflamed his desire.

Why had he never come back?

Afraid to face her? *Yes.* Afraid she'd gone on and built a better life without him? *Yes.* Too satisfied with his comfortable, no-commitment life? *Yes.*

A heaviness settled in his chest. Ten years ago, he'd had nothing to offer her. And he'd desperately wanted to leave Freedom. For good.

Aside from Keira, he had no ties to Freedom. His mother had left shortly after he graduated, swore never to return. Louise Dempsey had lived under a mantle of disapproval. A single mother who'd never been married, who worked nights at a rough-and-tumble bar to make ends meet. She had warned her son against getting involved so young, against ruining his life before even having a chance to live.

But Alec hadn't listened. At least not at first.

While Keira had agreed to leave, he knew a part of her would forever be tied to Freedom. They'd talked of having babies. Children he knew she wanted to raise on Fire Mountain.

She would have wanted to return eventually. While he wanted to burn bridges.

On the morning they were supposed to leave, Alec panicked, wondered if they were doing the right thing. Hell, Keira hadn't even graduated yet. She had six more weeks of school.

It had been so easy to talk himself out of it—to listen to his self-doubts, convince himself he was doing the right thing for both of them by not going back. Decision made, he'd joined the army and shipped out the next day.

Sacrificing Keira had nearly killed him. The harsh reality of boot camp made him realize what he'd given up.

At first, he'd missed her so fiercely he thought he'd die of loneliness. Of want. His mother told him Keira had contacted her. Relayed the message that she never wanted to see him again.

Actually, she'd wished him every evil short of death and promised to hate him forever. She did nothing lightly.

Alec had decided to go back to Freedom first chance he got. He knew the only way to make it right was in person. Besides, every time he tried calling, her grandfather hung up.

But as soon as Alec completed basic training, he went to Vegas on a two-day pass, drank his entire paycheck, and woke up married to a woman who swore he'd followed her to three different casinos, begging her to marry him. She'd had long red hair.

Divorcing her hadn't been nearly so easy.

While he regretted the rash marriage, he didn't regret his time spent in the army. Or the life he'd built since then.

If you could call it a life.

His undercover assignments usually entailed working round the clock for long stretches. Girlfriends either understood or they didn't. *Didn't* was less complicated. But sex without commitment was unsatisfying. Maybe that was part of the problem: He'd been celibate too long.

He tucked the blanket under her chin, ran a finger along her creamy cheek. She sighed in her sleep, made kittenish sounds.

Desire raged like wildfire. *Not good.*

He stood. He wasn't going to push those buttons again with Keira; he wasn't going to get involved.

He needed to remember the reason why he was in Freedom, remember it was just a job. And temporary.

He started gathering the clothes strewn about the room. He didn't like the idea someone had been in her apartment, had gone through her underwear, even as a prank.

He also hadn't been happy not to report the incident to the authorities, but he'd go along with it to stay on her good side.

He picked up the strapless bra she'd worn earlier and scowled. Every guy at the dance had ogled her in that dress. Alec included. Somehow, he'd managed to maintain control . . . until he'd found her in the hall in that underwear.

Until he'd kissed her. What the hell was he thinking?

And whom was he kidding?

This assignment would be more difficult than he'd dreamed.

Chapter Four

Keira awoke with a blistering headache. Whimpering, she rolled onto her side. Movement, however slight, was a big mistake.

"That bad, eh?" Alec's morning-rough voice surprised her.

Startled, she flipped over. Pain spiraled beneath her skull, intense and unbearable.

She groaned, feeling too rotten to ask him what he was doing in her bedroom. She had a vague recollection of asking him to stay, wanting him to stay. A frown grew as she tried to remember.

"How did you get in here?"

"Climbed through the window."

"I've got to replace those locks," she hissed. "Did I pass out?"

"Yes."

"Did you spend the night?"

"No."

Her eyes fluttered shut in relief. "Good."

Alec grinned in spite of her obvious discomfort. Probably three-quarters of the people from last night's dance were waking up with monster hangovers. He was only concerned about one.

"Take these." He pressed two tablets into her palm.

"What are they?"

"Aspirin." He helped her sit up, then held a glass to her mouth. "Drink this. It'll help."

This turned out to be a warm mixture of tomato juice and a few other things she couldn't identify. It went down surprisingly easy.

"Good girl. I'm going to ease you back."

Very gently, he lowered her against the pillows. Keira gritted her teeth, fighting dizziness as the room spun, afraid she'd be sick. Then a cold cloth was draped across her forehead.

The cloth felt so good she would have granted him any wish. Was glad he didn't ask.

"Go back to sleep," he urged. "You'll feel better."

Three hours later she awoke again, the headache absent. So, too, the nausea. Her eyes drifted around the room, confirming she was alone. The heavenly scent of coffee wafted on the air, a warning. *He* was still around.

Moving cautiously, she rolled from bed and headed to the bathroom. That she felt this good was a minor miracle. Whatever Alec had concocted with the tomato juice needed to be patented.

By the time she climbed out of the shower, she felt remarkably human. Until she spotted the hot cup of coffee sitting on the bathroom counter.

Alec.

He'd obviously crept in and out. In stealth mode. A note was written across the steam-fogged mirror, the letters bold masculine slashes: *Later, babe.*

She drew her hand across the words, erasing them. "I'm not your babe."

At least he was gone.

He was the last person she wanted to see just then. She'd behaved poorly the night before, and that morning when she woke she'd been wearing different clothes. Alec had obviously had a hand in that.

She had another hazy recollection of begging him to undress her, of being in his arms. Self-consciousness flooded her as her memory failed. Had anything happened last night after she passed out? Anything . . . sexual?

She'd dreamed of him that way. Dreamed she'd sleep-walked out the fire escape and into his bed. He hadn't disappointed. He'd ravaged. Long-banished memories had haunted her sleep. Kept her feverish.

With the dawn came a return of reason.

She wiped the rest of the steam from the mirror, shook her head at her reflection.

Last night she learned a twofold lesson: one, she wasn't immune to Alec's charm. She should never have let him kiss her. And she'd known he was going to, had seen it in his eyes. She could have avoided it.

In the past, she had always known when Alec was going to kiss her. Had always melted in the heat of anticipation. And their kisses rarely ended with only lip contact. They'd usually gone all the way.

She'd wanted to go all the way last night. If Alec hadn't stopped . . .

That one kiss had smoked her defenses instantaneously. The fuzzy effects of alcohol hadn't helped. She needed to watch how much she drank around Alec.

Lesson two: She still had urges. Nothing wrong with that. She just needed to find someone safe to explore those urges with. Maybe she'd rethink Franny's advice on dating.

It was painfully apparent she'd underestimated her reaction to seeing Alec again. Granted, she'd thought she still had a week or two before he showed up, thought she had plenty of time to work through any unresolved sensitivities.

But the old hurts surfacing had been a surprise. And the anger. Where had it all come from?

Alec Dempsey had left her ten years ago. She'd only been eighteen. A child. She'd gotten over it and moved on. Had never really considered seeing Alec again.

So why had her heart felt as if it would burst through her rib cage when she first saw him? Why the onslaught of mixed sentiment? Rage and excitement.

The last thing she wanted was strong feelings for Alec—good or bad. He was there for one reason only. Which was where she had to keep her thoughts focused.

It was nearly one o'clock when Keira reached her office. Even though it was Saturday, Tina, her office manager, sat at the desk, stuffing envelopes.

"What are you doing here?" Tina asked. "Isn't there a big reunion party at the pool?"

Keira nodded. Scarlet and Cissy had jammed a week's worth of events into the weekend. She'd obviously missed the pancake breakfast that morning, and that afternoon the reunionites were playing beach blanket bingo at the city pool, followed by a picnic and bowling.

"I'll meet them later," Keira said. "I've got a lot to catch up here. What are you working on?"

"Invoices and statements," Tina said. "There's a stack of checks on your desk that need signing."

Tina started a two-week vacation on Monday, and in her typical, extraordinary fashion, she was making certain all was in order before she left.

"I'd be lost without you," Keira said.

"Good. Don't want you getting too attached to Martha while I'm gone."

Martha, a part-time office assistant, had agreed to fill in during Tina's absence but had made it plain she didn't want Tina's job.

"I almost forgot." Tina handed Keira a phone message. "Walt Pelter's called twice. Wants to know if you'd be interested in taking on the Chevy dealership job. He pulled the bid from the Barry brothers and says he's hanging in the breeze."

"He pulled the bid?" That news surprised her, but not nearly as much as the fact Walt had called *her.*

Walt Pelter was a prominent general contractor who routinely ignored Keira's bids. If he had called her, he must be desperate indeed.

In the five years since Keira had bought out Jack Carson's electrical business she'd quadrupled profits and doubled the number of employees. But the larger jobs— like the dealership—evaded her. She knew why. Few women had penetrated the good-old-boy network dominating construction.

Never mind that she'd started working as an electrician's apprentice at sixteen. Or that she had a degree in electrical engineering. She lacked a penis.

She didn't lack balls, however, and she had feminine wiles in spades. If she could get her foot in the door, she'd kick it down. She'd show Walt.

"Did he leave a number?"

"Said he'll call back. Oh my!" Tina nodded toward the front door. "Hunk alert. Headed this way."

Keira spotted Alec walking across the parking lot. "Oh shit."

Tina's brow quirked up. "Was that a good *oh shit*, or a bad one?"

"A bad one."

"Want me to tell him you're gone?"

"No." Yes, she wanted her to, but doing so would only postpone the inevitable. Sooner or later, she had to face him again, and her office was probably the best place. Private, but not intimate.

The door opened, sounding a small buzzer.

"Hello, Alec."

Alec nodded at Keira, then introduced himself to Tina.

Tina's smile grew as she shook Alec's hand. "I recognize the name. You used to work here, didn't you?"

"Long time ago. When the sign outside said JACK CARSON ELECTRIC." He looked back to Keira. "Of course, Morgan Electrical Contracting has a nice ring."

Keira shrugged, trying to hide her pride. In her secret heart of hearts, she admitted she might have wanted to see Alec again. Just to show him she had prospered without him, that she was a successful businesswoman.

Alec studied the office. "You've expanded."

"Added a warehouse. And a ladies' room."

He grinned. "Got a minute to talk?"

She glanced at her watch, then walked over to the coffeepot. "I've got a few minutes. Want a cup?"

Alec helped himself, then followed Keira down the hall to her office. He closed the door.

"Feeling better?"

Moving to her chair, she nodded. "I want to know what was in that tomato juice. By rights, I should still be sick."

"That punch should have been outlawed. I suspect it was pure alcohol, with a package of powdered drink mix thrown in for color. Quite honestly, I don't know how you made it home."

She recalled the long walk to her apartment, remembered finding someone inside. Remembered Alec *had* helped her. Ugh.

The next words nearly choked her. "Thanks for assisting me last night."

The grin returned as Alec sipped his coffee. "My pleasure. It's not every night I get to help a gorgeous, inebriated woman into bed."

Keira winced. That wasn't what she meant, and he knew it. Still, the fact she couldn't recall the entire evening bothered her. She fished for information.

"At least tell me I changed my own clothes."

"You took off your bra."

At her look of misery, Alec laughed out loud. "Relax, Keira. Nothing happened. You were already pretty much undressed to begin with. It wasn't difficult."

She frowned, recalling how Alec had found her in her underwear. "Yeah, well, believe me, it will *never* happen again."

"I wasn't complaining."

Suddenly his smile annoyed her. His presence, too. "What do you want, Alec?" She pointed to the stack of checks Tina had left. "I've got a lot of work to get through."

Alec set his coffee aside. He'd talked with Miles Ostman a short time ago. Ostman admitted telling Keira a lie—that her grandfather had been threatened—the only way Ostman felt he could induce her assistance.

"It's obvious she's not real fond of you," Ostman had said. "What exactly did you do to her?"

Alec had ignored the question. "What did you tell Keira about my cover?" he asked Ostman instead.

"We didn't get that far. I told her I'd get back to her," Ostman said. "And, since you showed up early, it's your problem. Just don't blow it."

Alec watched Keira shuffle papers, knew his being there unnerved her. He hadn't yet decided how to handle the misconception that Griggs threatened Keira's grandfather.

To reveal at this point that Ostman had lied would only increase her distrust. And he needed to assure his place in town. It was the only way to establish a watch on Griggs. To protect her.

"We need to discuss my role here," Alec began.

Keira agreed. "You can start by telling me how you plan to protect Willis."

"Initially, Griggs will be restricted to the halfway house when he's not working. I'll keep him under close surveillance, wait for him to make his move."

"Do you really think he'll get his money and run?"

"Wouldn't you? He has no reason to stick around."

Neither did Alec, Keira reminded herself. "Sounds like your plan's complete then."

"Not quite. We still need to establish my reason for returning to Freedom."

"You told Franny you'd just been discharged from the army, though personally I thought the grenade-exploding story was overkill."

Alec grunted. "It won a lot of sympathy."

"Fine. So there's your cover." She shrugged. "I don't think anyone in town will question it. The last anyone heard, you had joined the army. No one's known—or cared—what you've done since."

She hoped he'd volunteer the information. Yeah, she was curious what he'd done all these years, but darn if she'd ask.

"It's not that simple. I need a compelling reason to stick around. Something with substance. Ian Griggs will be looking for weak links." He paused. "For starters, you need to hire me. Then you and I have to pretend we're involved again."

Keira nearly fell out of her chair. "What? That's as ridiculous as it is insulting."

He grimaced. "I understand how you'd feel that way. And believe me, I've tried to come up with an alternate. But given our past, nothing else fits. And it has to be 100 percent convincing. Griggs will find anything less suspicious. He'll be expecting traps, looking for the unusual, so we have to make it look sincere. Which also means making everyone in town think we've buried the hatchet and have rekindled our relationship."

Keira shut her eyes against the cruel bite of his explanation. She'd known from the beginning Alec would need a cover, a reason to justify his return. She would have never guessed this one.

And even as part of her recoiled in objection, part of her recognized the truth: Alec returning for her had the sort of fairy-tale quality people naturally wanted to believe. Which ticked her off.

"So you just show up out of the blue and beg my forgiveness, huh? And just like that"—she snapped her fingers—"I forgive you?"

"We'll let people think we've been corresponding by e-mail," Alec said. "I contacted you. You told me off, but in spite of the harsh words, we made a connection. And I've come back to prove myself."

How many times had Keira played that scenario over in her head ten years ago? It hurt just recalling it.

It also bothered her that everyone assumed she was available to play the part.

She crossed her arms over her chest. "What if I'm sort of involved with someone?"

"Sort of?" He scoffed. According to Scarlet, Keira hadn't had a steady boyfriend in over a year. Yes, he'd pumped Scarlet for information while they danced. "You'll need to *sort of* break it off for a while."

"What if I don't want to?"

Tough, he wanted to say. "It's temporary, Keira, remember?"

The words stung. "You and Scarlet were pretty chummy last night. She might make a believable cover." God knows she'd be willing.

"Not as believable as you and me."

Tina interrupted, coming across on the intercom. "Walt Pelter's on line two. Growling like a bear."

"I need to take this call," Keira said.

Alec stood, picked up his coffee cup. "One last thing. You've sworn Franny to secrecy, right?"

She would have loved to throw an indignant *"How dare you"* in his face. Instead, she nodded.

"We might need to clue Franny in so she can back up our story about the e-mail."

Franny would love that. "We'll see. I need to think about this."

"Fine. We'll talk more tonight."

"Tonight?"

"The reunion bowling party," he clarified.

Scarlet had no doubt invited him. "Maybe." She shrugged, noncommittal, and grabbed the phone.

And maybe she needed to have her head examined for agreeing to Miles Ostman's request in the first place.

It was dark by the time Keira pulled into the bowling alley. Judging by the lack of parking, she was probably the last to arrive.

The Pin Palace II was Freedom's sparkling new bowling alley. The original Pin Palace had met its demise two years earlier when a fire burned it to the ground, taking with it a small strip mall that housed the Church of Good Souls.

The church fathers and the bowling alley patrons had been feuding for months over the Pin Palace's desire to expand. The bowling alley wanted a bigger, full-service bar. The church wanted the alley's current beer-and-wine license revoked.

Under city law, no alcohol could be served within one city block of a church or school. But since the bowling alley had been there first, they were grandfathered in by a special proviso. Which the Good Souls' pastor claimed rankled the Lord.

Keira smiled. The Lord must have really been pissed when that same pastor was arrested for arson.

The new Pin Palace was twice the size of the old. A game room and pool tables had been added along with the new bar. Monday through Thursday, the senior citizens' bowling leagues ruled.

But on Friday and Saturday nights, the place converted as *Cosmic* bowling took over. The standard-issue, black house balls were replaced with neon-colored balls in pink, blue, yellow, orange, and green.

Panels painted with psychedelic Day-Glo designs unfurled from the ceiling. The fluorescent lights were shut off in favor of black lights and flashing strobes. Tiny racing lights chased up and down the side of the lanes, at different speeds and colors. Even the pins glowed under the black lights.

Short-skirted waitresses went from table to table on Rollerblades, while music videos blared from the same monitors that aired CNN during the day. The effect was electrifying, like stepping into a futuristic world.

That night the place was packed with the class reunion attendees. Several people wore fifties-style bowling shirts. Scarlet and Cissy had matching shirts, unbuttoned low, with the collars high.

Scarlet made a beeline for Keira. "Have you seen Alec?"

"Nope."

The other woman looked relieved, then checked her watch. "I'm sure he'll be here soon."

"That's what he said earlier."

"You did see him." Scarlet's brows drew together. "I'm only going to tell you this once. *Back off.* I saw him first." Then she stormed off.

"Knock yourself out," Keira muttered under her breath. Then she turned and headed for the far side of the alley.

Franny came up, looped an arm around her shoulders. "What took you so long to get here? Mabel was afraid we'd have to forfeit the game." Franny tugged her toward their lanes.

Bowling was Mabel's religion. She bowled on the women's senior league. Her booth at the salon sported a huge state championship trophy, plus several small trophies from league play.

"I had to write up a job for Walt Pelter."

"Walt Pelter? What kind of job?"

"He gave me the Chevy dealership."

"That's the second time this week hell froze over." Franny shook her head. "I thought the Barry brothers had that one?"

"Guess they tried to shake Walt down for more money."

"I'd love to see Eddie Barry's face when he hears *you* got the job," Franny crowed.

"He already knows, and Walt warned me he's pissed."

Keira bid regularly against the Barry brothers, another electrical contractor in town. They seemed to be personally affronted by a woman in their line of work and took special joy in harassing her.

"Any word from Alec?" Franny asked.

Keira filled her in on Alec's visit to her apartment the night before and to her office that morning.

"He wants to pretend you're lovers?" Franny rubbed her hands together. "Awesome."

"Not. I told Alec I was sort of involved."

"With who?"

"I didn't say."

"That's even better." Franny grinned. "Leave that part to me."

"Oh no you don't."

"Oh yes I do. I think it's an omen Alec's returned."

"Yeah. A bad one."

Mabel interrupted, tapping Franny's shoulder. "You're up next. Change your shoes."

Relieved Franny was distracted, Keira watched as Sally rolled a strike.

There were eight of them bowling on two adjacent lanes. Girls versus boys. Thanks to Mabel and Sally, the girls were ahead.

"Watch that hook," Mabel yelled, as Franny moved to take her turn.

Franny nodded and grabbed her ball.

All male heads within a ten-lane radius swiveled to watch Franny line up for her approach.

In keeping with the fifties theme, she wore a pointy Jane Russell bra underneath a tight, white cashmere sweater. She had on black pedal pushers cinched at the waist with a wide red belt. A red chiffon scarf at her neck completed the picture.

As a bowler, Franny could hold her own. However, her new designer nails wouldn't fit in the holes, so she simply tossed the ball with two hands.

The ball wobbled down the lane, barely taking out one pin. Everyone clapped. Her second ball hugged the gutter, but still everyone applauded. Especially the guys next to them.

"We needed the break," Fred, Mabel's husband, confided. "We're losing."

Sally's fiancé, Stan, and his brother were bowling on

the men's side. Keira's employee, Reggie Reeves, filled the fourth male spot. Reggie had been shooting pool and agreed to fill in for Darryl, who'd been detained at the fire station.

Both Keira and Reggie picked up their balls at the same time. Grinning slightly, he indicated she should go first.

Wiping her hands on her jeans, she lined up, found her mark, and tossed the ball. She took out seven pins.

While her lane reset, Reggie moved in to take his turn. Keira studied his profile, thoughtful.

As a worker, Reggie was reliable. More importantly, he did quality work. He had moved to Freedom the previous month when his lease expired in Hot Springs and had caused quite a stir among the town's single female population.

It was easy to see why. Reggie had shoulder-length blond hair and—as Franny called them—bedroom blue eyes. He also had a great tan and an equally great physique. Without a shirt, he was the penultimate fantasy construction worker.

Next to Alec.

Frowning at the thought, Keira narrowed her eyes, studying Reggie's shoulders. Maybe Franny was right. Maybe it was time to break a few rules, broaden her horizons. Reggie might not be a bad place to start.

Reggie's ball split the pins, leaving the two corner ones standing. He swore, then shrugged. "Your turn, boss lady."

Keira took her second turn, picking up a spare. She did a little victory dance as Sally and Mabel applauded.

Franny waved from the rear booth, catching her

attention. Keira nearly tripped when she saw Alec leaning down, talking to Franny.

"Alec was just telling me he's your new neighbor,"
Franny said.

Keira glanced suspiciously at her friend. Why was
she acting like this was news?

"Maybe you and Reggie could invite Alec to a cook-
out one night. Oh, there's Darryl!"

Finished causing trouble, Franny scooted out of the
booth and took off toward the entrance. Keira knew exactly
what Franny was doing—inventing her *sort of* boyfriend.

"Reggie?" Alec questioned.

"Reggie Reeves. Works for me."

"Surfer dude? Not your type."

His response irked her. "What's it to you?"

"Just checking the turf, babe."

"My turf is none of your business. Reggie's turf either."

Alec smiled. "Fifty bucks says you're not involved."
He leaned in close, brushed the hair back from her face
with a single finger. "I saw you checking out his ass, and
it wasn't a gee-I-know-that-ass kind of look. It was a
gee-is-that-as-good-as-other-asses-I've-known look."

Keira felt her cheeks grow warm. She used to brag
that Alec's backside was the best in the South. *A long
time ago.*

Damn him and his smug little look. "I've known
some bigger asses in my time. I wouldn't necessarily say
they were better."

Alec's hand closed around her upper arm, pulling her
close. His voice dropped to a whisper. "I'd forgotten how
cute you look when you're mad."

She tugged her arm away, remembering how Alec used to tease her. Just to rile her. "I'm not mad."

"Right. You look like you did at fourteen. When I gave you your first spanking."

Keira's eyes flared with the heat of unwelcome recollection.

When she was in eighth grade, she and Franny had followed the high school football team to their annual bonfire at Culverleaf Pond. The rumors were true—the football players all went skinny-dipping.

Unfortunately, they were caught spying by a couple of drunken seniors, who threw them in the pond, clothes and all.

Alec had come to their aid, driven them home. He wasn't happy. After they dropped Franny off, he had headed up Fire Mountain. Halfway there, he pulled over to lecture her on the danger she and Franny could have faced.

Keira made the mistake of sticking out her tongue and telling Alec nobody told her what to do. Alec yanked her over his knee and gave her a couple hard wallops, right through her wet jeans.

She'd been mortified then.

She was mortified he brought it up now.

Grinning, Alec pointed to the scoreboard where her name flashed. "Your turn again."

Red-faced, she huffed to the lane.

Reggie had just thrown his ball, scoring another split. He swore again. "Can you believe it?"

Keira lined up her ball. She looked at the head pin, envisioning Alec's smirking face. Aiming for his nose, she let the ball fly.

Pins exploded, shooting up in the air, spinning, then falling.

Strike!

She jumped, fist in the air, surprised.

Reggie grabbed her, spinning her around as the others clapped and hooted. When he set her down, she leaned into him. Then she reached up, looped her hand around his neck.

Drawing his mouth down, she pressed a kiss to his lips.

It lasted only seconds, and, when she looked up, everyone was staring at them openmouthed. Everyone except Alec. He was gone.

She glanced back at Reggie. "Sorry. Too much excitement, I guess."

He grinned. "No problem."

Franny, Sally, and Mabel converged on her when she walked toward them.

"Nice," Mabel said. "Excellent strike, too."

Franny scooted closer to Darryl, making room for Keira in the booth. "He's at three o'clock with Scarlet and Cissy. I think he saw."

Keira resisted the urge to turn around. She needed to get a grip. She had nothing to prove. Her life had been fine before Alec returned. It would be fine when he left. In fact, the sooner he left, the better.

The women won all three games.

When they finished bowling, Keira stopped by the bar.

Most of the reunion attendees were there. Many were leaving early the next morning.

It saddened her to think it would be another ten years before she saw most of these people, and it irritated her to realize she'd looked forward to seeing some of them, but hadn't because of Alec's presence.

Franny grabbed her arm, lowered her voice. "There's that guy."

Keira looked around, not seeing anyone she recognized. Alec and Scarlet had both disappeared too, she noticed.

"What guy?"

"The one I told you about last week. The creepy-looking dude shooting pool with Harold Harper."

Keira waited a few seconds, then looked.

Harold had the pool table closest to the jukebox. His opponent was backed against the wall, leaning heavily against his cue stick. The man was average height, average build, with dark hair slicked back in a stubby ponytail. His shirt collar hid most of the tattoo on his neck.

And he stared directly at them.

Keira felt an involuntary shiver run down her spine. Franny said he worked at Big Cheney's Grocery and had made an obvious effort to carry her groceries last week, then tried to hit on her in the store's parking lot.

"He's been staring at me since we walked in," Franny said.

"Make sure he sees you hanging on Darryl. He'll get the hint."

One of their former classmates came over to talk.

When Keira looked up again, the creepy-looking guy was gone. And it was nearly one o'clock. She motioned for their tab. "I'm heading home."

"We'll go out with you," Franny said. Darryl had his arm around Franny, kissing her as they walked.

When they reached Keira's car, she hugged them both. She started to climb in when something caught her eye.

She screamed and backed away.

Darryl was beside her in an instant, Franny right behind him. He peered in. "How in the hell did that get inside your car?"

"How did what get inside her car?" Alec demanded as he pushed up beside Keira.

Darryl carefully grabbed the thing off Keira's car seat— an eighteen-inch doll that had been horribly mutilated.

Stripped of clothes, the doll's plastic body had been punctured and burned. Both hands were chopped off, one leg ripped away at the hip.

Worst was the doll's head. Most of the hair had been cruelly hacked off, but several long shanks of dark red hair were left intact.

Hair the exact same shade as Keira's.

The eyes had been gouged out. BURN BITCH was scrawled across the doll's forehead.

Keira turned away, feeling sick. She recognized the doll.

So did Franny. "How did someone get her?"

"Her?" Alec looked at Keira.

"My grandfather gave me the doll." Keira's voice shook. "She sat on my dresser. I hadn't even noticed her missing."

Darryl had already summoned the alley's private security. The security guard knew everyone, but looked suspiciously at Alec. "Can someone vouch for him?"

Keira nodded. "He works for me."

"So what happened?"

Keira kept the explanation brief, still in shock that someone had purposely done such a thing.

"Not much to go on," the guard said. He grabbed the

doll. "I'll turn it over to the sheriff. And I'll ask around, see if anyone saw anything. Bet it's a prank, though."

Alec grunted. Any evidence the doll might have yielded was probably gone thanks to the inept handling by the security guard. "Prank? Not likely. Whoever did it broke into Keira's apartment last night."

The guard whistled, jotted down another note. "You get on someone's bad side lately?"

Keira's first thought was the Barry brothers. But she'd been on their bad side for years. Were they retaliating for the dealership job? "Lately? No."

As soon as the guard left, Alec reached for her keys. "I'll drive your car. You can follow in my Jeep."

Too shaken to argue, Keira accepted his car keys.

When they reached the apartment building, he walked her to her door in silence.

She looked at him, recalling last night. The kiss. His undressing her. *Her dreams.*

She suddenly felt awkward. Torn.

"Don't suppose you'll invite me in for a nightcap," he said.

"I'm pretty tired." She unlocked the door, opened it.

He stopped her. "You hate feeling grateful to me. For even the tiniest thing."

She looked away. He was right. It rankled. But worse was the feeling of being susceptible. Something she'd never admit to. She sought to cover her vulnerability with good manners.

"Thanks for driving my car home," she said stiffly.

"Lighten up, babe. If it will make you feel any better, I'm probably getting ready to piss you off again."

He clasped her chin, holding her gaze.

For a moment, she thought he'd kiss her again. For a moment, she wanted it.

Didn't want it.

Mostly it vexed her Alec assumed it would piss her off, making her want to prove him wrong. Maybe she'd enjoy the kiss just to confound him.

Alec trailed a finger down her cheek, leaned in close. Her bottom lip trembled.

"You left your car unlocked at the bowling alley tonight," he whispered softly. "Don't do it again."

She jerked away. "Don't tell me what to do!"

Stepping into her apartment, she slammed the door. And heard his laughter fade away.

Chapter Five

Keira was at the gym when it opened at eight o'clock Sunday morning.

After working out, she swung by the bakery and waited on a fresh batch of donuts before going to Franny's apartment, her usual Sunday morning ritual.

A pajama-clad Franny met her at the back door, squealing in anticipation. *Her* Sunday morning ritual. She snagged the bakery box and dashed back up the stairs.

"It's a good thing we only do this once a week. I'd be as big as a barn."

"You could meet me at the gym first," Keira teased.

Franny wrinkled her nose. Sunday was her morning to sleep in. Darryl typically stayed late on Saturday night but was gone by 5 A.M., which in Freedom meant he hadn't *technically* spent the night.

While more people thumbed their noses at it, cohabitation was still frowned upon by the city fathers. And since Darryl hoped to be appointed the next fire chief, he and Franny tried to be discreet.

Franny poured coffee. "Tell me what happened after you and Alec left the bowling alley last night."

"Nothing. He walked me to my door and left."

"That's it?" Franny's look could have soured milk. "Weren't you scared after finding that doll in your car?"

She hesitated, not wanting to admit having nightmares over the doll. Admitting fear gave it power. "Actually, it made me mad. The doll had tremendous sentimental value."

"We'll find another one just like it. You know me, the queen of shopping."

Keira smiled at her friend. "Thanks, but there's no replacing it."

"So Alec was a perfect gentlemen? What a drag. I thought he'd at least offer to spend the night."

"He lives next door."

Franny grew thoughtful. "Letting him spend the night would prime the rumor mill, though. Which would play right along with his cover."

Letting him spend the night would prime trouble. Aside from the problems Keira had with Alec's *cover,* she still hadn't figured out what to tell her grandfather. Willis needed to hear the reason for Alec's return from her first.

"I don't need those kinds of rumors floating around," she said. "It's bad for business."

"Not to mention it might scare Reggie off," Franny said. "And after that kiss you gave him at the bowling alley—well, I bet ole Reggie will be hot on your trail."

"I shouldn't have kissed Reggie. I'm already trying to figure out what I'll say when I see him tomorrow."

"Oh please! It wasn't that big a deal. Reggie probably doesn't get real excited over a kiss unless tongues are involved. I don't."

Keira shook her head. "Last night was a disaster. I should have stayed home."

"Do you think the doll incident is related to Griggs's return?"

"No. If Griggs were out already, it would be a different story. But he's still locked up for another two weeks."

Franny sipped her coffee. "Could it have been one of the Barry brothers? Getting back at you for landing the dealership job?"

Keira had wondered that, too. It seemed the only feasible explanation. "I wouldn't put it past them."

"I hope I'm around when those guys fall flat on their faces," Franny said. "Now, I'm starved. Let's eat."

Keira spread the Sunday paper out on the kitchen counter, then flipped open the bakery box and grabbed a warm, sticky glazed donut.

Franny muttered, "Eenie, meenie, minie, mo," while she surveyed the box, selecting her victim. She picked up the cruller, her eyes fluttering shut with the first bite. "Mmmmm. You know, I read somewhere that if you stand up while you eat, the calories do less damage."

Keira snickered, grabbed another donut. They always stood side by side, eating and reading the Sunday paper together. "Good. I'll start getting two dozen."

"Don't you dare."

Franny licked her fingers, then picked out a second donut before skimming the entertainment column. "Oh damn."

She pointed to a display ad for professional wrestling in Hot Springs. SOLD OUT was emblazoned across the ad in block letters.

"Why do they do that? Put in an ad when there are no

seats available?" Franny sighed in disappointment. She was a huge fan of the televised wrestling program.

So was Keira, when she had time to watch television. Yeah, it was campy. Maybe a little tacky. But it was hilarious. Fun. And the male athletes had bodies to die for. Tickets for the live events always sold out quickly.

Keira's cell phone rang.

It was Lacy Hicks, a friend of her grandfather's. Lacy ran the Lucky Nugget, a tourist mining attraction on the outskirts of town.

"Hate to bother you," Lacy said, "but the lights in the store won't come on. Customers won't buy stuff they can't see."

Keira sighed. Even though she did mostly new construction, there were a handful of her grandfather's friends who still called when they needed something.

She checked her watch. "I'm at Franny's. I can be there in five minutes." She hung up and explained to Franny.

Her friend laughed. "That old geezer thinks that just because he's friends with your grandpa, you have to jump whenever he calls."

"Yeah, and so far it works."

Alec woke up Sunday with an oddly familiar feeling: the urge to run. To leave town as fast as he could. The feeling passed, but left him feeling restless. Discontent.

He spent the morning driving around.

While Freedom had changed—for the better, he admitted grudgingly—the surrounding countryside was virtually unchanged.

The big barn at the edge of the field of old man Horton's farm was still rickety as hell. Looked like a strong wind would take it down. Mrs. Horton still hung shiny aluminum pie pans in her cherry tree to scare off the birds. The birds still hadn't fallen for it.

The fact that he recalled all the shortcuts and unmarked crossroads amazed Alec. Each new sight brought back a host of memories. Drag racing against members of the rival high school. Running moonshine across county lines. Getting drunk and camping out at Culverleaf Park.

Picnicking with Keira.

Swimming with Keira.

Making love to Keira.

He knew now why he rarely gave his hometown a thought. The memories weren't all unpleasant. To think of Freedom was to remember Keira. The innocence. The love. The lost, forgotten dreams that still haunted him on occasion.

Maybe coming back would proved cathartic.

He'd already had one major epiphany. In facing Keira, he realized what he'd been running from all those years ago: himself.

Maybe when this job was over, he'd leave with a true sense of closure, finally be able to put the past behind him and move on.

After he faced one more person, that is.

Keira's grandfather: Willis Morgan.

Alec stopped his car. His meanderings had ended at the single-lane gravel road that led up to Fire Mountain. A waist-high bush of black-eyed Susans nearly covered the hand-painted NO TRESPASSING sign.

Barely visible was the postscript VIOLATORS WILL BE SHOT.

Too late, the sound of gravel crunching alerted Alec someone had approached his car. He knew who that someone was the moment he felt the metal barrel of a shotgun press against the side of his neck, just below his left ear.

"Hello, Willis."

Not daring to move, Alec shifted his eyes, studying the profile of Keira's grandfather in his peripheral vision.

Willis O. Morgan hadn't changed. The "O" was for ornery, or so he told people. He was short, maybe five-five, wiry, and cussed stubborn. The older man had a full head of hair and a beard, both which had been white for as long as Alec could remember.

And while he couldn't see Willis's eyes, Alec knew they were even greener than Keira's. Right now he'd bet those eyes were sparking fire.

"Heard you were back," Willis said. "State your business."

A man of few words, Willis Morgan either liked you or he didn't. Alec knew exactly where he stood.

"Morning, Willis. I was just headed up to see you."

Both men knew it wasn't a social call. It was more a squaring off.

While Alec hadn't had contact with Keira since he'd left, he'd talked with Willis twice. The first time was ten years ago. Alec hadn't been allowed to make a phone call those first few weeks of army basic training. And all his letters to Keira had been returned, unopened. When he finally got to a pay phone, he'd called Keira, but Willis answered.

Willis had told him to stay away from Keira, refused to take a message. Alec realized it was Willis who had returned his letters.

"I don't want her getting her hopes up," Willis had

said. "Besides, any man that would walk out on my granddaughter doesn't deserve her."

Then Willis had delivered the *coup de grace*. "She's found someone else. Leave her alone."

The news had devastated Alec. He made plans to return to Freedom as soon as he had enough leave available . . . but the fateful trip to Las Vegas changed all that.

The second time Alec talked to Willis was five years ago. He'd read about the armed robbery and Ian Griggs's subsequent arrest. One of the papers mentioned Keira's part in his arrest, and when Alec followed up on the back story, he'd learned about Ian Griggs's attack on her. The assault had taken place before Griggs robbed the armored truck.

Alec had called Willis to see how Keira was. While Willis wasn't quite as bitter, he still insisted Alec stay away, that after all this time Keira didn't need to see him.

"I'll say it again." Willis nudged Alec's head with the gun. "State your business."

"I came back to see Keira, Willis. To set things right. I should have done it a long time ago."

"You seen my granddaughter already?"

"Yes. A couple of times."

"Guess the fact you're still walking says something." Willis lowered the gun, spat. "You sticking around this time?"

"Don't know."

Willis nodded. "I'm on my way to see Keira now. If I get the first inkling she ain't hunky-dory with your return, I'll expect you to leave."

"Fair enough."

For a moment, Alec thought Willis might say more.

He could tell the old man wanted to. And Alec would have let him. He knew Willis had felt betrayed ten years ago. Willis had accepted Alec into his family, had trusted him with his most prized possession: Keira. Alec's defection had hurt them both.

Instead, Willis turned and headed back to his old red truck. The tacit dismissal stung.

Revving his engine, Willis took off, spinning up rocks and leaving Alec in a cloud of dust and bitter memories.

Keira pulled up at the Lucky Nugget. The exterior, a façade of what appeared to be crumbling rock and rotten timber, was designed to look like an old mine entrance.

She ducked inside, nodding to Lacy's employees. The Nugget had a snack bar and store, but most of the attraction was an open-air maze of water chutes.

Starting at seven dollars, you could sluice through a giant bucket of sand and dirt, searching for gemstones. If you were lucky enough to find a large stone—and each bucket had a money-back guarantee—the Lucky Nugget could cut and mount the stone in its full-service jewelry store. For a price.

For the more adventurous—and wealthier—clients, there was Lacy's newest shtick, a fifty-dollar "mother lode" bucket. Ten gallons of dirt from a gold mine.

Large overhead boards gave instructions on how to sluice the sand—a handful at a time—through screened sieves. The boards also described the typical "finds." Amethysts, quartz, ruby, tigereye, and gold nuggets. The fact that few of the stones were native to the area didn't faze most buyers.

Just inside, Lacy held court with a Boy Scout troop. The scouts were most likely camping at nearby Culverleaf Park, and Lacy, ever the salesman, was repeating the tale of the Lost Confederate Gold—a local legend dating back to the Civil War.

Some historians had argued that the tale was completely unfounded, based on a similar Civil War tale.

Others embraced the notion of hidden treasure as gospel. Keira had grown up listening to her grandfather talk about the gold; knew Willis and *his* grandfather had searched for it when Willis was a small child. She'd heard the tale a hundred times.

But Lacy had the storytelling down to an art, embellishing it with dialogue, sound effects, and facial grimaces.

The Scouts listened, wide-eyed, as Lacy pointed to a big map on the wall and talked about Union soldiers advancing on a Georgia stronghold, and how a handful of loyal Confederate guards had taken off with the chest containing the Confederacy's treasure.

"Didn't want those damn Yankees getting their grubby mitts on their gold."

"Damn Yankees," the boys echoed.

Lacy coughed. "For years folks assumed it was buried in Georgia, till they found a letter one of the soldiers had written his mama. Told her he'd buried the gold in Arkansas, along with the body of a soldier who'd lost both hands protecting the treasure."

Lacy tapped a spot on the map. "They found a grave, here. The skeleton was wrapped in a tattered Confederate flag and both its hands were gone. Severed at the wrists."

Keira noticed the spot was suspiciously close to the Scouts' campground.

Lacy caught her frown, ignored it. "The treasure's never been found. Some say the ghost of that Rebel soldier still roams these hills, guarding the gold."

"I bet he's looking for his lost hands," one boy yelled.

"I don't know." Lacy scratched his chin. "You may be right. Why don't we ask Keira, here. Her grandfather has spent over seventy years looking for the gold."

Fifteen heads turned toward where she stood.

"Show 'em your necklace," Lacy urged.

Keira scowled, not wanting to be drawn in. But it was too late. Not wanting to disappoint the kids, she tugged the necklace free of her shirt. A large gold coin dangled from the chain.

"The treasure!" one boy whispered.

"I'm not sure it's part of the actual Confederate gold," Keira admitted. "But my grandfather claims he found it while out mining."

The coin, so worn the date was illegible, was probably not part of the treasure. She suspected Willis had made up the story to amuse her. And to humor him, she'd never debated it.

Most locals dismissed the story as myth—a myth the town fathers had learned to perpetuate in order to attract tourists—but Keira knew Willis still searched regularly for the gold. Her grandfather didn't believe the treasure was mythical.

She waited as Lacy sold fifteen miniature copies of the map and directed the boys toward the water chutes.

"Thanks for coming," Lacy said, motioning toward the jewelry shop. "Bet I've lost hundreds of dollars in sales."

She doubted that, since his only customers were the

Scouts. First thing Keira did was check the fuse box outside. Sure enough, a breaker was thrown.

"I swear, I checked it," Lacy grumbled. "Sorry to call you out on something stupid, but seeing as me and your grandpa are practically partners . . ."

That was Lacy's way of avoiding a charge for a service call. *Partners.*

She shook her head. Keira knew her grandfather collected rocks and crystals for Lacy's attraction when he was out looking for his gold. But she'd bet Willis's real partnership with Lacy stemmed more from the moonshine Lacy peddled after hours from the back room.

When Keira finally returned to her apartment, it was late afternoon. She was surprised to find her grandfather waiting. She hugged him.

"My, my," Willis said. "Maybe I need to stop by more often. Not every day an old coot has a pretty gal throw herself all over him."

"Stay for lunch?"

"Sure."

Keira made sandwiches while her grandfather complained good-naturedly about his garden. "Cutworms got half my tomato plants. Green beans are spotty, but squash will be plentiful."

Willis laughed when he heard about her visit to the Lucky Nugget. "I told him not to call you unless it was a real emergency."

"If Lacy thinks he's losing a ten-dollar sale, that's an emergency."

Willis shook his head, then sat at the dining room table, relating the details of his last doctor visit while

Keira poured iced tea. "Doc says I'm healthy as a damn horse."

"That's good to hear," she said. Willis Morgan was eighty-four, with the fortitude of a man half his age.

As they ate, he asked about her work in Hot Springs. Then he got to the real reason for his unannounced visit.

"I hear Alec Dempsey's back in town. How's that sitting with you?"

Keira gathered their plates and ducked into the kitchen to avoid her grandfather's direct gaze.

"It's okay," she kept talking. "He e-mailed me about a month ago. At first I didn't want to respond—but then I realized it was silly to hold a grudge this long."

"Ain't nothing wrong with a good grudge," Willis observed. "Or a swift kick in the keester."

She sighed. "It's been ten years, Gramps. I've gotten over it."

Willis shook his head. "Still wasn't right. Hope you at least told him off."

"I did." Keira snagged a bag of Oreos, hoping to distract Willis with his favorite cookie.

At the sight of the familiar cellophane wrapper, Willis grinned. He opened the bag, then took a cookie and twisted it apart before popping the half with all the creamy white filling into his mouth. "You'll tell me if he bothers you any?"

She smiled. Willis had been playing white knight since her parents died. While she had no recollection of them, she had lots of wonderful memories of life with her grandfather. Which made the thought of Ian Griggs's threat to harm him all the more upsetting. She would do anything to assure Willis's safety.

"I'm serious, gal. Say the word, and he's gone."

Willis popped the other half of the cookie into his mouth, then drew a single finger across his neck while making a strangled noise. "Lots of bottomless pits on Fire Mountain. His body would never be found."

Keira nodded. If Alec let anything happen to Willis, that's exactly what she'd do.

Willis finished his tea and stood. "I've got a business meeting with Lacy."

She knew he meant *moonshine* business. "You and Lacy are being careful, right? No selling to strangers."

Willis looked offended. "You forget who you're talking to. I invented careful." He pointed to his nose. "Besides, I can smell a revenue agent a mile away."

Halfway out the door, he turned. "Almost forgot."

He reached in his pocket and withdrew a small, battered pewter flask. "Brought you a little draeberry wine. Best batch yet." With a wink, he disappeared.

Shaking her head, Keira uncapped the flask and sniffed. *Draeberry wine* was yet another code name her grandfather had cooked up for white lightning. No such thing as draeberries, but most outsiders didn't know that.

She blinked and refastened the cap. The Morgan family had been making the mellowest 'shine in the state for over two centuries. The family recipe was closely guarded, handed down from father to son.

Keira had never been interested in operating a still, but maybe she needed to rethink that. It was sad to think that the secret recipe for Morgan Moonshine would die with her grandfather.

Keira put their glasses in the dishwasher. When she turned around, Alec stood in her dining room. She squelched a scream. He'd no doubt climbed in through her bedroom window. Again.

"Didn't your mama teach you to knock?" she asked.

"I knocked on the window. You were busy."

Which obviously hadn't stopped him from coming in. "How long have you been in there?"

"Long enough to know I better watch my step around your grandfather." Alec drew a finger across his throat.

"Willis would probably prefer to fill you full of buckshot."

"And dump my body in a bottomless pit."

Keira narrowed her eyes. "Guess your mama didn't teach you it's not polite to eavesdrop, either?"

Alec chuckled, walked over to the flask on the counter. He held it out in a "may I?" gesture.

She retrieved a shot glass.

Alec poured a small amount of the clear liquor in the glass. He sniffed it, then belted it back.

Grimacing, he shook his head. "Damn! Willis hasn't lost his touch."

He resealed the flask, savoring the warmth in his stomach. Willis Morgan had developed moonshine into a liquid art.

Since joining ATF, Alec had specialized in weapons smuggling and rarely had dealings with the division that oversaw untaxed liquor. He had already made up his mind before returning to overlook the moonshine operations going on in the Freedom area.

The big-time operators, the ones that produced thousands of gallons of illegal whiskey, were located much farther south, and were well organized. The local producers, like Willis Morgan and his cronies, had slowly dwindled in number and were relatively harmless.

Demand was low, nothing like fourteen years ago when Alec and his buddies made gas and party money by running moonshine from county to county one night a week. They had fast cars, could drive the back roads blindfolded . . . and at sixteen, they were minors. Not that any of them got caught.

He handed the shot glass back to Keira. "Is this a good time to talk?"

"As good as any." After visiting with Willis she was eager to hear Alec's plans for protection.

He helped himself to a beer from the refrigerator, held one out to her. She shook her head.

"There's two things we've got to settle," Alec started. "One is my working for you. It solidifies my staying. You'll need to add me to the payroll so it appears legit, but the Bureau will reimburse you. And you'll need to fabricate some jobs for me to work. *Alone.* Can't promise how much help I'll be, but I'll pitch in where I can."

"I wouldn't expect you to do any electrical work, Alec. Your job is to watch Griggs. Make sure he gets nowhere near Willis."

He grunted. "Afraid I'm rusty? I've kept up."

"Actually I'd be more concerned for the safety of the others working with you. I take my men's safety seriously."

"Ouch." He put a hand to his heart.

She ignored him. "So that's one thing. What's the other?"

"Us. I was serious about pretending to rekindle our relationship."

"Alec—"

"Especially after the incident at the bowling alley."

While Alec couldn't directly attribute the incident to Ian Griggs, he felt it was more than a prank. Someone had gone to the trouble of stealing the doll and mutilating it before returning it.

Alec had done a little checking, knew about Keira's problems with the Barry brothers. It hadn't been hard. Everyone in town knew about the fierce rivalry between Barry Brothers Electric and Morgan Electrical Contracting. Alec hadn't liked some of the stories he'd heard.

And while he hadn't eliminated the Barrys as suspects, it wasn't their style to skulk around in dark alleys. They were verbal Neanderthals, preferring face-to-face insults. The Barrys got their thrill in the moment. They'd want to deliver the doll, watch her face.

"In fact," Alec continued, "the sooner word spreads we're involved, the better."

She straightened at the word. *Involved.* "Isn't there another way?"

"None as instantly convincing. My presence won't raise any eyebrows if everyone thinks we're knee deep in an affair. It may also make Griggs think twice about coming near you when he returns."

"It's not me I'm worried about." She touched the pewter flask Willis left. "How convincing do we have to be?"

"In public? One hundred percent. We've got almost two weeks before Griggs arrives. We'll start off gradually." Alec moved closer. "In fact, since you were the injured party, most people would expect you to be more aloof—to hold back while I try to make up for lost time. To prove myself."

Keira stared into his dark eyes. It took a moment to recall that Alec was talking about their cover. Their lie.

She shrugged, looked away before he saw her confusion. "Whatever."

He reached out, touched her arm. "I don't think you fully understand. You have to act like you really want it, Keira. That you want *me*. Which means cooling it with Reggie Reeves."

Alec had watched her kiss Reggie the night before. Hadn't liked it.

Keira stepped back, a ready rebuttal on her lips.

Her phone rang. Alec stepped aside as she stalked over and grabbed it.

"Hello!" she snapped.

"Keira? It's Scarlet. Uh, you haven't by chance seen Alec, have you? I know he lives next door. We have a date tonight, and I'm afraid my sitter's running a little late."

Keira slid her eyes sideways, toward Alec. A date? "What time do you want him there?"

"Seven will be fine."

Keira hung up, crossed her arms. "Scarlet's changed your *date* to seven."

Alec started swearing. "It's not a date. She asked me to come over and install a ceiling fan."

Keira was unmoved. "Must be a bedroom fan. She's getting a sitter."

"It was hard to say no without blowing my cover as an electrician. Listen—"

She cut him off, reminding herself Alec was there to do a job. In the bigger scheme of things maybe it didn't really matter whether he feigned an affair with Keira. Or Scarlet.

Who was she kidding . . . of course it mattered.

"No, you listen. I suggest you get your story straight with Scarlet. Make sure she knows you're *taken*."

Alec threw a mock salute. "And ditto you, with Reggie."

Keira was out of her apartment before dawn on Monday morning, which wasn't unusual. The fact that she'd been up most of the night before was.

Typically a heavy sleeper, she'd tossed and turned, stewing. More than once she caught herself listening for sounds from Alec's apartment, wondering how late he'd stayed at Scarlet's.

She told herself she was only upset because it was Scarlet. There had never been any love lost between the two women.

Scarlet had been Freedom's self-appointed prima donna and everyone's rival in school. She'd been captain of the cheerleading squad, homecoming queen, and class president. She'd never had a pimple, never sweated, and probably never had cramps. And she looked down her nose at Keira because she worked in construction.

There were only two things Keira knew of that Scarlet had failed to achieve. She'd been furious when Franny showed up in sixth grade wearing the first bra.

She'd also never hooked Alec Dempsey, the star quarterback, the town's resident bad boy, and best-looking guy in high school. Oh, Scarlet had tried, but Alec had belonged to Keira, body and soul. Back when he had a soul, anyway.

If Keira had been smart, she would have let Scarlet have him back in high school.

By Monday evening, Keira felt like she'd moved mountains. Hard work had always been her panacea.

She'd have no problem sleeping that night. She stopped by the Burger Haven drive-through, taking supper home in a sack.

Shower, food, bed, she promised herself as she climbed out of the elevator. Halfway down the hall, she smelled the delicious aroma of cooking tomatoes. The heavenly scent almost overwhelmed her as she unlocked her apartment door.

Alec popped his head out of her kitchen. "Hard day at the office?" he quipped.

She started to yell at him, except her stomach held her tongue. "What's that?"

"Marinara. Homemade."

Alec reached down, grabbed the sack from her hand, and opened it. He extracted two fries, holding one out to her.

She opened her mouth. The lukewarm french fry tasted like old grease against the scent of Alec's marinara.

He stuck the other fry in his mouth, then dumped the sack in the garbage. "This will be ready by the time you're cleaned up."

She opened her mouth to protest. Damn it, they needed to establish some rules. She didn't want him waltzing in and out of her apartment like he owned the place.

Then she spotted another pan. Her resolve weakened. "Garlic bread?"

He nodded, turned on the broiler. "With cheese."

"Don't you dare eat it all before I'm out of the shower."

Alec laughed, shoving her toward the bedroom.

Five minutes later, Keira reappeared in shorts and a T-shirt. Her feet were bare, and she had a towel wrapped turban-style around her head.

Alec pointed to a chair, then brought over two plates loaded with steaming ziti, heavy with sauce and lots of freshly grated Parmesan.

Keira grabbed a piece of garlic bread. "I think this is the first time a meal's ever been cooked in this apartment."

"I'm not surprised. You can't cook. I had to go to the store for everything."

Keira took a bite of pasta and closed her eyes in pure bliss. Alec, on the other hand, was a phenomenal cook, thanks to an Italian mother who didn't want her only son marrying just to get a good meal. "I hope you made enough for leftovers."

Alec sipped his tea. He'd picked up a week's worth of groceries, most of which were in his apartment.

He asked about her day, then dished up a second helping of ziti. He stuck the last piece of garlic bread on the edge of her plate, watched her eat. Keira didn't have to watch calories, in fact she needed carbs to keep up with the demands of her job.

She insisted on cleaning up, a task Alec willingly ceded to her.

"I hate to eat and run, but I'm expecting a phone call," he said.

"Scarlet?" Keira regretted the words immediately. Alec seemed to find them amusing.

"My boss. Feel better?"

"No. I mean, it's none of my business."

"Sure it is. Just like it's my business to know that you're planning to go climbing with Reggie this weekend."

"Look—"

"Cancel it," he said. His cell phone rang. "Later, babe," he mouthed, and left.

*   *   *

What Alec had neglected to tell Keira was how he'd found out about her plans with Reggie.

Alec had reported to her office first thing that morning and filled out a stack of new employee papers. Martha, one of Keira's assistants, had explained payroll, health insurance, and the vacation/sick leave policy.

Alec then loaded a few supplies from inventory, careful to take common items that were plentiful. He'd sneak them back in later, after hours.

Reggie had pulled in just as he was leaving. Alec met the other man's stare. Returned it.

The animosity between them was immediate. Tangible. And boiled down to one issue: Keira. Reggie obviously had the hots for her and perceived Alec as a threat. Or at least that's the perception Alec wanted to perpetuate.

"Heard you used to work here." Reggie spoke first. "Hope you don't expect special treatment."

"Keira and I go way back," Alec replied. "Guess you could say I've got seniority."

"Well, we work on the merit system here. Skill beats familiarity. And old age."

"But I've got the home field advantage," Alec countered. "And I intend to use it."

"I didn't get the impression you had any advantage. In fact, just this morning Keira asked me to go climbing with her next weekend. Ought to be . . . fun." With that, Reggie strode off.

Alec had wanted to deck the man. Instead, he'd left, driven around until his temper cooled. Reggie and Scarlet were both problems that had to be nipped in the bud, to avoid interfering with Alec's cover. Period.

He tried calling Miles Ostman, eager to hear if Griggs's parole hearing had taken place as scheduled.

The parole board reminded Ian Griggs of fish. *In a barrel.*

He sat before them, back straight against the battered wooden chair, and tried not to appear too confident.

"You gotta look repentant, but not pious," his cell-mate had coached. *"And don't tell them you've found the Almighty and been saved. They hear that shit all the time."*

Ian cleared his throat. "Well, sir, one of the first things I hope to do when I get out, is to find my pa."

"Find him where?" The man flipped through a file, frowned. "Says here your father abandoned his family when you were in high school. After your mother filed abuse charges."

Which time? "He wasn't a nice man," Ian agreed. Life with Farley Griggs made time in prison seem like Club Med. "But he sent me a letter recently. Apologized. Said I'm all the family he's got left. Said he'll come to Freedom and make things right." Ian looked directedly at the man. "Guess I owe him a chance to prove he's changed. We all deserve second chances. Right?"

Two of the board members nodded slightly, which told Ian that his lie had seemed sincere. Of course, with his connections, he could tell them all to kiss his ass and he'd still get out. Lady Luck was on his side.

To keep from grinning, he stuck his hand in his pocket and fingered his good luck token. A shank of red hair . . .

* * *

Alec was in one of the vacant buildings that stood directly behind the halfway house Ian Griggs would soon call home.

Miles Ostman had located the owner of one of the buildings, a lawyer in Little Rock, and arranged a short-term lease. Alec would have free access to the building under the guise of rewiring it.

He hoped to keep his presence concealed. No sense calling attention to himself. The overgrown bushes surrounding the property would help.

He glanced out the second-story window, peering through the wide-spaced boards. From there, he had a perfect view of the halfway house.

He noted the windows, the entrances, the alley. The house was fenced with a small parking lot on one side. Using binoculars, Alec copied down license tag numbers.

According to Ostman's sources, Griggs would be assigned the first-floor corner room. Alec stared at the room. With the blinds up, he could easily see in the window. But what were the chances that Griggs would leave the blinds up?

Alec rubbed his chin. Griggs wasn't stupid. He'd know Big Brother would be watching. And Alec would bet that Joseph Ciccone would be sniffing around, too, but from a distance. The mob would have as tough a time as the FBI planting someone in Freedom.

And God knew who else would climb out of the woodwork once news of Griggs's release spread. The press. The amateur fortune hunters. The terminally curious.

Ostman was right about one thing. The sooner

Griggs got his money and left, the better his chances of doing so unobserved. This job might wrap up sooner than Alec expected.

Returning to his car, he drove a short distance and pulled into a gas station. In spite of the fact it was an old-fashioned, full-service station, Alec climbed out and began pumping his own gas.

The owner, a man Alec didn't recognize, ambled over, offering an untrusting smile while wiping his brow with a dirty rag.

"Another scorcher of a day," the man said. "The only good thing about the afternoon thunderstorms is that they cool things off."

Alec nodded, topping his tank before shutting off the nozzle. He pulled out a credit card and followed the man into the dingy shop.

"Hold on. I gotta find that dang credit card machine." The man scratched his head, bewildered.

Alec tugged out his wallet. "Is cash easier?"

The man nodded. "My help usually takes care of this stuff. I try to avoid paperwork."

"Shorthanded?" Alec tried to sound casual. "Are you hiring?"

The man punched the sale into the ancient cash register. "Nah. Got a new guy starting soon."

Ian Griggs. Alec knew the station had a contract with the halfway house to provide "employment training." Which basically meant that the station owner made money by employing parolees.

"Men's room around back?" Alec asked.

The owner handed Alec his change and a key. "I close in five minutes."

After using the toilet, Alec bought a lukewarm soda from the vending machine and left.

The building was straightforward, with no rear exits. He noticed the station didn't have an alarm system. The office had a television and a pay phone.

Between the expanse of plate glass windows across the front and the garage doors that were kept open during business hours, Griggs would be easy to watch while working.

Alec circled the block, checking out the surrounding businesses. It would be dark soon. He would park and walk back to the station to check it out more thoroughly.

A sheriff's patrol car cut in behind him, lights flashing. Swearing, Alec pulled to the curb, shut off his car, and had his driver's license in hand when the deputy leaned in his window.

"Feel funny having a legitimate license?"

Alec recognized the man's voice.

"Carl Winters." Smiling, Alec climbed out, shook the deputy's hand.

He and Carl had graduated the same year. They had played football, cut every class they could. Both made occasional moonshine runs. But mostly they were forever in search of fake IDs. Beer had been the beverage of choice among seniors.

Alec pointed to the star on the deputy's uniform. "Pay much for that badge? Almost looks real."

Carl leaned an arm along the Jeep's roof. "Heard you were in town. Back for good or just visiting?"

"Haven't decided." The lie stuck in his throat. He had returned to Freedom for one reason, then he'd leave.

Alec changed the subject. "When did you come back?"

"Six, seven years ago." Carl shrugged. "I know. We couldn't wait to leave this town, swore we'd never return. But when I ran out of wild oats, I found, by comparison, Freedom wasn't so bad. And after my daughter was born, well, hands down, it's a great place to raise a family."

Alec nodded. That was one reason he'd known Keira would have wanted to return.

"Everyone comes back sooner or later," Carl continued. "And they're all amazed by how much Freedom's changed. How much it's stayed the same. I figured it was just a matter of time before you showed up."

Before Alec could deny it, the two-way radio in Carl's patrol car squawked. "Unit seven, we got a one-eleven at the county park."

Carl responded to the call then turned back. "A one-eleven's a loud party. Damn high school kids."

"Are they as bad as we were?"

"Hell no. Which makes my job easier." Carl moved to his car.

"My wife and I own the old Hecklemeyer place on Elm. Stop by one night. We can catch up."

Alec watched Carl make a U-turn, tires squealing slightly.

For a moment, Alec remembered racing on Saturday nights, out on Highway 87. Nobody could beat Carl, though Alec had tried plenty of times. The men were friends. Comrades. Both bad news. They had joked about how the final race would be graduation night. The last one out of Freedom lost.

So who'd won?

Chapter Six

The following day, word of Ian Griggs's parole hearing made the news.

Most people in Freedom were outraged to learn that the chances of his returning to town were quite favorable. The local radio station urged listeners to write their congressmen in protest.

Alec reminded Keira to act surprised, not to give away the fact she had advance knowledge.

She was in her truck, on the way back from Hot Springs, when Willis reached her on her cell phone. Her grandfather was furious. "Dag-nab judges. What the hell are they thinking with? Their asses? Why, I got a mind to—"

"Settle down, Gramps. I know you're upset. I'm upset, too."

Even though she'd already known, it still unsettled her to hear it on the morning news. Besides covering the latest developments in Griggs's case, the station did the obligatory "look back" at the crime. The film clips made her ill.

Two reporters who zeroed in on the story about the assault charges being dropped had already tried reaching Keira for her "reaction." The buzzards were circling.

"Look," she said to her grandfather, "I'll stop by and visit. We'll talk."

"You do that. Just don't think you'll change my mind."

Keira hung up. She had no expectation of talking Willis out of his anger. He was entitled. So was she.

The best she could hope for was that Willis would vent the worst of his ire on her, then feel guilty. Which she could use as leverage to make him promise to steer clear of Ian Griggs.

Keeping her grandfather out of harm's way was her only concern.

Twenty minutes later Keira pulled into Willis's drive.

She climbed out of her truck, a familiar sense of ease settling over her as she entered her grandfather's cabin. *Home.*

The main room was over a hundred years old and was part of the old stone cabin erected by her ancestors after fire destroyed the original log structure.

Her grandfather claimed the fire started when a still exploded. No doubt the highly flammable moonshine was great fuel.

She found Willis around back, hoeing his garden. Grabbing another hoe, she moved in beside him as he attacked the soil with harsh chops. Sand and dirt gritted against steel as they worked in silent unison. Within minutes, Keira was perspiring.

Finally, he spoke. "Those lying good-for-nothings! They said he'd serve his full sentence."

"I know, Gramps."

"Back in the good old days, we would have dealt with it ourselves. Permanent rehabilitation. In a facility six feet under."

Keira sighed. "Do you think I like any of it?"

Once again, Willis's hoe danced furiously in the dirt. He didn't stop until he reached the end of the row.

Then he dropped the tool and mopped his brow with a blue paisley bandanna. "It ain't right he's being set free after what he did to you."

"I agree. But you know the one thing that keeps me going?"

Willis didn't respond.

"You told me a long time ago life wasn't fair, but we had to keep moving forward anyway." Keira raised her chin. "Those words kept me afloat through some tough times. And they'll keep me going now."

She knew by the slight slump of his shoulders that Willis had gotten over the worst of it. For the time being.

Once again, the thought that Ian Griggs wanted to harm her grandfather nearly overwhelmed her. As much as she resented the emotional intrusion of Alec's return, she was glad he'd be keeping tabs on Griggs.

"Hand me that watering can," Willis grumbled. "And lower your hackles."

By the time they finished tending his garden, Willis's mood was improved enough he thought he could nap.

Keira bid him good-bye, but didn't go far, not ready to leave the peace and quiet that was Fire Mountain.

Instead, she went just down the road, not far from her grandfather's place, where she was building a log cabin on the mountain's small lake. It was the same spot her parents had planned to build.

The view there was stunning. When the sun sank low on the western horizon, it set the lake on fire. Possibly the reason her forefathers had named it *Fire Mountain*?

She shut off her truck and eyed the site. Earlier in the spring, she'd hired a crew to raise the walls and complete the roof, but there was still plenty of finish work to be done inside and out.

Initially, she had planned to work on the cabin at her own pace, had no set deadlines for completion. But suddenly she had the urge to see it finished.

To be closer to Willis.

Alec pulled in behind her truck.

He'd gone by Keira's office and learned from Martha where he could find her. While he was at the office, a reporter phoned. He got the impression it wasn't the first such call. Martha's protectiveness didn't surprise him. Keira's employees were fiercely loyal.

Alec stared at the log cabin, mildly surprised. Though only the walls and roof were up, he knew exactly what the finished structure would look like. His eyes followed the soaring roofline.

Yeah, she'd changed a few things, but he recognized the plan. *Their dream cabin.*

He and Keira had drawn it together. In fact, he still had some of the rough sketches. Had always planned to build the cabin himself, but never found the right piece of land.

She had picked an ideal spot. The cabin fit perfectly with its surroundings. Forest encircled three sides of the house, but she had a pretty good clearing for lawn.

He felt a momentary pang of envy as he climbed out of his car. Keira was building a future, putting down roots with the quiet tenacity of a woman who'd always known exactly what she wanted. Even at eighteen, she'd had a single-minded determination few acquired in a lifetime. Hadn't that been one of the things he'd loved most about her?

He went inside, picking his way around the power tools and scrap lumber strewn on the floor. Without a breeze, the house was sweltering. The mercury had peaked at ninety-seven that afternoon.

He looked out the back door. The view rivaled a fantasy. Perched on a slight knoll, the cabin overlooked the lake. It was private, secluded, and surrounded by Morgan land.

For a second, Alec envisioned children playing in the yard, a young boy running up with a fish on a line. A young girl on a swing set.

He shook his head, banished the thought. "Keira!" He called out, sharper than intended.

When she didn't respond, he grew anxious, yelled out again.

Uneasiness pricked his spine. Dammit, where was she and why wasn't she answering? He drew his gun and stepped onto the unfinished deck.

He spotted a neat pile of clothes on the bank just as her head surfaced thirty feet out. Holstering his gun, he jumped off the deck and ambled down to the water's edge. Only then did he realize how fast his heart was pounding.

He stopped at the clothes, grabbed them. "Aren't you a little old to be skinny-dipping?"

Keira trod water, eyeing him. He had one knee straight, one relaxed, a hand on his hip. A deceptively sexy stance.

"Aren't you a little old to be stealing a girl's clothes?"

"Guess you never outgrow some things."

"Ditto. Now drop my clothes and go back where you came from."

Alec shook his head. "Never outgrew that part, either."

Keira ducked underwater, smoothed back her hair. His words triggered memories of being seventeen and skinny-dipping in this same lake. Alec would steal her clothes back then, too, refusing to relinquish them. Or he'd strip down himself and come in after her. Either way they always ended up making love.

For a moment she wished he'd come in, wished she could turn back time, recapture the sweetness. Without the heartbreak.

She ducked under again. Despite the heat, the spring-fed water was a little chilly for staying in one place.

"Drop 'em, Alec. I'm freezing."

To her surprise, Alec dropped her clothes. But he didn't step away. He cocked his index finger, signaling *come here*. Silently daring her.

She'd show him.

Swimming toward shore, she climbed out of the lake wearing a light yellow, one-piece strapless. Alec's gaze dropped, his grin widening as he held out a towel.

She looked down at her suit. Her nipples were contracted, poking through the damp fabric like little torpedoes. She snatched the towel and wrapped it around her.

"It's the cold water," she gritted.

"Hey, I didn't say a thing."

He didn't need to. His wolfish grin said it all. Grabbing her clothes, Keira headed back toward the cabin.

Alec followed, only to find himself banished while she dressed.

"This is going to be a great place," he told her, when she let him enter.

Keira started gathering up tools, putting them away quickly, in a hurry to leave. She didn't like Alec being there, in the house. Didn't want a memory of him to take hold to haunt her later, when he was gone. This was a part of her life untainted by him, and she wanted to keep it that way.

Stowing her gear in quick, efficient movements, she headed for the front door.

"When it's done it'll be nice," she agreed as she made her way to her truck.

"I recognize the floor plan."

Keira nearly stumbled. "Don't flatter yourself. It's not the same one." She had purposely changed several elements so it wouldn't look exactly like the house they'd planned together.

Alec followed her, carrying a toolbox. He swung it into the pickup's bed and secured it.

"You changed the exterior a bit," he said. "I like the porch and double doors. But the rest? It's everything we planned. I remember we didn't want a cook top on the kitchen island."

The better to make love on it, Keira recalled.

"We wanted the fireplace to take up most of one wall," he continued.

To keep them warm while they made love on cold winter nights.

"And we wanted a balcony off the master bedroom—"

To make love under the stars. She cut him off. "Coincidence, Alec. There's no sauna, no whirlpool on the patio."

His shrug said they'd be easy to add. "The plan turned out pretty decent considering we planned the entire thing around making love."

She slammed the tailgate. Hard. "Figures you'd think that. That *was* all you ever thought about."

Alec caught her arm, tugged her close. "Hey, you were the one who insisted we have an island in the kitchen. Because you were short. Or were you planning to become a gourmet cook?"

He was correct, but she'd die before admitting it. If making love was all Alec thought about back then, she was equally guilty.

She sighed, stepped away. "Did you come here for a reason? Or just to annoy me?"

He lowered his voice. "I was worried. I was at the office when a reporter called. Martha said you've been dodging calls from the press all day."

"They'll lose interest as soon as a bigger story breaks."

Alec didn't agree, but kept quiet. Once the press confirmed Griggs was returning to Freedom, they'd close in. "Are you headed back to your apartment?"

She looked at him, wanted to tell him to mind his own business. Except that sounded childish. "I've got to stop by the office first."

He moved toward his car. "I'll head to your place and start heating the ziti."

Her place? She frowned. They needed to have a talk about the way he pranced in and out of her apartment. She didn't like it, and would tell him so.

Right after they ate.

Keira purposely worked late, in Hot Springs, the next few days, avoiding the reaction and disbelief sweeping through Freedom as word of Griggs's upcoming return spread.

But no matter how late she worked, Alec was at her apartment when she got there. And he played dirty.

Tuesday, he used two-inch-thick pork chops, stuffed with apples, raisins, and bread crumbs, against her. Wednesday, he had fettucine Alfredo with grilled chicken breasts and fresh asparagus. It felt like she gained five pounds overnight.

By Thursday, Keira was ready to take her grandfather up on his offer to run Alec out of town. Too much of a good thing could be habit-forming. And Alec was a habit she couldn't afford to acquire.

Besides, Thursday was a special day—a sacred day.

Keira stopped by Franny's salon at four, just as it was closing. The place was deserted. "Mind if I clean up?"

"Avoiding Alec?" Franny asked.

She nodded.

"Go upstairs and shower, if you like," Franny said.

"No time. I want to get out there before it rains." Storms were predicted for later that evening.

Keira ducked into the rest room. When she came out, Franny was carrying a stack of magazines to the front reception counter.

"Don't look now, but Alec just rode by." Franny dropped the magazines and pressed her nose against the plate glass window, peering outside. "Yep, he spotted your truck. And he's doing a U-turn."

Keira started swearing. "Not today. Any day but today."

Franny nodded toward the back door. "Take my car. Keys are in it. How much of a head start do you need?"

"Thirty minutes." Keira checked her watch. She still had to stop by the florist.

Franny waved her off. "I'll try and buy you forty. Go."

*   *   *

When Alec walked in, he found Franny singing along with the radio as she swept around one of the chairs. Her hair was deep red, with a few strands of the previous week's blond mixed in.

Franny had been changing her look weekly for as long as Alec could remember. And no matter what the color, what the style, she looked good.

She also dressed to kill. She had an hourglass figure and a wardrobe that fringed on theatrical, but always showcased her looks and revealed a mile of A-1, prime cleavage.

Unable to help himself, he smiled.

She smiled back, winked saucily. "Hello, handsome." Franny had also written the book on flirting.

"Hello yourself. The red looks hot."

Franny curtsied at the compliment. "What brings you here? Or should I guess?" She rolled her eyes toward the stairs leading to her apartment.

Alec had spotted Keira's truck out front, knew she was upstairs. Probably hiding. He'd wait her out.

He looked around, pretended interest. "Nice place." The salon was decorated in shiny chrome and bubble gum pink. "Barbie would feel right at home here. Maybe even Ken."

Franny giggled. "Darryl feels uncomfortable here, too. Says it's too froufrou. I'll tell you the same thing I tell him: Get over it."

Alec raised his hands. "Done."

"Good. Now tell me what you think of the rest of the downtown district?"

District? A big word for a small town. He hesitated.

"It's changed." From what Alec had seen so far, much of the town had transformed.

"For the better?"

He nodded. "When did all the antique shops open?"

"Carrie Devlin, the mayor's wife, saw an article on a small town in Florida that transformed itself by adopting a specialty. She spearheaded a campaign and got the city to apply for federal grant money for revitalization, sent out notices to several large antique dealers, and *voilà!* A few years ago *Southern Style* magazine listed Freedom as one of the top ten antique spots in the country. Tourists have poured in."

Franny set the broom aside and patted the styling chair. "But enough about Freedom. Let's talk about you. Have a seat, big boy."

Alec recognized a command when he heard one. As soon as he sat, Franny draped a flowered cape over him, fastening it at the neck. Then she lowered the pneumatic chair.

"So you're divorced," she began.

"Eight years."

"Kids?"

"None."

"Pets?"

"None."

"Steady girlfriend?"

Alec smiled. "None. Do I pass?"

"With flying colors. Now relax. I've been dying to get my hands on this hair of yours," Franny purred. She ran her fingers through his thick, black locks, digging into his scalp. "You don't mind, do you?"

Mind? Franny's fingers felt divine as she skillfully

massaged his head. "If I was a dog, my leg would be twitching."

Franny laughed, cracked her knuckles. "This is your lucky day. I feel like showing off. Tip your head forward."

Alec obediently dropped his chin to his chest and closed his eyes as Franny's fingers dug rhythmically into his neck, forcing the tense muscles to liquefy. He groaned in near ecstasy.

"Lower," he begged. "Please."

Just before he slid bonelessly to the floor, Franny grasped his chin and brought his neck straight back, popping it. His joints creaked in satisfaction as tension released.

"Christ!" he said, moving his neck from side to side. "Where'd you learn that?"

"Trade secret. And you haven't seen anything yet."

She leaned forward, simultaneously tugging Alec back. She wedged his head squarely between her breasts as she started massaging the muscles on the front of his neck, just below his jaw.

His ears thought they'd died and gone to *ta-ta* heaven.

Franny tugged upward, straightening his neck again. More joints creaked. He hissed in gratitude.

"Will Keira be much longer?" he asked.

"Why? You thinking about leaving? I'm just getting warmed up. Besides, you're getting a haircut, whether you want one or not." Franny dug her hands into his shoulder muscles. "And it's bad form to argue with the salon owner."

Alec groaned again as Franny's hands moved down to the spot where his neck met his shoulders. Years of tension and stress seemed to melt beneath her agile hands.

"We need to talk anyway." Franny continued rubbing and stroking. "About Keira."

He sat forward, alert. "What about her?"

Franny yanked him back, her fingers clamping on to his ear. "You hurt her again, you'll be singing soprano. On crutches. With a broken nose."

Most men might have looked at Franny and laughed at the threat. Alec knew better.

"Yes, ma'am."

"The same applies if you let Ian Griggs get anywhere near her grandfather."

"Okay."

Franny released his ear. "Now that that's out of the way, let's get down to business." She tugged his neck back between her boobs again and shimmied slightly, adjusting. "Loosen up. They don't bite. And believe it or not, it keeps the muscles warm."

Sometimes the better part of valor was surrender. Alec closed his eyes and leaned back.

He was unabashedly a breast man. And while he wasn't physically attracted to Franny—Keira was the only woman his libido was interested in—he could still appreciate the fact that Franny was a gorgeous, well-endowed woman.

"Of course, you breathe a word of this to anyone, and I'll stab you with my scissors," Franny said. "Then I'll dump your body in a bottomless pit."

"Funny. There's a lot of that going around."

Keira stared at the smooth, gray granite headstone. Willis Morgan Jr. and Mary Ellen Morgan. Her mother's date of birth was three years later than her father's, but the dates of death were identical.

Twenty-five years ago to the day, her parents had been killed when their small sightseeing plane crashed over Niagara Falls. It had been her parents' fifth wedding anniversary, and they were celebrating with a honeymoon they hadn't been able to afford when they first married.

Mary Ellen had just learned she was pregnant again and knew with a baby on the way it would be a while before she and her husband could get away.

Kneeling, Keira arranged the roses she'd brought. Yellow. Two dozen, specially ordered. Her grandfather claimed they were her mother's favorite.

A pot of white mums sat beside her roses. She glanced at a nearby headstone, seeing an identical pot of mums on her grandmother's grave. Her grandfather had no doubt been up earlier.

She heard a noise and stopped, but the sound didn't recur. She shrugged, brought a fragrant yellow bud to her nose.

This part of the cemetery was enclosed by an ancient wrought-iron fence that marked the Morgan family section. It was oddly peaceful there.

For as long as she could remember, she had been coming here on the anniversary of her parents' death. When she was younger, she and Willis had come together, often packing a lunch and spending the day.

He'd tell her stories about her father as a young boy. They'd visit other tombstones, and Willis would relate stories he'd been told by his grandfather, that had been told to him by *his* grandfather.

But for once the tranquillity was imperfect. Seeing

the graves made her worry about Willis, what Griggs might do to him. An eye for an eye.

She looked at the far-flung scattering of headstones where generations of Morgans were laid to rest.

Not the first blade of grass was untrimmed, thanks to her grandfather, who felt like the county's maintenance was inadequate. At least for his kin.

Keira knew at Willis's passing, the task of maintaining the family plot would fall to her. And at her passing . . .

She dashed away a tear. For their losses. Past and future. Her grandfather frequently referred to the two of them as the last of the Mohicans. She would be the end of the line.

It was hard to believe that at one time she'd considered leaving it all behind to follow Alec.

Just as she'd always known she'd live and die on Fire Mountain, Alec had always known he'd leave Freedom. Keira knew he'd grown up listening to his mother bewail small-town life. As a young, single mother, she couldn't afford to leave. But as soon as Alec finished high school she'd packed up and taken off.

Keira could hardly blame her. Louise Dempsey couldn't find peace in Freedom. She'd been labeled a loose woman: first, for having a child out of wedlock; second, for rumors she was having a string of affairs with married men. In classic double-standard style, no one blamed the men.

After he graduated, Alec had moved to Hot Springs, returning every weekend to see Keira. She could remember how long the weeks felt back then. They couldn't afford long-distance telephone calls, so she lived for the weekend and spent every available minute with Alec, often sneaking out and meeting him again after her grandfather had gone to bed.

Keira knew Alec was counting the days until she could leave. They talked of it constantly. After she finished school, they were going to St. Louis, where an uncle of Alec's promised to get him on with the union. Keira, too.

The thought of leaving her grandfather, leaving Fire Mountain, nearly overwhelmed her. But she knew she couldn't live without Alec.

So she made her choice, made peace with leaving. She'd bid farewell to her parents' graves and talked to her grandfather—who was actually quite supportive.

She remembered thinking that once she and Alec were married and away, she would eventually convince him to return to Freedom, which made saying good-bye seem less final.

Of course, Alec never came back. So it had all been a moot point.

She shook her head. Maybe it was time to make peace with that past, too. *Bury it here and now. Forever.*

A breeze ruffled the warm air, stirring up more strange noises. The iron fence squeaked in protest of the approaching storm.

She bent to rearrange the roses one last time.

She sensed someone behind her. Startled, she turned. *No one was there.*

Straightening, she scanned the rest of the cemetery. The place was deserted. Yet it felt as if someone watched. Goose bumps skittered up her arms in spite of the heat.

The wind kicked up, peppering her with grit and sand.

She looked at the sky, heavy with rain clouds. Maybe the changing air pressure was what felt odd.

Running her fingers over the smooth headstone one last time, she stepped toward the gate, swung it open, then carefully closed it.

Since her ancestors had been among the first to settle in the area, the Morgan section of the cemetery was in the farthest corner, a pretty good walk back to the parking lot.

A small copse of woods bisected the back half of the cemetery. Nicknamed Deadman's Forest, the ancient thicket hid several pre–Civil War graves and an ancient, spooky, half-buried crypt.

Actually, the concrete-and-stone crypt hadn't been used in ages and had fallen into disrepair, making it even creepier. Rumors of rattling bones abounded. In high school it had been a favorite *I dare you* spot for boys to prove their manhood.

As she hurried past the woods, she once again had the sensation that she wasn't alone. Of being followed.

She heard a twig snap, felt the ground shake with a footfall.

She spun around. "Damn you, Alec!"

The words faded as she came face-to-face with Ian Griggs.

Franny had just finished cutting Alec's hair when Mabel sailed through the salon's front doors.

Winded, Mabel paused. "Keira here? Her truck's out front."

Franny mouthed the word "no" from behind Alec.

Mabel grimaced. "I saw her at the florist earlier. I thought maybe I could catch her."

Alec turned, pinned Franny with a frown. Immediately he realized he'd been bamboozled. "She's not upstairs?"

"She's got my car, so she'll be back."

"Did she go out to the cemetery?" Mabel interrupted.

Alec's gaze went to the calendar hanging on the wall as he remembered what today was.

"Is something wrong, Mabel?" Alec pressed.

"Well, I'm not sure. I talked to Fred a few minutes ago," the older woman said. "He's a county supervisor, you know. Anyway, he said one of the maintenance men had reported finding something weird at the graveyard this afternoon."

Alec stood, yanked off the cape. "What was found?"

"A fifth of Jack Daniel's, three shot glasses, and a pair of women's underwear. Perched on one of the Morgan headstones. But by the time Fred got there, they were gone. Sounds sorta sick to me."

Franny grabbed for Alec's arm. "Keira may still be out there."

But Alec was already at the door. "I'm on my way. Just do me a favor and call the sheriff's department. Have a deputy meet me there."

Chapter Seven

Five years in prison had not been kind to Ian Griggs. Harsh lines creased his face, and his nose was flattened, crooked, as if broken more than once.

She wanted to scream, but her throat felt paralyzed. She wanted to run, but her feet were locked in place. Like in an unending nightmare.

"Hello, Keira. Long time, no see."

With Herculean effort, she managed a single, micro-step backward, too afraid to turn her back on him, too afraid to blink.

She tried again to speak, but no sound came out.

"What's the matter? Cat got that snotty little tongue of yours?" Griggs laughed, then started coughing. "How 'bout a hug for old times sake?"

A trembling started deep within her psyche.

"What are you doing here?" Her brain skittered to make sense of his presence. According to Alec, Ian wasn't supposed to be released for another week.

"Why, I'm doing the same as you. Paying respect to my dearly departed kin. You remember my two brothers, don't you, Keira? They're buried in the pauper section. What's left of them anyway. Fire got most everything."

Griggs eased forward a step. "Don't suppose you've ever been to the pauper sites before, what with your family having its own section. No fancy headstones for my brothers. Just little brass plates with numbers: 167 and 168. Wanna see?"

Revulsion twisted Keira's stomach as she managed another step. Away. Thunder rumbled overhead as the wind gusted. "Stay back."

"My mama's over there, too." Ian wheezed, ignoring her request. "You know they wouldn't let me out when she was dying. Not even to go to her funeral. Too bad I didn't think to bring my mama any of those pretty yellow roses."

Her knees threatened to disintegrate at the realization he'd been watching her the whole time. Earlier, while at her parents' grave, she'd had a feeling someone was there.

She tried to rally. "You don't scare me."

"I don't?" Griggs smiled, eyes wide, feigning surprise.

He looked away, and when he turned back, the expression on his face was one of sheer hatred. "Guess I'll have to try a little harder."

Keira ducked sideways as he lunged. His fingers caught the sleeve of her shirt. Fabric ripped as she swung around, twisting free of his grip.

"Bitch!" he snarled.

She took off running at full speed, glancing over her shoulder often, afraid to turn her back completely on him. If he caught her . . . she knew what he'd do.

No. No. No.

The ground was slippery, the scent of recently mowed grass heavy. Nauseating.

She looked back again, tried to judge the distance, get her bearings. Make certain he wasn't gaining on her.

Pain erupted down her left side as she crashed into something solid. The blow knocked her backward, causing her to lose her footing.

Too late, she realized she'd run into the small crypt tucked into the edge of the woods.

She fell head over heels across the stone ledge, then stumbled down the moss-slickened stairs leading to the crypt's subterranean entrance. With a scream, she crashed against the rusted iron grating stretched across the door.

She struggled to her feet, her arm aching. Her leg, too. She glanced down at her torn pants, the bruised flesh, knew it was nothing compared to what she'd suffered the last time at Ian's hands.

Ian appeared at the top of the stairwell, blocking what little light remained in the face of the encroaching storm.

She heaved, wanting to vomit, afraid to take her eyes off him. "I said, stay back."

"Still bossy as hell." Griggs laughed and sat on the top step, effectively trapping her in the stairwell.

Fighting nausea, she tried to draw in oxygen. From behind her, from the crypt, the moldy smell of death permeated the fetid air. Something scurried under the pile of debris at one side.

"Probably just a couple of spiders," Ian called out. "We had 'em all the time in prison. Big ones. You ever been to prison, Keira?"

She eased away from the pile but couldn't quite manage to ignore it. She looked up at him, could barely see him in the darkness. *Keep him talking*, her mind ordered. "You know I haven't."

"Prison ain't so bad. Kinda like a big frat house. Problem is they let anyone in. Can't keep the riffraff out." Griggs casually picked at his ear. "First thing I did when I landed there was stab someone. Let 'em know who's boss."

Model prisoner. Good behavior.

"You bastard," she lashed out, sickened. "They should never have set you free. You should have rotted in that damn prison."

"I like it when a woman talks dirty. Means she really wants ya." Griggs coughed, looking away briefly as he clawed at the ground with one hand. "You know how they rape you in prison? They get broomsticks. The size of baseball bats. And guess where they stick 'em? It ain't pretty."

Her muscles tensed. A rustling noise again caught her attention. Something was definitely under the debris. She moved back, away. Felt the metal grate press into her spine.

"Come 'ere spider, spider, spider." Griggs laughed. "Oh, I'm sorry. I just remembered. You hate spiders."

Keira bit her lip, tasted blood. Some people feared snakes. Others heights. She had a spider phobia.

"You're awful quiet down there," Griggs tormented. "Want company?"

"No!"

"Ah, come on. Did you find a little present in your car the other night?"

Keira's mind reeled. A present? *Her doll.* When had it

been left in her car? Five, six days ago? "That was you? How did . . ."

"How did I what? Get to the bowling alley from prison? Demonic powers. The kind that lets me be any-where, anytime." He spat. "The kind of power you get when you sell your soul to the devil."

"You never had a soul," Keira shot back.

Griggs laughed again, the sound dark, fiendish. "You scared, Keira? Afraid I might fuck up your life like you fucked up mine?"

She fought for a shred of courage. "You damned well better let me go. Now."

"Go? I ain't touched you." He held up his hands. "Hell, I'm just sitting here visiting. Reminiscing about old times. You do remember where we left off, don't you?"

How could she ever forget?

"Scream, Keira." His command was low, eerie, seem-ing to originate from the crypt behind her. "Scream for me."

Those were the same words he'd used five years ago when he'd attacked her. Beaten her. Tried to rape her. Re-vulsion clawed through her veins.

"No!"

A crash of lightning burst across the sky, followed by a huge boom of thunder.

Griggs stood. "Yes. And when I'm through, I'll stuff your body in one of those old coffins. Maybe bury you alive. Or cremate you."

Frantic, Keira turned in circles, searching for an es-cape route. Behind her, the crypt's door was padlocked against vandals. She grabbed the metal bars, shook them uselessly, before turning back to where Griggs blocked the stairwell's entrance.

To her horror, he took a step forward.

She braced herself, drew her hands into fists. She'd charge him as he came down the stairs. If she could hit him hard enough and slam him against the steps, perhaps she could get a head start and escape. If not, she'd fight to the bitter end.

But Griggs had stopped, wasn't even looking her way.

"Gotta go for now, Keira. We'll talk later. You and me got a lot of catching up to do." He threw something down the stairwell at her. "Don't forget. I owe you one."

She flinched sideways. A large earthworm landed on her shoe.

"Get used to 'em," Griggs sneered. "That and maggots are all you got for company when you're dead."

Another flash of lightning erupted, slicing open the heavens and releasing a blinding rain. When the lightning faded, Griggs was gone.

Was it a trick?

Demonic powers? Did he wait for her at the top of the steps? The trees just beyond? Was he trifling with her, trying to lure her out in the open? Ready to attack?

I owe you one.

Oh, God . . . what if Griggs was on his way to see Willis? An eye for an eye.

The rain rapidly filled the stairwell, and with the rising water, the debris around her came alive, as rats and other vermin scurried toward the stairs to higher ground.

Keira screamed and dashed upward, felt her feet slip

on the wet stone. She cleared the steps and kept running blindly, through the woods. Faster now.

She ducked to avoid a limb. Her side ached with a cramp, but she didn't dare slow. She drew in air, fighting the urge to be sick.

Griggs could be anywhere. Waiting to grab her. To finish what he had started five years ago. Did he plan to get her first, then go after her grandfather?

A hand closed over her shoulder. Cowardice rose like bile in her throat. She screamed, threw a punch as she spun around.

Her fist connected with Alec's chest.

"Keira! It's me."

It took a moment for his voice to register. Another moment before she could stop struggling. She tried to talk, but only incoherent sounds came out.

Alec drew her close, shielding her as best he could from the rain. She was wild-eyed, hysterical, frightened.

"It's okay, babe. I got you." He kept his voice low, soothing, giving her a chance to catch her breath. "Nod if you're okay."

She nodded, straightening, noticed Alec had a gun.

"Ian Griggs," she wept. "Back there."

The rain came down in torrents now.

Alec caught her chin, forced her eyes to meet his. He noticed that her shirt was torn at the shoulder, her jeans ripped as well.

"Did he hurt you?"

She shook her head. "But . . . Willis. What . . . what if he's gone to get my grandfather now?"

Alec's guilt mushroomed. "Come on. We'll call from my car."

"Why didn't you tell me he was getting out early?" she accused, misreading his guilty expression. "I—"

He tugged her toward the parking lot. "I didn't know."

Keira stopped short. Then she spotted movement.

Alec saw it, too, and stepped in front of her.

A sheriff's deputy moved toward them, wearing a yellow rain slicker, flashlight in hand. The deputy had his gun drawn as well. Alec quickly tucked his gun at his back, not wanting to raise questions.

"You found her." Carl Winters had responded. "What happened? Miss Franny called, screaming for help."

"Ian Griggs accosted Keira," Alec said.

"Griggs? What the hell is he doing out already?" Carl turned to Keira, taking in her torn clothes. "You okay?"

She nodded.

"Where is he now?" Carl asked.

"I don't know," Keira said. "He took off. Toward the back."

A burst of lightning struck a nearby tree, splitting it. The awful *crack* made all three of them duck.

"Christ! This storm is getting worse," Carl said. "Let's get back to the station."

Ian Griggs watched Keira disappear into the rain. He knew someone had arrived; he'd watched headlights sweep into the parking lot minutes earlier. The timing had been perfect.

Did she think she'd been *saved*?

He laughed, which triggered a hacking, coughing fit. Stupid bitch. She'd been *spared*. By the grace of Ian.

If he'd wanted to hurt her, she'd have been hurt. If

he'd wanted her dead, she'd have been killed. Years ago. But where was the fun in that?

I had no intention of harming you . . . today.

Or tomorrow.

Or the next day.

Beyond that, I'm not making any promises.

Being locked up had taught him the art of prolonging terror. Stretching it to its limits just to see how far it would go.

He coughed again. Spat. Then took a swig off the bottle, stared at the shattered shot glasses. He picked up the pair of underwear, rubbed them on his face. Oh, Keira owed him. Big-time. But Ian wanted his payback in increments. On demand, with interest.

He closed his eyes, groping his crotch as he savored the fear he'd seen on her face. *I bet she even peed those fancy little underpants she's so fond of.*

The thought squeezed his groin, made his balls snap and release. He looked at his trousers, saw the growing wet spot as he lost control.

Sure, in the end she'd come around, tried to be brave. Nothing wrong with that. He preferred a struggle. In fact, it would make her ultimate fall all the sweeter.

And she'd die screaming his name . . .

Alec and Keira spent the next hour at the sheriff's department. Keira had reached Willis, who was at the Lucky Nugget, helping Lacy.

In the end, she didn't mention the incident at the cemetery, not wanting to alarm her grandfather. She'd have to tell him eventually, but not until she had a chance to talk privately with Alec about stepping up the plans to safeguard Willis.

Carl Winters took her statement and promised to call as soon as he located Ian Griggs.

When they reached Keira's apartment, Alec steered her straight for the bathroom. She was shivering from being in wet clothes so long. He started hot water running in the tub to keep from stripping off her clothes himself. He wanted to see exactly how bad her knee was, to see if she had any marks on her from Griggs.

He had desperately wanted to go with Carl Winters to see Griggs. The need to even the score—for now, for five years ago—burned in him.

"Soak," he suggested when the tub was full. "It'll warm you up. I'll fix something to eat."

"I'm not hungry."

He didn't argue. "I'll be in the living room if you need anything."

As soon as the bedroom and bathroom doors shut, Alec reached for his cell phone, called Ostman.

"What the hell is going on?" he demanded when Ostman answered. "Why wasn't I notified Griggs was released early?"

Ostman seemed surprised. "You didn't know? Phelps was supposed to get ahold of you yesterday."

"Yeah, well, fuck Phelps. From now on, I expect you to keep me informed."

"I'll handle it."

"So why is he out?"

"We thought springing him early would give him a chance to make a run for the money, before a bunch of reporters invade Freedom." Ostman's voice dropped. "Have you made contact with him already?"

Alec tightened his grip on the phone. "He accosted Keira Morgan today."

Silence stretched across the connection. "Is she okay?"

"No thanks to your incompetence."

"Did she file a complaint?"

"Of course."

Ostman swore. "Can you keep her under control? The last thing we need is for Griggs's parole to be violated."

Alec's blood pressure spiked. "If his parole gets violated, it's his own doing."

"Don't forget your priorities."

"*My* priorities?" Alec wouldn't allow Keira or anyone else to be harmed for the sake of the assignment. "Let me tell you about my priorities—"

Ostman cut him off. "Look, I'll check on a few things and get back with you. In the meantime, keep an eye on Griggs."

"I'd have kept an eye on him already if Phelps had let me know."

Alec hung up, frustrated. Not for the first time, he questioned why he had taken this job. Understood why he could not have refused it.

He paced to the bedroom door, listened, but heard nothing. He thought about going in, checking on her. Except he was too damn mad. At Griggs. At Ostman. At Phelps. Hell, even at himself.

When she appeared ten minutes later, wearing a thick terry bathrobe, he felt more in control.

"Feel better?" He grasped her hands, found them cold. "Come on. I made soup."

He steered her toward the living room sofa, then handed her an oversize mug of tomato soup.

In spite of her earlier claim of no appetite, she took a deep sip. Then another. He had fixed it the way she liked, with milk and lots of pepper.

Alec had first-aid supplies on the coffee table. While she ate, he examined her knee. The scrape wasn't as severe as he'd initially thought, now that it had soaked. It probably stung like hell, though.

He bandaged her knee. "More soup?"

She shook her head.

When he stood, she reached out and grasped his hand, stopping him.

"Thanks. I mean it."

Alec shrugged off her gratitude, knew he didn't deserve it. "I know you may not feel like talking, but I need you to tell me what happened out there."

While Carl Winters had taken the statement from Keira, Alec had gone to reassure Franny that Keira was safe. He knew the basics of what had transpired, but he wanted specifics. He wanted to know how she felt; what she thought.

Keira grew quiet, then, "I took flowers to the cemetery."

It was June 26. Keira always visited the cemetery on the anniversary of her parents' death.

"And Griggs surprised you?"

She nodded. "As I was leaving. I'd had a feeling of being watched, but I ignored it. I'll never make that mistake again."

"He did this?" Very tenderly, Alec brushed the small bruise on her cheek, vowing silently to seek revenge.

She shook her head. "I ran into the old crypt. I wasn't watching where I was going."

Alec filled in the blanks. She had probably been running from Griggs, looking over her shoulder. Terrified. It had to have been gruesome to be accosted in a cemetery. Especially at the old crypt.

"Did he touch you?"

She knew what he meant. "No. He trapped me in the stairwell." She hesitated remembering his words. Words she'd heard before. *Scream, Keira.* "And he scared the hell out of me."

Alec wondered at her pause. "How'd you get away?"

"I didn't *get* away. He let me go, Alec. And all I could think was that he was going after Willis. That I wouldn't reach my grandfather in time." She pinned him with worried eyes. "We have to come up with a better plan. I don't think just watching Griggs is enough to protect my grandfather."

Remorse washed over Alec again. "Griggs won't bother Willis."

"But Miles Ostman said—"

"Griggs's threats were made against *you*, Keira. Ostman lied to get your cooperation."

Keira's head whipped from side to side in denial. Her eyes widened as the full implication hit. "And you knew that?"

"Not until after I got here. He lied to me, too."

"But you've been here almost a week. When did you plan to tell me? Or did you?"

Alec met her gaze, recognized that once again—however unintentional—he'd hurt this woman.

"I had planned to tell you before Griggs was released.

I came to Freedom early to give us a chance to work through our past differences." Alec ran a hand through his hair. "To be honest, I didn't expect you to agree once you knew it was me they wanted to send in. That should have been my first clue. When I discovered Ostman had lied, well . . . I thought I still had time. It's a lousy excuse."

She looked away, briefly, shifted. Feeling used. Miserable. "So be straight with me now. The FBI is really just after the money, aren't they? My safety, my peace of mind, don't figure into the big picture at all, do they? On second thought, don't answer that. If the FBI would lie about my grandfather being threatened, I don't think I'd believe anything else they had to say."

Once again, Alec found himself lumped in with the FBI. Once again he faced difficult choices. He looked away, battling with his conscience.

The FBI wanted more than the money. They wanted Joseph Ciccone. But there was more at stake than just the high-profile arrest.

Before accepting, Alec had studied every file he could on Ciccone, found the man was even nastier than he'd thought. Taking out Ciccone would virtually shut down the south-central drug network. Not to mention putting a serious dent in extortion, prostitution, and murder for hire.

He briefly debated telling her the truth about Ciccone. Except the chance that she'd let something slip to Franny or her grandfather was too great. And if Ciccone ever learned that she knew, her life, Willis's life, would be forfeit.

Alec sighed. "Your safety and peace of mind mean a

lot to me. You're also the only reason I took this assignment."

Ironic she was also the only reason he'd considered not taking it.

The phone rang. Grateful for the interruption, Alec answered.

It was Carl Winters.

"I just interviewed Ian Griggs," Carl said. "Get this: He denies the entire incident. And the halfway house records show he arrived early this afternoon and hasn't left. His roommate claims they've been together since one o'clock." Carl grunted, "Worse, Griggs says he'll look into taking legal action if Keira makes another 'false' claim about him. Says he knows she's out to get his parole violated."

Alec swore.

"My sentiments exactly," Carl said. "I'll head out to the cemetery, look around."

The men talked a few more minutes, then Alec hung up. Keira looked at him expectantly.

"Carl spoke to Griggs, but he denied it. His roommate provided an alibi." Alec would check out Griggs's roommate in the morning.

She lost color. "He's lying."

"We know that. At least now, he knows we know. But that's not all." Alec repeated Griggs's allegation against her.

"That's ridiculous. He's—" Keira searched for words.

"A lunatic. I know. Carl knows it, too. Carl also suggested you get a restraining order. Said he'll have a copy of his report ready for you tomorrow."

"A restraining order?" Her voice flattened derisively. "Won't that support Griggs's claim I'm out to get him?"

"It's not a perfect answer, but it might make Griggs think twice once he realizes breaking it could violate his parole." And Alec would love to see the man behind bars again, with or without Ciccone.

Alec sat back down on the sofa. "In the meantime, you need to rethink your schedule, your routines. Griggs got the upper hand today because you were alone."

"Griggs got the upper hand because I didn't know he was free. It won't happen again."

"Especially if you keep someone with you. At all times."

"I don't want to let fear dictate my life again," she shot back.

"A little fear can be healthy. And admitting it doesn't make you less of a woman, you know."

"It diminishes me as a person. You weren't here, Alec. You don't know what it was like. I was afraid to leave my apartment, I was afraid to go to work. It was awful, and I swore I'd never again let anything restrict my life like that."

He knew she was talking about the first time Ian Griggs assaulted her. Alec had reviewed those case files as well. He knew she'd ended up hospitalized with broken ribs, internal bleeding.

The report had been a cold, straightforward chronology of the events. But it couldn't begin to cover the true horror and pain.

Particularly in an attempted rape.

He picked up her hand, clasped it in his. He lowered his voice, to a plea. "I want to know what happened five years ago, Keira. Will you tell me?"

Ian's attack from years before came howling back into her consciousness. She closed her eyes and took a deep breath, pushing back the abhorrence, reminding herself it was in the past.

When she opened them again, her eyes were resolute. Distant. "Ian and I both worked for Jack Carson back then. Everyone knew Ian drank on the job, but he had a nasty temper and no one wanted to cross him. We were on a site in Hot Springs. Ian improperly wired a box. Another man was electrocuted because of it. I found Ian's lunch thermos full of moonshine and gave it to the owner. Jack fired him."

Keira shivered, remembering. "A few days later, Ian showed up at the office, drunk. I was there alone, pulling supplies in back, and didn't hear him come in. He caught me off guard. I fought, but the alcohol seemed to increase his strength. He'd started with his fists, then picked up an iron pipe. Said he wanted to hear me scream his name."

Alec squeezed her hand. He knew from the reports he'd read that she hadn't screamed. Even when Griggs told her she'd still be conscious when he raped her.

"Jack Carson arrived before he could carry out his worst threat," she continued. "Ian ran. The sheriff issued warrants, but he disappeared. A month later he and his brothers knocked off that armored truck. You know the rest of the story."

He nodded. In an uncanny twist, Franny and Keira had been shopping in Little Rock and spotted Ian Griggs at a liquor store. They called police to have him arrested on the assault warrant, unaware of his connection to the robbery.

Until that day, the Griggses had almost pulled off a

perfect robbery. They'd left a baffling trail of leads that pointed to the armored truck's driver and guards. They weren't even suspects.

In the end, Ian's brothers died in a fire following a shoot-out with police. The three men had barricaded themselves in the store, swearing they wouldn't be captured alive. But at the last moment, Ian leapt through a window to escape the flames.

There hadn't been a trial. Griggs pleaded guilty to robbery and went to prison.

Alec also knew that Griggs had never been tried for assaulting Keira. The local district attorney had opted to let those charges drop since Ian had been convicted on federal ones.

"They assured me Griggs would serve his full sentence. Life in prison. That a second trial was a waste of money and would save me from having to recount my ordeal in court." She stared at Alec, her voice stronger in her anger. "Do you understand why I have so little faith in the judicial system? It failed me once. I won't give it a second chance."

Alec skimmed his fingers down her cheek. He wanted to erase her distress, soothe every hurt Ian Griggs had caused. His regret over not being there five years ago was profound.

And while he couldn't go back and change the past, he could do something in the present. He would stay in Freedom until Griggs was behind bars.

"Would you believe me if I told you I won't let him harm you again?"

Believe him? The irony stung. Alec had failed her once, too. She'd learned over the years to depend first and foremost on herself.

She avoided answering, instead asked a question of her own. "In the beginning, Ostman said he expected Griggs to get the money and run. Was he telling the truth?"

Alec couldn't attest to Ostman's honesty. "If I were Griggs, I'd get the money and head for the border. Once word spreads that he's free, people will be watching him. It will be tougher to make his move. With or without help."

Keira recalled the treasure seekers who had swarmed into Freedom after Griggs's arrest five years ago. Everyone looking for the two million. She also recalled the influx of journalists, each one out for a unique angle.

"You think there are many people still following this?"

Alec shrugged. "A few. There's still a reward for the recovery of the money."

"Great," she muttered.

"Actually, the more people around watching Griggs, the safer you'll be."

Keira mulled over his words. Of course, she hoped Griggs would leave soon. Which would mean Alec would leave soon, too. She felt a dull edge of pain. That wasn't good.

All the more reason she needed to get through this on her own. Because in the end that's where she would be: On her own.

She looked at Alec, saw his proffered strength. *Dammit, right now I don't feel like playing superwoman.* Her knee still stung, and her cheek ached with a dull throb. The fear left her feeling hollow.

"Can we talk about something else?" she asked.

Alec nodded and stood. He disappeared into the kitchen. When he returned, he had two beers and a bag of pretzels. He held out a beer, then pointed to her video collection. "Feel like a movie?"

She nodded. "You pick."

Alec loaded *Dances with Wolves* because it was a three-hour movie.

Snagging the remote, he moved back beside her on the couch and wrapped an arm around her shoulder, hugging her close.

Keira started to say something, but it felt too blasted good. Instead, she grabbed more pretzels. Just for one night she wouldn't question, she wouldn't debate.

She fell asleep about an hour before the movie ended. Alec shifted her head onto his lap and lowered the volume, letting the video play out as he watched her sleep.

The burning need to even the score with Ian Griggs had passed. Actually, it had only been postponed, allowing him to think more clearly.

That was where things would start to get tricky.

The fact Griggs had a ready alibi for the afternoon proved he had people willing to help him. And he had a big ace in the hole: Two million could buy a lot of loyalty. A lot of favors. Which would make Alec's job all the more difficult.

The movie finished.

Alec punched the power button on the remote and looked down at the sleeping beauty. Keira had her head on his thigh, her knees drawn up close to her chest. His heart slowed as he watched her dream.

So, what's it going to be, Dempsey? The couch? Or the bed?

He'd already decided to spend the night. Plan A had

been Keira in her bed, him on the sofa. Plan B had included her on the sofa, stretched out beside him.

At the moment however, he was formulating Plan C. Both of them in her bed.

After all, the couch wasn't big enough for two. And the thought of her in one room, him in another didn't sit right.

Mind made up, he carefully tucked her in his arms and stood. She didn't move. In the bedroom, he held her in one arm and tugged back covers with the other. Then he deposited her in the center of the bed.

"Don't leave," she murmured, groggy.

"Shhh. Go back to sleep, babe. I'm not going anywhere."

She calmed. Alec padded through her apartment, checking doors and windows and turning off lights.

Back in her bedroom, he peeled off his shirt. His hand paused on the button of his jeans. *Underwear.* He'd leave on his underwear.

He climbed in her bed, scooting close, drawing her near. They were both on their sides, her back spooned against his belly. The terry bathrobe she still wore was warm and smelled faintly of honeysuckle.

She was restless, her feet kicking, arms twitching. *Bad dreams*, he thought, soothing her with low sounds.

She quieted but soon grew restless again. She tugged at the robe, clearly not used to sleeping in something that bulky.

With a tight sigh, Alec rolled her over, lifting first one arm, then the other free of the robe. Beneath it, she wore a pair of cotton bikinis with a matching camisole that hugged her figure like a second skin.

He tossed the robe to the foot of the bed and picked her up, sprawling her across his chest. Immediately she quieted.

Alec had been fighting an erection since first climbing into bed with her. With the press of her thinly covered breasts against his chest, he lost the battle. His flesh swelled. Her nipples had contracted in the cool night air, felt like little buttons against his chest. Twin taunts.

His rock-hard cock pressed against her abdomen, separated from her flesh by their underwear.

Unbidden, memories swirled back. Their first kiss. The first time he saw her bare breasts. The first time she'd touched his penis. The first time they'd made love . . .

There was a time when they wouldn't have tolerated any clothing between them—like this—in a bed. When the press of flesh on flesh was something sacred, something precious.

But he'd violated that bond by leaving. Now he could only look at her and wonder who else had loved her.

Reggie Reeves?

He frowned.

The thought of any man loving Keira sent a knife through his gut. And yet, Alec had no claim on her. No right to challenge anyone.

His home, his life, were fifteen hundred miles away, in Seattle. He'd left them for this job, would leave them again for the next one. Their lives had separate paths.

Keira wriggled, snuggling farther up on his chest. Her leg drew up between his, nudging his already painfully tight testicles.

He shook his head.

Maybe he should have stayed with Plan A.

Chapter Eight

Keira awoke to the sound of pans clattering in the kitchen. The delicious aroma of coffee. Familiar, warm feelings.

Alarms sounded in her head. *Familiar* wasn't good. Neither was *warm*.

Alec.

Sometime during the night, she'd become aware she was lying on top of him. That he'd stripped down to his briefs.

It hadn't bothered her at the time. In fact, she'd relished the moment.

Through drowsy eyes, she had watched him, felt his abdomen rise steadily against hers. Even in sleep he had his arms wrapped tightly about her, making her feel secure.

She'd also felt his hard-on, wondered if it was simply a nocturnal body function . . . or an honest-to-God reaction. Did he desire her?

She had been tempted to touch him. *There.*

It had been ten years since she'd made love to Alec, yet her body remembered as if no time had passed. Heat pooled. Moist, hot, and low.

Tears collected in her eyes at the bittersweet memories.

She hadn't wept in years, but since Alec's return, it seemed she wanted to every day. *Enough.*

She had learned the hard way that in spite of the love in her heart, in spite of desire, she and Alec weren't destined to be together. Nothing had changed. History was merely repeating itself.

The heat and passion were still there, the physical attraction stronger than ever. But just as in the past, there'd be no happy ending.

She threw back the covers and climbed free of the bed.

Alec heard the bathroom door shut and poured coffee.

He'd been awake since four, unable to fall back to sleep. Actually, he'd lain there for a while, content to hold Keira as she slept.

She'd stayed on top of him all night. Belly to belly. Then his erection demanded an unfair amount of attention. *Do or die.* He had to get up. Or forever forfeit his right to be called a gentleman. Which at the moment felt like a vastly overrated title.

When Keira came out moments later, she was fully dressed and ready for work. He noted that the redness on her cheek had virtually disappeared.

He handed her coffee. "How are you feeling?"

"Fine." She gulped the hot liquid.

He had obviously showered recently. His T-shirt clung to his shoulders, his abs. She looked at his still-damp hair. She'd noticed last night it had been cut, knew who had cut it. Franny had left it a little longer in the back, but tapered the sides and front. As if he needed to look hunkier.

"I can't stay," Alec said. "What are your plans for the day?"

Keira's relief was tangible. "I'm going by my attorney's to see about a restraining order, not that I believe it will do much good. Then I've got an appointment in Little Rock to pick up blueprints for a new job I want to bid."

While the news she was seeing an attorney relieved him, the idea of her going to Little Rock bothered him. "If you'll wait I'll—"

She held up a hand, cutting him off. "I'll get Jake to ride with me."

"Jake?"

"My senior crew chief. He was in an auto accident and was just released for light duty." She'd reconciled herself to the fact it probably was smart to keep someone with her, at least until she had a restraining order issued.

"One last thing." Alec placed a gun on the table beside her coffee cup, a small thirty-eight snub nose in a brown leather holster.

He removed the gun, showed her the cylinder with five shots. "When was the last time you fired a gun?"

"Years ago." Probably squirrel hunting with Willis when she was twelve.

"We'll go out this weekend to do some target practice. In the meantime, keep this in your car. Just in case."

He didn't stop to consider the pros and cons of his advice. His only concern was keeping her safe. God only knew what Griggs could have done yesterday if Alec hadn't shown up at the cemetery.

He finished his coffee. He needed to make a few phone calls before starting surveillance.

"You'll be okay?"

She nodded, then looked up at him. "Thanks for being here last night."

Unable to stop himself, Alec brushed a kiss across her cheek. "See you tonight."

Keira went by her attorney's office and spoke with his secretary. Since it was Friday, the secretary couldn't promise they'd get a judge to hear the request, but she promised to try.

She met Franny for coffee, to assure her friend she was unharmed, then spent the morning in Little Rock, with Jake. It was early afternoon by the time she returned to her office to help Martha process billing and sign payroll.

Martha held up two pink phone message slips. "These are for the new guy. Alec Dempsey. Any idea if he'll be back in later?"

Keira glanced at the messages—noticed both were from Scarlet. The woman was determined. Or had a lot of ceiling fans to be installed.

"If he doesn't call by five, stick them on his locker."

All her employees carried cell phones and called in for messages during the day. Of course, Alec was the exception since he wasn't really working a job site.

Franny called midafternoon, excited.

"You'll never guess what just happened!"

"What?"

"I won front-row tickets to wrestling in Hot Springs! Plus autographed T-shirts."

"How'd you do that?"

"I was the twenty-fifth caller on ROCK-FM. They've been giving away tickets all week."

Keira laughed. "Congratulations. I know how much you wanted tickets."

"Actually, I was hoping you wanted to go. On such short notice, Darryl can't get off in time."

"You mean it's tonight?" Keira glanced at her watch. It was nearly three o'clock.

She thought about Alec, wondered what he'd say, then grew vexed for thinking that.

Alec's main concern had been that she didn't go off *alone*. And she wouldn't. She'd be with Franny. And a crowd of nearly twenty thousand rabid wrestling fans. The event was televised to millions of home viewers.

"Sounds like fun. Count me in."

Franny squealed with delight. "Come by the shop, and we'll get ready here."

Alec talked with Miles Ostman twice during the day.

As suspected, Griggs's roommate, Beau Watson, had served time with Griggs. Watson had a rap sheet a mile long, starting with grand theft auto at age thirteen.

Watson worked at Big Cheney's grocery store, a half block from the gas station where Griggs was employed. Griggs didn't own a vehicle, and, according to parole files, didn't have the money to buy one. But Watson had a car to lend.

Alec bet it rankled Griggs to be penniless, with his movements restricted, when he had access to two million. Hopefully, those same restrictions would fuel the need to make a break.

Alec slipped by the grocery store, picked up a few items, and planted a tracking device on Watson's vehicle.

Then he went and watched Griggs pump gas.

When Griggs clocked out, Alec followed him back to the halfway house. Even though he didn't need to, Alec slipped into the abandoned building and watched the house for another hour.

As part of his parole conditions, Griggs had a strict curfew. During the first few weeks, he was only allowed to leave the house to work. Even his court-mandated counseling sessions were held on the halfway house premises.

Alec doubted Griggs would stay around long enough to make the first session.

By six, Alec was home. He knocked on Keira's door, then let himself in, having kept the key from the plant stand. The apartment was quiet.

The light on her answering machine flickered, showing two new calls. He played them back.

One call was a business client, the other was from her attorney confirming a restraining order had been issued. The news, while far from perfect, pleased Alec.

He went next door and checked his own answering machine. The first three messages were from Scarlet. Then he had a call from Keira, informing him she'd gone to Hot Springs to watch wrestling with Franny. Darryl had left a message inviting Alec to watch the match with him later, at the bowling alley.

Frowning, Alec replayed Keira's message. The fact that she was with Franny didn't make him feel better. Actually, the only time he felt secure was when Keira was with him.

After changing clothes, Alec headed downtown. He grabbed a sandwich from a drive-through and ate it while watching the halfway house. A little after seven, Griggs returned to his room, turned on television, and closed the blinds. There was nothing more to see.

Alec left the warehouse and headed to the bowling alley, knowing Griggs was locked up for the night.

The bar at the Pin Palace was jammed.

Sally and Mabel had spread the news around town, telling everyone Franny and Keira would be at wrestling that night. The manager had even put a message on the front marquee: "Franny and Keira take on Pro Wrestling—Live at 8:00."

The bar had twelve television sets, half of them big screens. Usually there were at least six different sporting events on the televisions. But for once all twelve were tuned to wrestling.

The place erupted into screams when the show opened with a live shot of Franny and Keira waving to the camera.

Alec grinned in spite of himself. Two gorgeous, buxom redheads. The cameraman was no fool.

Keira wore a short, tight, T-shirt that showed her midriff; Franny a black leather bustier that barely contained her.

As the opening theme music roared, Franny leaned forward and brushed her hair back, behind her shoulder, revealing a wrestling-logo body tattoo on the swell of her breast. The camera zoomed in tight, filling the screen with nothing but the tattoo and cleavage.

The crowd in the bar cheered as fireworks flashed on the TV screen. The announcer claimed to be having heart palpitations after the opening shot.

"Big hooters always do that to you," the other announcer quipped.

Clearly used to Franny's antics, Darryl smiled good-naturedly as people slapped him on the back.

Even Alec was laughing before the night was over, as Franny manipulated the cameramen. The wrestlers, following the crowd's cue, fell over the ropes and proceeded to fight it out right in front of Franny and Keira. Headlocks and cleavage shots.

Keira got her fair share of camera time. The tight T-shirt didn't hide her curves, and her firm, flat stomach was sleek and sexy as hell. Alec noticed her nipples stabbing through the T-shirt, knew he wasn't the only admirer.

By the time the program went off the air, the bar was standing-room-only. Franny called Darryl as the program wrapped up and promised to come directly to the bowling alley.

"They'll be here within an hour," Darryl said.

"In that case, we challenge you to a bowl-off," Mabel said. "Losers pay."

Sally and Mabel scurried off to reserve a couple of bowling lanes.

Alec pulled out his wallet. "Guess I better hit the ATM."

Even though the telecast ended promptly at ten, the action went on another fifteen minutes as a free-for-all broke out center stage.

To everyone's delight, all the wrestlers from backstage poured back into the ring for one last, heart-stopping bit of drama. The crowd went wild.

The referees finally broke the wrestlers apart, but not before they split into two factions, with threats tossed back and forth from one set of gleaming muscles to the other.

"Tune in next week," the announcer said. "To see if the Doom Brothers pick up the gauntlet."

As the crowd started a mass exodus, Keira turned to watch Franny, who still held court with two cameramen. She gathered up their programs. As she straightened, she caught a glimpse of a man staring at her from several rows up.

He looked familiar . . . yet not. Then she remembered the fellow Franny pointed out at the bowling alley. The "creepy-looking" guy. Was it him?

The man met her stare, then stepped backward, disappearing into the crowd. But not before nodding to a second man. A man she didn't see clearly. *But who looked like Ian Griggs.*

Keira drew a sharp breath, felt as if she'd been punched. She frantically scanned the crowd.

"What's wrong?" Franny asked.

"I thought I just saw that guy. The one you said worked at the grocery store. At least I think it was. And for a moment I—" Keira shook her head, uncertain.

"You what?"

"I thought I saw Ian Griggs."

Franny's eyes widened. Both women searched the rapidly dwindling crowd but saw no familiar faces.

"How sure are you?" Franny pressed.

"On a scale of one to ten? One. Or less." Now Keira felt foolish. "Maybe I'm getting paranoid."

Her friend shrugged. "I think you're entitled after the incident at the cemetery. But didn't Alec say Griggs isn't allowed out of the halfway house after dark?"

At Keira's nod, Franny held up their tickets. "Then we're safe. And don't forget, we've got backstage passes. By the time we leave, everyone else will be long gone."

They were escorted backstage, where Franny received her autographed T-shirts and collected a number of other autographs as well as snapping a lot of photographs.

When Keira finally pulled her away, Franny was floating.

"Can you believe it? I got a picture of the Smasher kissing me *and* his autograph! Woo-hoo!"

They left through a rear exit. The parking lot was deserted, but well lit. One of the security guards spotted them and accompanied them to Keira's car.

Franny showed off her autographs, then demonstrated her version of the Smasher's signature move—the Death Bomb. "Of course, I can't really drop you over my knee—might kill you," she giggled.

The guard, who looked well past seventy, laughed. "I can think of worse ways to die."

As they left the coliseum, Franny dug out her cell phone. "I've got to call Darryl again." She flipped her phone open, then groaned. "Wouldn't you know! Dead battery."

"And I didn't bring my phone since you had yours," Keira reminded her. "But we'll be home in no time."

By then, traffic was nonexistent. As soon as Keira cleared the Hot Springs city limits, she sped up. She made the drive almost daily and felt like she could navigate it blindfolded.

Franny rifled through her CDs, selected one, and

cranked up the volume. Windows down, they sang along with Garth Brooks.

When Keira stopped singing, Franny looked at her. "What's wrong? Don't tell me you forgot the words."

Keira shook her head, eyes flicking to her rearview mirror. Another car had come up behind her and was closing in fast.

"Tailgater." Keira sped up, but so did the driver behind her.

Franny twisted in her seat. "What's his problem?"

Keira glanced at her speedometer. She was doing a little over eighty, which was as fast as she felt safe driving at night. The road had a few turns, and while it was currently deserted, another vehicle could come up at any time.

The car behind her turned on its high beams, nearly blinding her, as the bright halogen light reflected like magnified solar flares off her rearview and side mirrors.

Temporarily blinded, Keira looked away, flipped the rearview up to break the reflection. Then she pushed her side mirror out. Franny did the same.

Blinking, Keira swerved slightly then started swearing. "I'm going to slow and let him pass." She removed her foot from the accelerator and tapped her brakes.

But instead of passing her, the car behind her slowed.

Keira straightened her side mirror cautiously. As she watched, the headlights disappeared completely.

"Whew! We lost them."

"What a jerk!" Franny craned her neck backward, confirming no other lights were visible on the roadway. "Lucky for him we didn't stop and kick his ass. He doesn't want any of this—"

No sooner had the words left Franny's mouth than they were hit from behind.

Keira's Blazer jerked, then fishtailed as she accelerated to get away.

The other car's headlights suddenly came on, and Keira realized the other driver had been following them all along, but without lights.

"I'm going to floor it."

Keira sped away from the other car. This stretch of road was a straightway. If she could pick up speed, she had a decent chance of losing them.

But the car stayed right on her bumper, forcing Keira to maintain her high rate of speed even as they approached more curves.

"Where's a cop when you need one?" Franny yelled.

They were rammed from behind again. Both women bounced against their seat belts as Keira tried to get her car to go faster. But the Blazer was maxed out.

"He's passing us," Franny said.

Keira caught a glimpse of headlights in the side mirror as the car overtook them. With sickening clarity, she knew the other driver's intent.

"He's going to run us off the road."

At that moment, the vehicle banged hard against Keira's car door. She got a clear look at the vehicle, a black pickup with tinted windows, could scarcely make out the silhouette of the driver and a passenger.

"Look out!" Franny shouted the warning.

Keira looked up and saw another car coming straight on. The truck was in the wrong lane, which meant the driver would ram her again to get out of the other car's path. The oncoming car started swerving as well.

"Hold on!" Keira hit her brakes, but it wasn't enough.

The truck rammed her yet again, knocking her car off the road as it shot out and cut in front of her. She skidded, fighting to keep control, fighting to avoid going into the opposite lane and hitting the third car.

But the forward momentum was too great.

As her right front tire spilled off the edge of the road, the tire blew, spinning her vehicle directly toward the oncoming car.

By eleven-thirty, Alec was watching the door. The program had gone off the air at ten. Traffic would have been heavy getting out of the sports arena, he figured. They should arrive at any time.

After another fifteen minutes, he quit bowling and paced outside, trying Keira's cell phone. No answer.

He went back inside to tell Darryl he was going to go looking for them when Darryl's cell phone rang.

Alec watched him take the call.

"Franny! I was worried." Darryl moved toward a quieter part of the bowling alley, his face serious. Alec followed.

"We're on our way." Darryl snapped off his phone. "They were in an accident. They're unharmed, but Keira's car is totaled."

"Come on." Alec headed out the door.

Darryl recounted what little he knew as Alec drove. The news that the women had been purposely run off the road enraged Alec.

They reached the emergency room in Hot Springs in

record time. Keira and Franny were in an alcove near the lobby, talking with a police officer.

Franny stood as soon as she spotted Darryl and launched herself into his arms.

Alec walked straight up to where Keira sat motionless. She looked pale and upset, her brow furrowed.

He was torn between wanting to scoop her up and kiss her, versus shaking her for not being more careful. Logic didn't apply, and it didn't matter that it wasn't her fault. It only mattered that she remain safe.

"You're okay?" he asked, voice tight.

She nodded, avoiding his eyes.

Physically, she and Franny had been extremely lucky. She'd narrowly missed the oncoming car, but ended up crashing sideways into some trees. The fact they didn't hit head-on or flip was a miracle. They could have both been seriously injured . . . or killed.

Alec bent low, catching her chin gently in his hand. Dark eyes scanned green ones. He recognized the fierce look she used when tears threatened, knew she was emotionally shaken.

She'd had two traumatic incidents, back to back. Griggs at the graveyard, now this. He pressed a kiss to her temple, then straightened as the policeman quickly recounted the facts of the accident.

The third car had skidded, unharmed, into the ditch. The driver quickly hurried to render aid to Keira and Franny as the black truck sped off in the night.

"Unfortunately, they weren't able to get a tag number," the policeman said.

"Anybody get a look at the driver?" Alec asked.

"Too dark. Miss Morgan thinks there were two

people in the cab. We've put out an APB on the truck, and we'll see what happens." The policeman's shrug said *don't hold your breath.* "In the meantime, these ladies are free to go."

Keira stood, her arms wrapped tightly across her chest. Alec put his hands on her shoulders and squeezed. When she didn't resist, he pulled her close and followed Darryl and Franny outside.

Alec drove, Keira beside him in the passenger seat. Franny recovered her voice first. "Did you see us on TV?"

Darryl laughed. "Couldn't miss you, honey. Half the town saw you, too."

"Our seats were awesome. And I got the Smasher's autograph."

Franny talked about the match most of the way back to Freedom. Alec noticed Keira remained quiet—as if lost in thought.

They drove to Franny's first. "To hell with propriety. I'm spending the night," Darryl had announced, as they climbed out.

When Alec and Keira finally reached her apartment, she stopped outside the door, fumbling for her keys.

"Is there something you're not telling me?" he asked.

Keira paused, then looked at him, debating whether to voice her worry. Uncertainty gnawed at her. "I thought I saw Ian Griggs tonight—but he couldn't have been there, right?"

Alec leaned close, pressed for details. "Did you get a good look at him?"

"No." Now that she thought about it more, she regretted mentioning it. "Actually, I only saw the back of a head. Crazy, I know. I'm not even sure it was Griggs. Or the other guy."

"What other guy?"

Keira described the creepy-looking guy.

Alec's frown deepened. "Sounds like Griggs's room-mate, Beau Watson. Works at the grocery store. Neither one of them *should* have been there."

If Griggs had found a way to circumvent the halfway house security system, he posed an even bigger threat to Keira.

But at the same time, Griggs would be a fool not to take advantage of the breach and escape undetected—with his money.

Alec reached for her keys, but Keira pulled them back.

She didn't want him following her inside. She felt too needy, too fragile. If he came in, she wouldn't want him to leave. And if he stayed . . .

He could guess what was on her mind. The same thing that was on his.

They'd slept together last night—platonically—but he knew she'd been aware of him. The sexual tension between them simmered even when they were unconscious, asleep. She'd caressed him once in her sleep, slipping her hand inside his briefs. The minute her fingers had closed over his rigid flesh, she'd awoken and withdrawn, startled.

He'd lain there in misery, pretending to sleep, fighting the urge to ejaculate, holding back.

He hadn't mentioned it that morning, knowing it would embarrass her. And tonight, well, he didn't want to make her feel uncomfortable by staying. Not after what she'd been through.

Besides, he needed to check on Ian Griggs and his

roommate. Beau's car was a beat-up, rusty Toyota—not a black truck—but Alec would still look for clues.

"I won't stay," he said, taking her keys from her hand. "Just let me check your apartment."

Unlocking the door, he did a quick walk-through. "All clear," he announced. "Can I do anything before I leave?"

She rubbed her forehead. "No. Thanks."

He moved to the door. "We'll talk tomorrow. If you need me, call my cell phone."

"You . . . you're going out?" While she didn't want him staying with her, she didn't want him anywhere else either.

"I'm going to check the halfway house," he said softly. "I should be back within an hour. I'll come check on you, if you'd like."

Her cheeks flushed. "No. I'll be fine."

Alec stood outside her door until he heard the dead bolt and security chain slide into place.

Stopping momentarily in his apartment, he grabbed a flashlight. He didn't like the thought of leaving Keira, but he had to go check on Griggs.

The halfway house was dark when Alec drove by; only four cars were in the parking lot, including Beau's. No battered black pickups with paint scrapes matching Keira's car.

Still, he circled the property several times before parking and watching from the vacant building, wishing he'd catch Ian Griggs sneaking in or out. Or his slimy little friend, Beau.

All remained quiet.

In the morning, Alec would have Ostman check the house records to see if Griggs had indeed been accounted for that night. Alec also wanted to know if Griggs had made any other friends, besides Beau, at the house. Anyone who might cover for him, help him.

Convicts didn't make friends, per se, but the criminal honor code did allow favors to be bought and sold. With two million stashed away, Griggs could buy a lot of sordid favors.

And while Alec had a copy of Griggs's work schedule, which days and what hours he was scheduled at the gas station, what he needed was a similar schedule for Beau Watson.

When Alec returned to his apartment a short time later, he was unable to sleep. He moved about in the dark, restless.

The harder he tried not to think about it, the more his mind replayed the officer's description of the accident. That the women hadn't been killed was miraculous.

While Keira might very well have imagined seeing Griggs at the wrestling match earlier, there was no doubt in Alec's mind about who was behind the accident. Ian Griggs had sworn in prison to extract vengeance for his brothers' deaths.

Why didn't the bastard just get his damn money and run? Hell, Alec would help him retrieve it. At least initially . . .

If Alec could catch Griggs with the money, he'd be busted for possession of stolen property, which would violate his parole and get him back behind bars.

Alec would also do what he could to make sure Griggs got the book thrown at him for every conceivable charge, to make certain he stayed in prison a very long time.

Because as long as Ian Griggs was alive, Keira would

be in danger. And Alec wasn't always going to be there, watching over her shoulder.

He frowned at the thought.

When this job was done, he'd go back to Seattle, to another assignment. Typically, he looked forward to a new job. Undercover operations suited his workaholic tendencies, fit well with his single lifestyle.

So why did the thought of *this* job ending seem so . . . unsatisfying?

He paced from room to room. Was seeing Keira again what made him feel restless?

Moving to the bedroom window, he climbed onto the fire escape. *He just wanted to check on her.*

He tried her window, perturbed to find it unlocked. What would it take to get her to remember to lock these? Maybe he needed to weld the damn things shut.

He shoved the window open and whispered her name so he wouldn't startle her if she was awake.

When she didn't respond he poked his head inside, his eyes seeking her bed.

The slight form didn't move, but she mumbled lightly in her sleep. By the way her sheets were tangled, he guessed that she was having a fitful night.

He sighed and stepped through the window. In moments, he was stripped down to skivvies.

He was already hard. Not that it made a difference. As much as he desired her, he knew he couldn't let himself get involved. It was wrong on so many levels, he didn't even want to contemplate it.

He looked at her small silhouette, his eyes following the full thrust of her breast, the curve of her hip. His groin tightened uncomfortably with need. He welcomed the ache.

In a warped sense, his denial was punishment for past deeds. Holding her and not *having* her was a painful form of self-flagellation.

Climbing into the bed, he touched her shoulder, softly calling her name.

With a cry of confusion, she came up from her dream. She blinked in sleepy recognition, then snuggled up to his side.

She wore a short tank top and panties. Alec moved her onto his chest, slid his hands under her shirt, skimming his palms down her smooth skin. She rubbed her nose, yawning, and fell back into a deep sleep.

Alec kissed her head, hugged her tight, and fell asleep himself.

Chapter Nine

Keira awoke alone.

Instinctively she knew Alec wasn't in her apartment. No smell of coffee. No scent of male.

She remembered his moving her off his chest, onto the mattress. He'd cuddled and kissed her, whispered something about seeing her later.

As much as she hated to admit it, she had slept better in his arms. She'd been having awful nightmares, claustrophobic dreams of suffocating, of being burned alive. While Griggs laughed.

But as soon as Alec had climbed into her bed, the macabre images vanished. She'd slept peacefully. Maybe her subconscious felt safe enough with him around to shut down.

Too bad her libido hadn't shut down.

Twice during the night, she'd awoken with thoughts of making love to Alec. Hot, steamy fantasies of slow hands, wicked touches. Her body melted at the recollection.

Both times she'd felt his thick shaft heavy against her belly, had ached to touch him. With her hands. And her mouth. To encourage him to touch back—with his hands, his mouth. She'd been wet. On fire. Trembling with the memories of their past.

Alec had been a superb lover. Not that she'd had a lot to compare to back then. He'd been her first. He'd been special. He'd been patient, considerate. *Daring.*

Alec had taught her how to seek pleasure, encouraged her to accept it. He'd also let her pleasure him, taught her the magic of receiving joy by giving it. Their lovemaking had been wild and uninhibited.

She shivered in recall.

She knew Alec would renew their physical relationship if she gave the word. Yet something held her back.

A lot actually. At one point in her life—ten years ago—she'd have done anything to have Alec Dempsey.

Now . . .

Well, now it was a muddy jumble. Did she want him or not?

Not if it would hurt.

And it would hurt eventually. When he left.

With a sigh, she slowly eased out of the bed. Her neck and back were sore reminders of the accident. A hot shower would feel good.

Halfway to the bathroom her phone rang. She crawled across the mattress to grab it.

"This is Martha. I'm at the office."

Keira closed her eyes, ordering her pulse to calm. She'd expected it to be Alec. "What are you doing in?"

"I came by to drop off the work I took home last night. And while I was there, a call came in from the contractor at Hot Springs. Vandals hit the site last night. Wants to know if you can send a crew up."

Keira frowned. Unfortunately this type of thing wasn't uncommon. What surprised her was that vandals usually picked easier targets. The site was fenced and fairly secure.

"Call a couple of the guys. Anybody that wants overtime should be there in thirty minutes."

Keira hung up and called Franny, eager to know her friend suffered no delayed injuries after their accident.

"I've got a bruise from the seat belt. Damn thing worked well," Franny said. "You going car shopping today?"

The last thing Keira wanted to do was look at new cars. She wasn't in the mood to deal with salesmen. Or her insurance company. "For now, I'll use one of the trucks from work."

"Well, be careful! You might not like Alec telling you what to do, but this time I have to agree with him: Keep someone with you."

"That really helped last night."

"I meant a *male*. Someone with a weenie, not someone who acts like one," Franny said. "My money says Griggs is basically a chicken. You and I don't scare him, but he might think twice about showing his ass with some real muscle around."

Alec spent the day following Ian Griggs.

Actually, he spent most of it sitting in his car, doing nothing, because Griggs didn't leave the halfway house until almost ten o'clock. Then he reported to the gas station for work. According to his schedule, he'd be there until four.

Ostman did some checking, and, according to the house records, both Griggs and Beau had been in their quarters Friday night when Keira's accident occurred. The lack of solid leads left Alec frustrated.

When he got no answer at her apartment, he called

Keira on her cell phone. He could tell by the background noise she was in her truck. She also wasn't alone.

"Thought you'd sleep in since it was Saturday," Alec said.

"Job site was vandalized. I'm taking a crew up to assess damage."

He frowned. "In Hot Springs? Want me to meet you there?"

"No. I've got Ray, Tommy, and Byron with me."

"Will you call me when you're through?"

Silence greeted him. Then Keira said, "We'll see," and hung up. He knew she resented the intrusion, knew she was still angry over Ostman's deception.

At that moment, the homing device on Beau's car indicated movement.

Beau didn't have as strict a curfew as Griggs did and was allowed some unsupervised time. Alec watched the screen on his laptop. Where was Beau going?

Easing his car into gear, he took off.

Beau spent two hours driving in circles around the county. He stopped once to drive through a fast-food place. And a second time for gas.

While Beau's meanderings seemed aimless, Alec did notice that he passed Culverleaf Park several times. In fact, when Alec checked the route on the map, he noticed Beau had circled the entire park boundary three times. Too much for coincidence.

Was he scoping something out for Griggs? Had Griggs taken on a partner? Alec made a note to get some park topography maps.

When Beau returned to the halfway house, Alec went

back to the gas station to check on Griggs. He parked in an alley, behind a large commercial trash container, and climbed out to stretch.

An hour passed, minutes oozing slower than frozen molasses, reminding him why he hated surveillance work. He watched the station and tried not to think about how hot it was.

A short time later, a familiar-looking truck pulled into the gas station.

Alec sat forward, watched as the driver apparently fumbled with something on the seat. He squinted against the glare. That looked like Willis's old red Ford—the same one he'd had for over twenty years.

The truck's door opened. Willis Morgan climbed out, rifle in hand.

"Shit!" Alec started his car, jammed it into DRIVE, and sped off toward the station.

By the time he got there, Willis was already inside.

Griggs was behind the counter, his back to the wall, both hands in the air. Griggs had the phone clenched tightly in one hand.

Alec could hear a voice from the phone, but not what was being said.

"You don't want to do this," Alec said calmly.

"The hell I don't. I heard he attacked Keira at the graveyard," Willis said. "And I got twenty bucks says he was behind her car wreck last night."

"You got no proof of either, old man. Ask Dempsey." Griggs nodded toward Alec. "I'm sure Keira told him the sheriff came to see me."

Alec ignored him. "Give me the gun, Willis."

"Bet your granddaughter's behind this," Griggs taunted. "She's out to get me. Wants me bad."

A muscle in Griggs's cheek flinched as Willis drew back the bolt to chamber a round. "Go ahead. Shoot me."

Alec took a step closer to Willis. "I know it's tempting, but you shoot him, you go to jail. And where does that leave Keira?"

Willis blinked, hesitated, which was all the opening Alec needed. "You're all the family she's got. Don't do this."

Seconds ticked by, the air explosive.

Finally, Willis lowered the rifle. Griggs dropped his arms.

"Don't make me come back here," Willis said. "Next time you won't be so lucky."

Two sheriff's patrol cars pulled up outside simultaneously, lights flashing. Alec knew whoever Griggs had been talking to on the phone must have called in an alarm.

Griggs grinned and quickly raised his hands. "Help!" he yelled, as the deputies approached.

Willis shook his head in disgust and handed his rifle to the first deputy.

"Afternoon, Bob. Carl. It ain't loaded. Just delivering a message."

Griggs's face turned red as he lowered his hands once again. "Isn't there a law against threatening people like that? How was I supposed to know it wasn't loaded?"

"If I wanted to shoot you, you wouldn't be standing there whining right now," Willis spat.

Carl Winters looked pointedly at Alec, then at the other deputy. "Take 'em down to the station. I'll get the statement there."

Willis pointed to Alec. "The boy didn't do anything."

"He's a witness," Carl said.

Willis ducked out of the door, but not before swapping glances with Griggs. Alec didn't miss the exchange. Griggs had been smiling.

The deputy let Willis drive his truck to the station.

Alec followed and sat patiently while Willis gave his side of the story. Willis recounted the events exactly as Alec had observed.

When questioned about his presence, Alec claimed coincidence. "I drove by and spotted Willis getting out of the truck with the rifle."

Carl Winters came in just then, shaking his head. "Willis, you know better than to pull a fool stunt like that."

Willis sat forward. "Would you have done any different if it were your kin?"

"Much as I'd have wanted to, I can't." Carl pointed to his badge. "This star means I have to uphold the law. Equally. And Griggs wants to press charges."

"Maybe I shouldn't have left my bullets at home," Willis grumbled. "Could have made it worth his time."

Carl sat in a creaking chair and thunked his head with the heel of his hand. "God, you're bullheaded. I have to charge you with something. Public display of a firearm is probably the weakest thing I can come up with."

"I'll post bond," Alec said.

Willis nodded. "I'm good for it." Then he turned back to Carl. "If that's it, can we hurry it up? I'm meeting Lacy at the lodge. Gotta beat the crowd. Tonight's meat loaf."

Alec talked with Carl while the other deputy processed Willis's bond agreement.

"I didn't want to mention this in front of Willis. God knows that old fart is crazy when it comes to his grand-daughter—but Griggs accused Keira of putting Willis up to threatening him today," Carl said. "Griggs wanted to file a complaint against her. I told him there was no evidence to support it, but I'm seeing a pattern here. He's out to implicate Keira, get to her any way he can."

Carl grew silent when Willis walked up. Alec exchanged glances with the deputy. Both men understood that Griggs was also trying to make himself look innocent by making Keira look guilty.

Willis frowned as Carl warned him against approaching Griggs again, then walked with Alec to the parking lot.

"I appreciate what you did in there," Willis began. "But it doesn't make up for what you did to my grand-daughter ten years ago."

"Nothing does."

Willis climbed into his truck. "And I don't think Keira needs to know about this little incident today."

Alec met Willis's gaze and nodded. "She won't hear about it from me."

He made it back to his surveillance point just in time to see Griggs leave the station. The conversation with Carl replayed in Alec's mind. Griggs's pressing charges of any kind against Keira was especially repulsive since Griggs had never even been charged with his attack on Keira. And certainly, Griggs knew that.

After following him to the halfway house, Alec called Keira.

He was eager to talk with her and see how things had gone at the vandalized job site.

He was surprised to reach her as she was leaving her office. "You're back already? How bad was it?"

"We were lucky. Most of the damage was to the Sheetrock, not the wiring. I left two men to help out."

"Any idea who's behind it?"

Keira pursed her lips. She was fairly certain the Barry brothers had instigated this one. STUPID CUNT had been spray painted on one of the walls. Eddie Barry knew she despised that particular four-letter word and seemed to relish using it around her.

"My signal's breaking up," she said, avoiding answering. "I can't hear you."

"Where are you headed now?"

"To my cabin."

Alec checked his watch. It was still early. "Mind if I meet you there?"

"I'm just dropping off supplies. I won't be long."

"Actually I thought we could do a little target practice. Do you have the gun I gave you?"

"You really think that's necessary?"

"Yes." If for no other reason than it made Alec feel better.

"I'll see you there then."

Shutting off her phone, Keira pulled onto the private road leading up to Fire Mountain and tried not to think about the unsavory events of the last few days.

She stared out the truck's window, at the tapestry-like section of valley spread out below, and savored the quiet. At times like this, she realized just how busy her life had become. Only in the perfect silence did she realize how much background noise she'd grown accustomed to, on the job, in her car, in her apartment.

She also realized the noise was a crutch she used to blot out the deep, soul-searching thoughts. When she moved up to her cabin, would she be forced to confront those thoughts?

By the time Alec arrived, she had the supplies stored.

First thing, Alec showed her a mug shot. "This the creepy-looking guy you saw at wrestling?"

Keira took one glance at the photo and nodded. It was the same guy Franny had pointed out at the bowling alley that night.

"Who is he?"

"Beau Watson. He's on parole for robbery. Works at Big Cheney's grocery. He's Griggs's roommate at the halfway house. They also served time together." Alec was checking on all of Griggs's former cellmates.

"You think Beau's helping Griggs?"

"I'd bet on it. Come on."

She followed him down to the clearing near the lake, watched as he set up empty soda cans on a large boulder less than twenty feet away.

"Think I'm that bad?"

Alec shook his head. "The thirty-eight's got a short range. It's good close in."

Checking the cylinder, he sighted the gun and shot down two cans in quick succession. "Your turn."

She took the pistol, felt its weight in her hand. If she'd had this at the cemetery, could she have shot Griggs?

Alec slid behind her, a welcome distraction. He put his hand over hers, showing her how to unlatch the cylinder. The act suddenly became intimate. Her pulse stepped up.

"I know how to shoot," she said.

"Every gun is different. I want you to know what this one feels like. How it responds to your touch. In an emergency you're not going to have time to think about any of those things."

Alec brought the gun up, his hand over hers. "Sight it and squeeze. I don't care if you hit anything. For now, just feel the way it fires."

Keira's first shot went way off.

"We're shooting hollow points, so it kicks," Alec said. "Try again."

Keira raised the pistol. Alec let go of her arm, only to rest his hands on her shoulders. Discomfiting.

She fired twice more, then flicked the cylinder open, dumping the cartridges on the ground. He handed her a box of ammunition, watched as she reloaded the pistol and prepared to shoot again.

"Don't lock your elbows," he reminded, running his hands lightly over her extended arms.

This time Alec settled his hands on her waist. She could feel his body pressed against hers. She forgot about the gun, remembering the feel of his bare chest pressed against her as they slept. Thoughts of making love flooded her memory. For a moment she was tempted to turn, ask him to kiss her.

Except it was pointless. Would only lead to trouble. If she were willing to settle for a one-night-stand type of relationship, she could take her pick of men. Alec wouldn't be one of them.

She fired the gun, emptying it in rapid succession. Cans flew off the boulder. Dead.

"Nice shooting, babe."

Babe. Years ago the endearment had been special. Now she wondered if he used it for all women.

She scowled, realizing how little she knew about him now. Franny had relayed the news he didn't have a steady girlfriend. Keira imagined that was a temporary state. It was difficult to envision Alec unattached for long. He was too damn handsome. Too damn virile.

Of course, maybe in his line of work he was cast in the role of protector enough that he didn't need a regular relationship. The thought was especially irritating.

"I'm not your *babe* anymore, Alec. Can't you get that through your head? I've moved on."

He bristled. Moved on? Did she consider herself Reggie's *babe*? The thought goaded him. "You couldn't prove it last night. You were snuggled pretty tight in my arms. Which reminds me . . . your window was unlocked."

"I put my plants on the fire escape during the day," she defended. "And if I happen to forget to lock them, it doesn't give you, or anyone else, the right to climb in uninvited."

"Didn't feel uninvited. In fact I felt very welcome."

Spurred on by the ugly recollection of her kissing Reggie at the bowling alley, he lowered his voice. "You make these little come-on noises in your sleep, *babe*. Drives me wild. But not half as wild as your touch, the way you rub against me. Makes me wonder what you're dreaming about. Or whom."

She glared at him. "Don't push it, Alec. I've got a gun."

He caught her eyes, held them. "But you'd never use it against me. I think deep down inside you still care,

Keira. In spite of what I did. And that bothers you enough you wish you could shoot me."

Shoving the gun at him, Keira turned and stalked away.

Later that evening, Alec knocked on Keira's door.

When she answered, he thrust a huge bouquet of daisies and baby's breath forward.

"Forgive me?"

Keira eyed the flowers—her favorites—then the man. "Typically one apologizes before asking for forgiveness."

"Then I apologize."

"For?"

"Everything. Famine. Global warming. Nuclear armaments. Being a dickhead." *Leaving you ten years ago.*

Keira accepted the bouquet. "I was thinking *insensitive jerk*, but dickhead works."

Alec edged closer when it became apparent she had no intention of inviting him in.

"Do you have plans for supper?" he asked.

"Frozen dinner."

"I was going out for pizza. Care to join me?"

The daisies had already eroded her resolve. "Mama Towers's Pizza?"

He nodded. Mama Towers made the best pizza in the state.

"Let me put these in water."

Ten minutes later they were seated in the downtown pizza parlor. Alec looped an arm around her shoulder as they walked in. He winked. "We're supposed to be involved, remember?"

An act. She frowned.

They placed their order, then discussed work, a safe subject.

"The car dealership's right on schedule," Keira remarked, then told him about two new jobs she'd landed in Little Rock.

"You've done well for yourself," he observed. "Who'd have thought ten years ago that you'd be one of Freedom's largest businesses?"

"What about you, Alec? What all have you done since leaving Freedom?"

She took a sip of beer, trying to mask her curiosity. She knew bits and pieces. Not much. And frankly, most of her curiosity was about his personal life. His marriage. His relationships.

"You already know I joined the army."

"Is it true you were in Special Forces?"

He nodded.

"Bet your mother was proud?"

Alec snorted. "She hated it. Thought it was too hazardous."

"Then I'm sure she still worries. You're not exactly selling encyclopedias door to door. What made you join the FBI?"

For a moment, Alec thought about correcting her. Telling her he was with ATF. Except he didn't want to take the chance she'd withdraw. Even slightly.

His being an ATF agent wouldn't be a plus. The Morgan family tree was steeped in moonshine. Where other kids grew up with stories of the Big Bad Wolf, Keira had grown up hearing tales of her relatives doing battle with the Big Bad Revenuers.

The odds were already stacked against him on several levels, and she'd been misled once by the FBI. He didn't need to add to it.

"Army life got old after a while, but I liked the idea of law enforcement," he began. "I finished my degree while stationed in DC, got recruited there." *By ATF.*

"And your mom?"

"She's married and living in Reno. She's gone from hounding me about being careful, to badgering me about settling down and producing grandchildren."

Keira set her beer down, harder than intended, and sought to shift the conversation. She didn't want to hear about Alec's plan to fulfill his mother's wishes.

"Where did you go to school?'

Alec didn't answer, his attention focused on a man who had just entered the restaurant. The man was dressed casually, in jeans and a plaid shirt. His sandy hair was receding, but Alec guessed his age at thirty-five. Reporter?

The man had been staring at Keira longer than was polite. Or acceptable. Alec stiffened when the man headed toward them.

"Excuse me for interrupting." The man held out his hand to Keira. "Miss Morgan? I'm Lance Parks from the *National Truth*. May I ask you a few questions?"

Keira's face closed, displaying no emotion. But Alec recognized the angry sparkle in her eye.

"No, you may not," she said. "Now if you'll excuse us."

Parks ignored her dismissal, had surely expected it. *National Truth* was a sleazy rag with no ethics. A story was a story, to be had at any cost.

"Surely you have some reaction to Ian Griggs's

release. Do you believe he's back to retrieve the money?" Parks persisted. "What about the story of your grandfather's arrest this afternoon for threatening Griggs? Do you have any idea when his court date is?"

Alec stood, wedging himself between Keira and the reporter. "The lady said 'no.' And if you're smart, you'll leave her grandfather alone, too."

Parks looked like he wanted to argue until he took in Alec's height and breadth.

"I'll be in touch," he said, and took a table on the far side of the restaurant.

Alec touched her hand. "Want to get our pizza to go?"

Keira ignored him, fumbling for her cell phone.

Alec knew whom she called. "He's not home. He's at the lodge with Lacy."

Her hand froze over the SEND button.

"And you know that *how*?" She eyed him suspiciously. "Out with it, Alec. What's going on? Was Willis really arrested?"

Having no other choice, Alec explained briefly what happened. "Willis planned to tell you himself."

The news distressed Keira. She should have known how Willis would react. And while Alec had already admitted Griggs's threat had been against her, not her grandfather, she now realized her grandfather's actions could change that.

"Do you think Griggs will come after Willis now, in retaliation?"

Alec shook his head. "Griggs is more interested in harassing you. But if he can use Willis to get to you, he will."

She glanced at where Lance Parks sat. His arrival

didn't surprise her. She knew sooner or later the press would appear.

But maybe this time they'd be a blessing and follow Griggs—keep him in line.

Away from her.

And her grandfather.

Chapter Ten

Early the next morning, Willis met Keira for breakfast.

"I already know," she began. "So don't try to soft-soap me."

She waited patiently as the waitress poured Willis a cup of coffee, then watched as he added four packs of sugar, took a sip, and added two more. Defiant sparks lit his eyes when he finally looked up.

"Can't believe Alec ratted me out," he said. "Should've known I couldn't trust him. I probably should've shot him last week when I had the chance."

His words perturbed Keira even more. Exactly how many run-ins had her grandfather and Alec had?

"And you had a chance when?"

Willis compressed his lips. Mr. Mute. Grandpa Mime. Keira narrowed her eyes.

"I heard about your arrest from a reporter, Gramps. Alec had the nerve to try and defend what you did."

Willis's cup stopped halfway to his mouth. "He did? Guess I better pay him back that bail money after all."

She raised an eyebrow. "Alec posted your bail?" He hadn't mentioned that part either. "You make sure and pay back every cent. I don't want to feel indebted to him."

"Thought you two had kissed and made up."

"That doesn't mean I want to owe Alec, or anyone else, anything. And quit changing the subject. We were talking about you getting arrested."

Frowning, Willis set his cup down, sloshed coffee. "It wasn't right what Griggs did, you know."

"Doesn't make what you did right, either." Keira lowered her voice to a stage whisper. "How do you think I felt hearing about it from someone else?"

" 'Bout the same way I felt hearing about Griggs bothering you at the cemetery. You should have told me yourself, gal."

She leaned across the table. "This is exactly why I didn't tell you. Afraid you'd take matters into your own hands."

Willis shifted in his seat. A sure sign of guilt.

She pressed her advantage. "So tell me what you did to Alec, Gramps? Did you threaten him, too?"

"We had a little prayer meeting. Two grown men, coming to Jesus." Willis shrugged. "Not much to tell."

His obtuseness riled her even as she realized he was being purposely evasive about his run-in with Alec in hopes she'd forget the matter of his arrest. She'd get the truth out of Alec later.

The waitress brought their food, winked at Willis.

"I think she's sweet on me." He watched her walk away. "Been thinking about asking her to dinner one night."

"You've been thinking about that for years. Don't think you're off the hook. I want your word you won't go near Ian Griggs again."

Willis picked up a piece of bacon, shook it at her. "I ain't a kid."

"Then don't act like one."

Neither of them spoke for a few minutes. Keira busied herself with spreading jelly on a piece of toast while Willis sulked.

Finally, he sighed. "Okay, I'll give you my word. I'll leave Griggs be."

"On Grandma's grave," Keira pressed.

At that moment, the front door of the restaurant swung open, hitting the wall with a noisy bang. Everyone looked up as a crowd of men shoved through the door.

Keira recognized Lacy Hicks and two of her grandfather's other friends. The rest were refugees from the old folk's home down the street.

"Oh great," she muttered.

"There he is!" Lacy pointed to Willis. The men made their way across the diner, canes thumping on the tile floor.

One of the old men slapped Willis on the back. "I checked the post office to see if they had you on the most-wanted list."

Lacy shook his head. "Those are fugitives, Earl. Willis ain't on the lam. Yet."

"So tell us what really happened," Earl demanded. "Heard you shot someone."

The entire restaurant went quiet as everyone waited for Willis to respond.

Keira rolled her eyes. This wasn't going to get any better.

"No one was shot," she announced to the room at large. "He didn't even have bullets in the gun."

"Had 'em in my pocket," Willis defended.

Grabbing the ticket, she stood. "I've got to get to work. But remember: your word. On Grandma's grave."

Willis nodded as his friends crowded in to take seats around the table.

She paid the bill and cast one last look at her grandfather holding court.

Alec had promised he'd keep an extra close eye on Griggs. It galled her to think that in some ways—thanks to Willis's little trick—Alec was now looking out for Griggs.

She was also pissed off Alec hadn't mentioned posting bail for Willis—or that he and her grandfather had already had a run-in.

What else was Alec hiding from her?

Keira scarcely saw Alec during the early part of the week. He stopped by her apartment in the mornings to give her an update on Griggs's activity, then left.

So far, Griggs had done nothing but go to work and return to the house, the model parolee. His roommate Beau, however, had made two more trips to Culverleaf Park. On the last one, he'd taken a camera.

She also received word the black pickup truck that had run her and Franny off the road had been found. As suspected, it had been stolen and yielded no clues.

Alec's nocturnal excursions through the window and into her bed had ceased. Monday and Tuesday nights she'd been too tired to care. Wednesday night had been a different story.

It felt as if she'd been up every hour, on the hour. More than once she'd been tempted to climb out on the fire escape and crawl through his window. Give him a taste of his own medicine. Except she didn't trust herself.

Her dreams of late had been erotic. Highly charged visions of Alec making love to her, dominating her sexually as she dominated him emotionally. She begged for his touch, he begged for her heart.

Thursday night she locked the window.

Friday was the Fourth of July. Like most of the general contractors she worked for, Keira shut down for the three-day holiday weekend.

The town's annual Fourth of July festival was held downtown and kicked off a weekend of celebration. The city put on a parade, followed by a Sadie Hawkins–style race and a charity softball game. The afternoon festivities were followed by a huge fireworks display after dark.

Then on Saturday, there was a reenactment of the Battle of Freedom at Culverleaf Park. Mabel's husband, Fred, played the Indian chief every year, so Franny and Keira usually joined the campers and spent the night at the park campground. Since the fire department would be on hand for the reenactment, Darryl camped there, too.

Friday's weather promised to be picture perfect, with clear skies and temperatures in the eighties.

Keira met her grandfather downtown for lunch. Since Lacy's shop was closed for the holiday, Willis and Lacy were planning to do some rock hounding.

"I checked with his probation officer," Lacy joked. "Got permission for him to leave town."

"You're not funny," Keira said.

Willis kicked her under the table. Hard.

"What was that for?" she demanded.

Willis turned red. "Sorry. That was meant for Lacy. Feel free to pass it on."

Lacy patted her hand. "Don't worry. Your grandpa's safe with me."

By one o'clock, Keira was at City Park. She and Franny shared a paper cone of cotton candy as they watched the parade, then they made their way to the middle of the crowded park.

Mabel and Fred had lawn chairs set up and a blanket spread out on the ground. Mabel pointed to two identical wicker baskets. "Your lunches, ladies. Now go register for the race."

Franny peeked inside one basket. "Fried chicken and lemon pie. Darryl will love you."

Fred laughed. "We all know who Franny will catch this year. But what about you, Keira? Anybody in particular you're angling for?"

Keira shook her head. "Somebody slow."

Last year she'd caught Tina's husband, since Tina just had a baby and didn't feel like cooking, much less running.

In the race, the men had a fifteen-second head start. They wore numbers on their shirts, and the women merely had to chase them long enough to tear the number off.

Traditionally, the men kept running to see who could be first to circle the town square. The winner of the race got a trophy and year's worth of bragging rights.

While the man paid an entry fee to join, the woman had to bring a picnic basket for two, and was expected to feed the man she "caught" and entertain him for the afternoon.

Since neither Keira nor Franny cooked, Mabel always made their baskets.

Cissy and Scarlet were already at the registration table when Franny and Keira walked up. Scarlet turned her nose up and left without speaking.

"Who you going for this year?" Cissy asked Keira sweetly. Too sweetly. Flies were swarming. "Of course Alec practically begged Scarlet to catch him."

Keira smiled back. "I heard he's not as fast as he used to be."

Franny eyed Cissy over the top of her sunglasses. "And who are you planning to take out this year?" At last year's race, Cissy had tackled Jeb Marlow and fractured his collarbone in the process.

Cissy looked indignant. "That was an accident. Someone tripped me."

Darryl walked up, tickled Franny's side. "Mabel got your basket?"

Franny nodded.

Cissy huffed. "I don't know why you bother. You don't ever chase anyone but him." Cissy pointed to Franny's sandals. "You can't run in those."

"It's for a worthy cause," Franny purred. "And I run a little."

Ten or twelve feet, Keira thought. The crowd loved it. Franny was Freedom's glamour queen. No one expected her to break a sweat. Her job was to look good. A role she took very seriously.

Alec came up, shook hands with Darryl. He bent close to Keira. "Is it true you've got one of Miss Mabel's picnic baskets?"

She shrugged. "Maybe."

He smiled. "Good. I'll let you catch me."

Cissy latched on to Alec's arm, yanking him away before he could step closer to Keira. "Scarlet's been looking for you. Wait till you see her basket. Got your name all over it."

Keira frowned. Obviously, Cissy and Scarlet weren't clear on the concept that Alec had returned for Keira.

Having no choice but to follow, Alec disappeared, towed by Cissy.

The mayor's voice crackled across the loudspeaker, instructing the race participants to line up.

Keira moved with Franny toward the staging area.

Fifty-seven men participated, against an equal number of women. Keira looked at the crowd, noticing several of her employees ready to run, with their wives or girlfriends ready to chase.

The mayor stood on the makeshift stage and called for the crowd's attention. "Remember, men, once your number's been pulled, you can either drop out and go eat, or you can finish the race. We've got a special prize package for this year's winner."

The mayor pointed a starting gun in the air. A boom sounded, and confetti sprayed. A cheer went up.

The men surged forward, but not too fast. It was more like they were simply spreading out. Jostling for position.

A second gun fired and with a collective squeal, the women shot forward. Within the first minute over half the men were captured and dropped out.

Darryl actually jogged in place while waiting for Franny to catch up, which brought a roar of applause from the onlookers.

Alec dashed in front of Keira. "I'm all yours, babe."

Just then, Cissy ran into Keira, knocking her down.

"Here he is, Scarlet. I got him!" Cissy yelled.

Thrown off-balance, Keira tried to regain her steps but couldn't. She broke her fall with her hands, skinning her palms on the asphalt as she fell.

The other runners simply swerved to avoid a collision. All knew somebody from the crowd would step in to help. Someone always took a fall in the race.

Keira rolled, trying to prevent further injuries, and landed against the curb.

"You okay, boss lady?" Reggie Reeves bent down in front of her.

She nodded, looking up just in time to see Alec head her way.

Scarlet intercepted him by flinging herself into his arms. Alec frowned as Scarlet triumphantly ripped the number off his back and waved it to the crowd.

Accepting Reggie's help, Keira climbed to her feet. Her palms burned from the scrapes. "I'm fine."

Reggie grasped her hands gently, swearing as he inspected her bloody palms. Reaching around, he tore off his number and handed it to her.

"Feed me lunch and we'll call it even."

Keira nodded, taking Reggie's number and waving it overhead. Everyone clapped as Reggie helped her limp off toward the picnic area.

Leaving Keira on the closest bench, Reggie went and collected her basket from Mabel.

When he returned he unfolded a plaid blanket on the grass, then unpacked the basket while Keira washed her hands with bottled water.

"Everyone says Miss Mabel makes the best fried chicken in town," Reggie said, offering her a plate.

"She makes the best of everything," Keira said. "Thanks for helping me."

Reggie winked, then bit into a drumstick. "You sure you're okay? I swear it looked like that big lady knocked you down on purpose."

"Cissy takes no prisoners."

"Actually, I was afraid that Scarlet chick would catch me. Glad she nailed Dempsey."

Keira wasn't glad, but rules were rules. You were stuck with whoever caught you in the race. She changed the subject. "So how are you liking Freedom?"

"To be honest, I don't know if I'll adapt to small-town life. Awful quiet."

She nodded. At least Reggie was honest. Freedom was growing, but it would never be large. You had to like it for what it was or leave. There was no middle ground.

Scarlet and Alec walked by. Alec's shirt was soaked; he'd obviously finished the race. And Scarlet strutted around like a queen bee looking for a hive to invade.

Scarlet spied Keira and Reggie.

"Here's a perfect spot," she announced.

Unfolding her own blanket, Scarlet spread it out right across from Keira.

Scowling, Keira set her plate aside.

Reggie looked at her thoughtfully. "Something wrong?"

"My hands hurt a little."

Setting his plate down, Reggie scooted closer and took her hand. "Let me see."

Surprised by his gentleness and concern, Keira allowed him to examine her abraded skin.

"You've got gravel in there." Reaching for a clean napkin, Reggie wet it with water. Looking up, he met her eyes. "This will hurt."

At Keira's nod, Reggie moved even closer, tugging her hands into his lap. Then carefully, slowly, he worked the small bits of dirt and rock from her skin.

It stung, but she knew it would feel better when he finished.

She looked away, caught Alec staring. Glaring actually.

His reaction made Keira feel a tiny bit better. Until Scarlet grasped his arm and thrust a plate into his hands.

Keira looked back at what Reggie was doing. He finished her right hand, stuck ice against it, and reached for her left hand. That one wasn't nearly as bad.

"Is it true you and Dempsey were engaged once?"

Reggie's question caught her off guard. "Yes," she answered bluntly. "But it was so long ago it doesn't count. We were both too young." *And stupid. And naive.*

"I hear he's back to try again."

Remembering the cover story, Keira nodded.

"Obviously Scarlet's trying to convince him otherwise," Reggie observed.

Keira looked at Scarlet. The other woman held a fork of food out to Alec. For a moment cartoon lovebirds flew around them. It shocked Keira to realize she was jealous.

"Scarlet caught him in the race. He's obligated to her for the next few hours."

Reggie grinned. "Guess that means you're obligated to me." He released her hand and stood. "Come on. Let's go find some antiseptic and Band-Aids. Gotta have you patched up for the big softball game this afternoon."

He pulled Keira to her feet just as a squealing patch of kids raced past, chasing a Frisbee-toting German shepherd. Reggie tugged her against his chest, held her until the stampede passed. Then he pulled her toward the first-aid station.

Alec watched Reggie fawn over Keira's hand. If Scarlet hadn't interrupted, Alec would have given the younger man a different hand to contemplate. *His fist.*

Alec had all but thrown himself at Keira. Stubborn little minx. He should have done what Reggie did—just ripped his number off and handed it to her.

He'd watched Cissy Odum run into Keira, knew Scarlet was hot on his tail. And in those precious few seconds when he'd stopped to try and help Keira, Scarlet had nailed him.

And Reggie got Keira and the chance to eat Alec's fried chicken!

When Reggie and Keira stood and walked off, Alec almost followed. Then his watch beeped, reminding him he needed to check on Ian Griggs.

He handed Scarlet his plate and made an excuse to go find a rest room. Scarlet pouted momentarily, then smiled.

"The softball game starts in an hour," she said. "I'll meet you there, okay?"

Alec nodded, distracted, as he watch Keira and Reggie disappear into the crowd. Then Scarlet wrapped her arms around him and pressed a kiss to his cheek before backing away, acting coy.

"See you soon," she gushed.

Alec hurried to his car and slid behind the wheel. He needed to establish some ground rules with Scarlet. He'd told her he wasn't interested . . . yet she still persisted.

He turned on Main Street, pulled down the alley. Griggs was scheduled to work until five that afternoon, but Alec still planned to do spot checks.

The gas station was deserted, but he could see Ian behind the counter, watching television.

Alec also noticed that Lance Parks, the reporter, had his car parked a block from the station. It hadn't taken Parks long to establish his own surveillance of Griggs. It was unlikely Griggs would do anything with the reporter watching.

Returning to the festivities, Alec looked around the park, at the families, the happy faces. Music drifted through the air from the bandstand. Delicious smells of barbeque, candy apples, and popcorn permeated the air. Smalltown, USA.

He passed the kiddy contests. The corn-eating contest had just ended. Next up was the watermelon-seed-spitting contest. Several entrants practiced dutifully.

Alec remembered participating in the same contests himself. The feeling of nostalgia washing over him was surprisingly warm.

He shook it off. For every good memory of growing up in Freedom, there was an equally bad one.

He'd picked his first fight in third grade, when he'd learned the real meaning of the word *bastard*. Had too many fights after that to remember.

In junior high, the guidance counselor had labeled

him delinquent, predicted a dire future. A future that had altered when he started dating Keira in high school. For the first time in his life, Alec had wanted to impress someone. Favorably. Keira had never asked him to be anyone other than himself—which made him stop and look at himself. He hadn't liked what he saw.

The distressful cry of a child caught his ear. He turned, and found a small girl at his knee, crying inconsolably. He bent over.

"Lose your mom?" he guessed.

She looked up, tears tracking down her cheeks. At first, she didn't say anything, clearly remembering her mother's admonition not to trust strangers. Then she nodded, crying harder.

Alec looked around, seeing the world from the child's three-foot-tall perspective. He saw legs and knees, no faces, no landmarks.

He smiled. "How about I lift you up on my shoulders so you can look for your mom?"

The child nodded and stepped into Alec's arms. Her trust humbled him. Very carefully, he swung the child up.

"Somebody lost her mother," he called out loud.

Immediately a woman yelled, relief evident in her voice. "Becky!"

"Mama!" The child started sobbing anew.

Alec made his way toward the distraught woman, swinging Becky into her mother's waiting arms.

"Thank you," the woman cried. "I would have never found her with all these people."

Nodding, Alec started to move on. The woman stopped him. "Becky wants to tell you thanks."

He turned, caught off guard when the child reached

forward and hugged his neck, then pressed a tiny, wet kiss to his cheek.

At that same moment, he caught Keira's gaze on the far side of the crowd. If Alec had stuck around, he and Keira could have had a little girl just like Becky. Hell, in ten years' time they could have had a half dozen. The thought wasn't unpleasant. Or scary. Now *that* was dangerous.

"Thank you," Becky hiccuped, releasing him.

"You're welcome." Alec looked back just as Keira turned away, with Reggie's arm draped around her shoulder.

Chapter Eleven

Keira had volunteered to help at the Fireman's Barbecue after the softball game. Afterward, she joined Franny and Darryl at a picnic table to eat. "I'm starved."

Scarlet and Alec materialized out of the crowd, Cissy right behind them.

Scarlet smiled brightly when she spotted Keira. "Oh, look, there's space at this table."

Keira picked at her potato salad, suddenly not so hungry. She felt a hand drop to her shoulder and looked around, just as Reggie Reeves set a plate beside hers.

"I've been looking all over for you." Reggie nodded at the others, then locked eyes momentarily with Alec.

Reggie looked away first, but not before squeezing the top of Keira's hand. "Great game this afternoon. We might have to organize a rematch."

"What about tomorrow, at the camp out at Culverleaf?" Cissy asked. "Who all's going? Besides me, Scarlet, and Alec, that is."

"I'm going," Reggie volunteered. "Been wanting to do some camping up there." He glanced at Alec. "I hope Keira will show me the old fire tower I've heard about."

Alec felt heat build behind his eardrums. The old fire tower in Culverleaf Park was the first place he and Keira had made love. The thought of anyone but him going there with Keira made Alec feel short-tempered.

"The fire tower's off-limits," he said.

"Yeah, the Forest Service will have it blocked tomorrow," Darryl interjected.

Reggie shrugged, winked at Keira. "Another time, then."

Dusk was rapidly setting in, and people began moving toward the huge expanse of grassy lawn to await the fireworks.

Reggie stood, grabbed Keira's plate. "I'll dump these, then let's go find a good spot to watch the fireworks."

He found a spot and spread out a blanket. "I heard Freedom puts on quite a fireworks display."

"They have to, or everyone goes to Hot Springs," Keira explained.

Darryl and Franny came up and spread their blanket beside Keira. Then Keira heard the squeal she was beginning to hate.

Scarlet.

She claimed the space right in front of Keira.

Keira looked off to the side, to where three young boys danced around, begging their parents to let them light sparklers. It couldn't get dark soon enough for her either.

Scarlet had managed to monopolize Alec the entire day. She must have thought catching him in the race gave her exclusive rights.

Of course, Reggie hadn't wandered far from Keira's side either. In all honesty, she'd done nothing to discourage his attention, so she could hardly blame Alec.

Still—

To her surprise, she felt herself bodily lifted onto Reggie's lap. "Come here, darlin'. I've been waiting all day for this."

Tilting her back in his arms, Reggie proceeded to kiss her.

It was a long, drawn-out kiss, short kisses in between longer ones. Keira couldn't have been more shocked. Recovering her wits quickly, she tried to lose herself in the kiss.

Unfortunately, her mind kept making comparisons. And while Reggie was definitely skilled, he wasn't Alec.

He didn't evoke mind-blowing emotion or passion. Reggie's kisses didn't make her want to rip his clothes off. They didn't even make her hungry for more.

They made her miss Alec's kisses.

Damned if she was going to let that happen.

She tried to block Alec from her thoughts by throwing herself fully into the kiss. She wrapped her arms around Reggie's neck, leaning in.

"That's better," Reggie mouthed against her lips. "Now, let me show you what you've been missing."

He took control of the kiss, his tongue sweeping into her mouth. He tasted vaguely of mint . . . not unpleasant. She felt his fingers creep along her lower back, teasing along the waistband of her jeans. Testing. She drew a sharp breath, unsure. He tugged her closer, his fingers stroking across her abdomen.

And still her mind was on Alec.

Enough.

She ended the kiss only to find everyone staring in the fading twilight. Franny had her mouth open. Darryl winked.

She turned and saw that Alec and Scarlet both watched, too, Scarlet in envy, Alec in anger.

Just then, the skies erupted in color.

She moved off Reggie's lap, disconcerted.

Luckily, the roaring fireworks kept everyone's attention elsewhere for thirty minutes. As the sky grew bright with the finale, the national anthem started playing on the scratchy public address system. When it ended, everyone clapped.

The park lights came back on as families gathered their belongings and tired children. Tomorrow many of the same families would watch a second, smaller fireworks display at the reenactment battle.

Keira kept her eyes averted, concentrating on folding the blanket. Scarlet and Alec disappeared in the sea of people heading toward their cars.

Keira bid Darryl and Franny good night, then walked with Reggie toward her car.

When they reached her truck, Keira stopped, not certain how to proceed. *This* was exactly why she didn't mix business and pleasure.

"I know what you're going to say," Reggie started. "You don't date employees. Except Dempsey." He let the words hang. "Give me half a chance, and I'll change your mind."

"Look, Reggie, right now . . ."

He cut her off with a wistful smile. "If now is not good, there's always later. This means I'm not fired, right?"

"Right."

"Good. Can I follow you home? Make sure you arrive safely?"

Keira shook her head. "Thanks for offering. See you tomorrow."

Traffic leaving City Park was congested, but Keira managed to ease into the flow of cars. She wondered where Alec was and if he was with Scarlet.

He probably was. And after her little show with Reggie, she had no right to be mad.

Yet . . . the thought of Alec with someone else stung.

Feeling restless, she turned at Main Street and headed out of town. The last thing she wanted to do was go home and wonder what Alec was doing with Scarlet.

Maybe she'd take a quick ride out to Fire Mountain, make sure her grandfather had gotten home safely. She debated taking a back road, then decided to stay on the main highway.

Traffic had thinned, the dark road deserted. She drove along mindlessly, her thoughts on Alec. Playing those what-if games. Wishing it had been Alec she kissed tonight, not Reggie.

A pair of headlights came up quickly, growing close in her rearview mirror. With a sick sense of déjà vu, Keira recalled the night she and Franny were run off the road. Panic clenched her stomach.

At least tonight she was in a powerful truck that could outrun almost anything. Alarmed, she floored it.

Alec was a gentleman and followed Scarlet home. Then he spent twenty minutes getting away.

Scarlet tried everything to get him to come in, practically undressing right in her driveway. She'd blatantly groped at his crotch, tugged at his belt. To Scarlet, *no* meant try harder.

"You can't be serious about rushing back to Keira after tonight," Scarlet huffed. "Not after the way she threw herself all over Reggie."

Actually, Reggie had thrown himself on Keira—not that Keira had offered much resistance. Reggie had warned Alec he'd push his advantage wherever he could.

It had taken every bit of control Alec possessed not to slug Reggie. He'd almost lost it when the other man had kissed her.

Alec also suspected Keira was upset with him for being with Scarlet all day. Like it was his fault Scarlet had caught him in that damn race.

When he finally arrived at his apartment building, the first thing he noticed was Keira's empty parking spot. His hand tightened on the steering wheel. Had she gone home with Reggie?

It would be easy to throw his car in reverse and drive by Reggie's apartment. He knew where the other man lived.

But what if Keira's truck *was* there?

The thought of her with someone else clawed at him.

Obviously, there had been others in her life. She was too passionate, too gorgeous. And Alec had been gone ten years. It was stupid to think she'd been a nun.

Yet recalling Reggie kissing her tonight drove Alec crazy. Was he jealous?

He resisted answering his own question. His days in Freedom were numbered. Any involvement with Keira had to be limited to maintaining his cover.

Slamming his car door, he went inside. He stopped when he reached the third-floor landing.

Outside Keira's door was a large white box with a bow on top. It had obviously been hand-delivered.

Approaching the box cautiously, he kicked at it. Nothing happened.

Alec kicked the box again, harder, dislodging the lid. Then he peered inside. What he saw disgusted him.

An unidentified creature, obviously long dead, lay in a bloody heap at the bottom of the tissue-lined box. The animal had been skinned.

Moving closer, he spotted the note on her door.

NO LESS THAN YOU DESERVE.

He yanked the note down, careful to minimize his own fingerprints.

Drawing his gun, he let himself inside Keira's apartment and quietly checked it. Nothing appeared out of order.

He took the box and its gruesome contents down to the trash. Jumping in his car, he rode by Reggie's apartment but didn't see her truck. Reggie's truck was gone, too. Were they together? Next, he went by Franny's, then Keira's office.

Growing worried, he tried her cell phone.

No answer . . .

Where the hell was she?

Keira had pulled onto a side road, thankful when the other vehicle zoomed by. Only then did she realize how frightened she'd been and grew annoyed by her sense of suspicion. What was wrong with her? Every car in the night wasn't after her.

She stared at the skyline, saw the distant lightning backlight a bank of black clouds. A storm was brewing. No sense getting caught in it.

Turning her truck around, she hurried home. Alec's car was gone. She knew where he was. At Scarlet's.

And he probably wouldn't be back anytime soon.

What did she expect after kissing Reggie earlier? She'd known Alec watched. Had she hoped to make him jealous? Or prove she was unaffected by his return?

To be honest . . . she had just wanted Alec. Wanted him to *want* her. She should have been sitting in the park making out with Alec, not Reggie.

And, God help her, with Alec she would have demanded a lot more than kisses.

She opened her apartment door, locked it. Loneliness closed in. Feeling sorry for herself, she turned on the stereo, grabbed a beer, and climbed onto the fire escape, brooding as she watched the approaching storm.

The air was heavy, charged. Change was coming. A bluesy love song played, but she didn't have the energy to climb back inside to turn it off.

She sipped her beer, tuning out sound, trying not to think. Not to feel. *Not to care.*

Watching Alec with Scarlet had forced her to admit she still had feelings for him. Deep ones. Complex ones. Their intensity surprised her.

She looked up at the sky, searching for an answer to the one question she'd avoided asking herself since Alec returned.

Did she love him?

She'd never stopped.

The realization was painful. Shocking.

She tried to deny it, but couldn't.

She'd always loved Alec Dempsey. Oh, she'd covered it up, ignored it. Learned to live with it. But seeing him again had brought it all out in the open.

He was the only man her heart had ever wanted. Period. And he would never be hers.

Yeah, the sparks were still there. Lust arced between them. She wanted Alec so badly sometimes it hurt. But it was like lighting candles in a fume-laden kerosene factory. Hazardous. And foolhardy.

They had no future. He wouldn't stay. She'd never leave.

She'd been willing to once, but now she realized she could no more leave Fire Mountain than she could stop breathing.

This was her home.

The sound of a window slamming open behind her startled her. She jumped, skittering to her feet, as Alec climbed through her window. Ire vibrated from him.

"Where in the hell have you been?"

"What business is it of yours?" she shot back. "And what are you doing in my apartment?"

"Looking for you." He drew closer, towering over her in the darkness. "And Reggie."

Keira refused to back up. "Well, I'm home—you can scurry back to Scarlet."

Alec grabbed her upper arms, shook her. He caught a whiff of Reggie's cologne. The scent enraged him. "Where were you?"

"I went for a ride."

"Did you take Reggie out to the fire tower?"

"I left Reggie at the park," she snapped. "I was alone."

"Damn it, Keira! What have I told you about going off by yourself?"

She looked pointedly at his hands. "You're overreacting. It was a short ride, and I wasn't gone long."

Alec drew a deep breath and relaxed his punishing grip. "Overreacting? Someone left a package at your door tonight."

"Where?" She hadn't seen anything when she came in.

"I disposed of it."

At his tone, Keira felt a shiver run up her spine. She knew it was awful, but had to ask. "What was it?"

He described the contents. Her eyes grew wide, and her hand went to her mouth. The anger that had moments ago buoyed her, fled. Leaving her feeling defenseless. Frightened.

Seeing her horror, Alec reached out again, gently this time. He drew her close. He had debated not telling her, but she had to know how serious the circumstances were. How sick the person behind all this was.

"Do you think Griggs did it?" she asked after a few minutes.

"I think he arranged it."

Alec had driven past the halfway house, seeing nothing out of the ordinary. The place was dark. While he couldn't see through walls, Griggs should have been inside. Beau's Toyota was parked and nothing appeared out of order. How was Griggs doing these things? It was obvious he had outside help.

"Why doesn't he just get his money and leave?" Her voice rose in frustration.

"Because right now he's enjoying toying with you. But he's up to something, Keira. I feel it in my gut. And when he makes his move, he'll strike fast, then disappear. All the more reason you've got to be careful."

She tried to shrug off his embrace. Couldn't. "I'm not a bad person. I don't deserve this."

"No, you don't." His anger had faded, slowly giving in to relief. Relief that she was safe. *Gratitude that she hadn't gone home with Reggie.*

When he couldn't find her, a million things had gone through his mind. The worst was the thought of not seeing her again. Not touching her again. *Not making love to her again.*

He shook his head. "Take a vacation. Hell, I'll watch over the business for you. Once you're gone, Griggs will lose interest."

"I can't leave Willis."

"Then let me move in, to protect you." He tightened his arms.

To protect her.

God, she was tempted. To give in. To give over. Just to lose herself in someone else's strength. What was so wrong with that?

Moments ago she'd realized she still loved Alec.

Now she realized it was more than that. She wanted him in a physical sense. Craved him. And admitting her neediness gave it power. Desire swelled, overwhelming her.

Suddenly, she felt feverish. It had started out as an awareness, but being this close, being held in his arms, pushed her over the edge.

Thunder rolled in the distance, low, powerful, yet subdued. The air carried the promise of rain.

The promise of seduction.

She whimpered.

"Shhh," Alec soothed. "I'm here."

He rocked her slowly in his arms. She felt his mouth brush across the crown of her head. It wasn't enough.

She met his eyes. "Kiss me, Alec. Please."

His response was immediate. He lowered his head, caught her lips.

Keira groaned as his tongue swept boldly into her mouth. His hands moved up, grasping her face, angling it slightly as he deepened the kiss.

When she sighed, Alec caught her breath, sealing her lips until she grew light-headed. Then he breathed into her mouth. Giving air. Taking her will.

This was a kiss. This was heat. This was passion.

And if it was wrong, then it was wrong, and she was about to be very, very bad.

She was weary of struggling, weary of debating herself. No one would ever move her heart, her soul, like Alec. The knowledge frightened her. And excited her.

Her fingers unbuttoned his shirt, hands greedy to feel bare flesh, hard muscle.

Alec didn't discourage her. He broke the kiss long enough to peel her T-shirt over her head. She wore a plum-colored bra. The low-cut cups molded her breasts, lifted them.

He ran a finger along the lacy edge of fabric, outlining the generous cleavage, fascinated by the rise and fall of her flesh as she breathed. Slowly, his hands curved, petting, admiring.

With a flick, he unsnapped the front hook, swept the cups aside.

"Jesus!" He'd forgotten how perfect she was. He cupped her breasts, rubbed his thumbs over her nipples. The small pink aureoles puckered tightly, like two plump, sun-kissed raspberries. Responsive, begging for his touch.

He felt Keira's hands on his chest, her fingers raking

muscle, moving lower. He caught her lips in a brutal onslaught and groaned in encouragement as she fondled
him through jeans that were uncomfortably tight. He felt
her fumble with his belt, felt the zipper lower.

Alec growled with approval when she shoved roughly
at his pants, tugging them down his hips. He shook as
she freed his flesh, her touch tentative at first. Then finally her hand closed over his throbbing penis.

He had never desired a touch so desperately in his life.

He jerked, breaking the kiss. Looking down, he
watched her fondle him. She knew how to touch him, remembered he liked a firm grip.

He lowered his mouth, eager to show he remembered
what she liked, too. He caught a pointy nipple gently between his teeth, tugging. She hissed, bucking her hips
slightly. In need.

Stepping back, Alec unfastened her pants then eased her
jeans lower, aware that they were still outside. Aware that
to stop would break the spell. Aware that he couldn't wait.

He checked their surroundings quickly, confirming
that no one could see them. There were no floors above
them, and the balcony faced a windowless building in the
alley.

He slid a finger between her legs, found her blistering
hot. Dripping wet.

She moaned.

"Here. Let me—" His thumb sought her clit, massaging it as his mouth once again closed over her breast.

He started sucking, pulling the tight nipple farther
into his mouth as his thumb increased the pressure.
The results were immediate as she bucked with a
swelling orgasm.

Alec quickly covered her mouth with his when she came. Even as he swallowed her scream, he kept his fingers busy. Rubbing, teasing, taunting, until he'd coaxed yet another orgasm from her. Her responsiveness inflamed him.

Keira trembled, beyond rational thought, wanting only to feel.

Thunder rolled again, but she paid it no heed, her mind centered solely on one thing: *Alec.*

She had to have him. Here. Now. Knew she wouldn't be satisfied until every hot, heavy inch of him was inside her. Making her whole.

But first . . . she wanted to make certain he was every bit as turned on as she was.

She dropped her gaze, teased him unmercifully with her hand. His erection was long and painfully hard. Superb. She ran her fingers down its length yet again, marveling anew at his size and heat. Anticipating. She'd forgotten how magnificent Alec was. Endowed. *Blessed.*

She pressed a kiss to his chest, intent on dropping to her knees and taking him in her mouth. Alec stopped her.

"You go down on me and I won't last ten seconds," he warned.

"But don't you—"

"Oh, yeah. I want it. Bad." He punctuated his words with a kiss, wedged his hand between her thighs. "But I remember that sweet mouth of yours too well. Just the thought makes me want to come."

Keira's eyes closed as Alec's finger began yet another dance of torment. Fire raged in her veins, building toward an explosion. They were both on the edge, both beyond waiting. An anguished cry escaped her. "I need you, Alec. *Now*."

Her words hit Alec hard.

Now meant there was no time to duck inside to find a bed, a chair. *Now* meant no second chances.

Now meant finding a position good for both of them. Fast.

Before she changed her mind.

Swearing, Alec turned her around, until she faced away from him. He placed her hands on the railing, his lips brushing her shoulder, his teeth grazing the soft skin.

He slid his hands down, sliding around her abdomen. Then he tugged her hips back, leaving her bent at the waist.

His hands glided over her buttocks, teasing along the firm crevice.

"Please," she begged.

"Shhhh." He touched lower, found her heat, and quickly fitted the head of his shaft against her. "Is this what you want?"

Keira felt a hot, heavy pressure from behind. "Yes." She strained backward, eager.

Alec pressed into her, but just barely. He grasped her hips, holding her steady as he worked in another inch. Her body was unnaturally tight. It was obvious she hadn't been with anyone in a while. Which pleased him. And made him even more eager to possess her. Mark her.

He drew back. She cried out at the loss. "No!"

"Hush." Alec leaned into her once more. "Just changing angles, babe. Hold on."

He pressed forward with a speed and strength that shocked Keira. She bit back a sharp cry as he buried himself to the hilt, then withdrew, before plunging forward yet again.

The relief she felt was fierce, hot. And temporary. When he drew back she resisted, only to surrender with each stroke. It was madness.

Keira was lost, as a thousand impressions melted over her heated skin like glaze. Sensation overwhelmed her.

Tender torture.

Exquisite relief.

Thunder crashed, growing closer. The heavens let loose with a downpour.

Oblivious to the rain, Alec moved against her, over and over. His hands came around, teasing at her nipples, tugging.

She writhed, the raindrops seeming to sizzle as they hit their overheated skin. Then his hand dropped lower, relentless, as he coaxed her to the brink.

"You are mine," he shouted hoarsely, struggling to be heard above the thunder. "Admit it."

She fought to deny his words. But it seemed as though Alec controlled her flesh. Her will. Her heart.

She shook her head from side to side, striving to control the feelings he evoked.

At her silence, Alex growled, refusing her denial. He locked an arm around her waist, holding her still, while he pulled back, nearly withdrawing. In complete control.

"Say it, Keira. *You are mine.*"

It felt like life or death hung in the balance.

As if he now also commanded the elements, the wind picked up, the rain howled, lashing her already sensitive skin, her exposed emotions.

"You are mine," she cried. "Finish it."

Unable to stop, Alec shoved forward, impaling her yet again. And lost himself to her.

He leaned over, covering her completely, as he battered away, shattering the last of her defenses, granting her that final release before he surrendeered.

Keira felt Alec stiffen, felt his shuddering climax spraying deep and hot inside her.

As the rain fell in torrents around them.

Chapter Twelve

A brilliant flash of lightning brought Keira's head up. Until then it had only been raining, the thunder distant.

"Come on!" Alec opened a window, scooped her into his arms, and ducked inside his apartment.

He set her down, then moved to snap on a lamp. The low-watt bulb cast the room in shadow.

While Keira knew Alec's floor plan was a mirror image of hers, his apartment was unfamiliar. She let her eyes drift. Curious.

Furnishings were sparse. Dresser, television, nightstands. A king-size bed. Unmade. The room smelled vaguely of his aftershave. Of him.

She shivered as the air-conditioning kicked on. Only then did she realize her jeans were still bunched around her ankles. Her bra and shirt were outside. Or so she hoped. She prayed they hadn't dropped to the fire escape below hers.

She watched as Alec leaned out the window, snagging their wet stuff. He had obviously toed off his shoes and stepped out of his jeans while her back was turned.

She admired his backside, the way his broad shoulders tapered down to a narrow waist and slim hips. He still had a fine ass. Tight, well chiseled, the cheeks pale in comparison to his tanned back and legs.

Then she noticed the scars on his left leg—faded but recent. Her heart twisted. He had been injured.

Alec dropped their wet clothes, shut the window.

"Your leg," she said. "I thought the grenade story was just part of your cover."

"I embellished it to make it fit."

Alec's last assignment had involved infiltrating a group of mercenaries buying stolen military arms. When ATF raided the compound, one of the mercenaries decided to blow up a munitions bunker as his last great act of defiance. Alec had been injured by shrapnel from the blast, while trying to stop the man.

"What really happened then?" Keira pressed.

"On-the-job injury," he said finally. "Comes with the territory."

She sensed his reluctance to discuss it, didn't want to shatter the fragile truce. "Will you tell me about it later?"

"Later," he agreed. "For now I want you to strip out of those clothes. You're shivering."

Keira kicked off her sneakers but found the wet jeans harder to work free. The soggy denim clung stubbornly to her skin.

"Let me." Alec dropped to one knee, tugging her pants as she lifted her leg.

She was keenly aware of how close his mouth was to her. Of how much she still wanted him. Making love outside had only whetted her appetite.

When he moved away to toss her jeans onto the pile of wet clothes, she once more admired the play of muscles across his shoulders.

But when he turned back, her line of vision was

drawn lower. He was hard again. And his sheer beauty made her ache.

Fully erect, Alec's penis jutted out from a thick, dark thatch. The stalk was long and wide, slightly curved. Wicked. And topped with a bulbous crown that was bloated, the outer flange stretched.

Her heartbeat accelerated. In awe. In anticipation.

In the confusing aftermath of life without Alec, Keira had quickly learned no male equaled him. In physical prowess, skill. Before Alec, she'd had no basis for comparison. Afterward, she naively assumed all men were alike.

She'd quickly chosen celibacy. Would go back to it when he left.

But for now she'd gorge herself on the experience of a perfect lover.

Alec watched her stare, felt himself grow even harder. The storm raged behind him, rain slashing the glass, thunder swelling, lifting, seeming to empower him with an elemental magic.

He reached down, drew his hand along the solid length of his cock, comfortable with touching himself. He flicked his fist once, pumping his flesh.

"I want you again," he rasped. "So bad it hurts."

The sight of Alec's need was erotic. Her voice was a raw whisper. "Come here. I'll make it better."

Alec jerked. The seductive rub of her words, her blunt invitation, nearly caused him to lose it. *Jesus, what this woman does to me.*

He stepped in and gathered her close against his chest. She felt cold.

"Hot shower?" he offered.

"Maybe later." She kissed his shoulder, nipping his skin with her teeth.

Bending, Alec picked her up and crossed the short distance to the bed. He looked at her, dark eyes dilated, and gently laid her down.

Reaching in the nightstand drawer, he withdrew a box of condoms, dumped the entire contents onto the table. Twenty-four foil packs. Wouldn't last long.

Grasping her chin, he forced her to look up. "I didn't use anything outside." That was a first. Alec never had unprotected sex.

Keira met his gaze. "I think we're okay." It was late in her cycle.

Alec wanted to make her promise she'd tell him if she got pregnant, but there'd be time to discuss it the following day. Just then, he wanted to love her. *All night long.*

He leaned in, kissed her again. His hand reached out, catching her breast, squeezing the full globe. She whimpered, indicating pleasure. She'd always had sensitive breasts, had always enjoyed intense foreplay.

He felt her fingers close around his swaying erection and reveled in the feel of her solid grip.

Pushing her back onto the bed, Alec took her mouth, kissing her leisurely, his tongue sweeping in. Gradually, he shifted his mouth to her neck, savoring the soft skin of her throat before moving lower.

She smelled fresh, like the rain. He licked the drops still sprinkled along the curve of her breast, then kissed each pouty nipple, teasing with his tongue until she groaned for more. He latched on and suckled.

She arched beneath him. He drew back slightly,

catching the tip between his teeth. Tugged. Her hands knifed through his hair, encouraging.

After he'd thoroughly laved that breast, he switched to the other, taking his time, loving, sucking, teasing, as she writhed beneath him.

He ran kisses down her ribs, lapped the rain in her navel, and pressed lower, his teeth grazing along the tender skin inside of her thigh.

She cried out, voice wild. "Alec. I—"

"I know. And I'll make it better."

Moving slowly, he kissed his way down one leg, to her foot. He sucked on her little toe before inching back up her other leg.

At the juncture of her thighs he paused, drew back, and spread her legs wider. He slipped a single finger inside her moist heat. Her flesh resisted. He coaxed, felt the slight give. The surrendering of her body.

If he had anything to do with it, she'd be sore tomorrow. Sore, but satisfied. Well loved.

He eased a second finger inside of her, felt the squeeze of her body as it adjusted against the welcome intrusion.

"You're hot, babe," he whispered. "For me?"

"For you."

"Good. Now hold on."

He lowered his mouth. His tongue darted between the moist folds, locating her swollen nub. Keeping his fingers inside her, he started sucking her clitoris.

Keira's hands went to his head, guiding, encouraging. Holding him in place.

The pressure built, and she quickly climaxed, but still Alec pressed on, unmerciful, stopping only to change rhythm—teasing, driving her mad in slow, sensual degrees.

Just before she came a second time, Alec shifted, moving back up, kissing his way from her abdomen to her breasts.

Condoms flew off the night table as he scrambled to grab one. He quickly sheathed himself, then settled between her legs, urging her knees up.

His blunt, throbbing erection nudged her slick opening. Keira moaned, still on the edge. She wanted him inside her. All the way. Hard and fast.

But Alec had other ideas. He pressed home slowly, slowly, easing his thickness into her. She shook her head, wanting him to go faster, digging her nails into his hips, scoring his skin, begging without words.

He caught her hands, holding them still as he continued his tortuous descent, refusing to be rushed.

Keira felt stretched to the breaking point with him atop her, his weight driving, pinning her.

Then, finally, he was in, filling her. Completing her.

"Wrap your legs around my hips," Alec urged.

She did and found he slid in even deeper. She closed her eyes, opening them abruptly as Alec began rocking very slowly, barely moving.

"God, you feel good," he managed.

She arched against him, shuddered, knew his words would shatter her. Worried *she* might say the wrong thing. "You talk too much."

She drew his mouth down, capturing his tongue and sucking on it. She felt his shaft withdraw, nearly coming out, before sliding back in. His penis was burning hot, felt too thick, like he wouldn't fit. Yet it did, tightly. Fiery flesh dragging on raw need.

Alec did it again, and again, that agonizingly slow withdrawal, going deeper each time, until Keira was mindless with sensation.

She shifted, moving her legs up, around his waist. The new angle caused him to sink even deeper. She drew a sharp breath. Of pain. Of desire.

Alec gritted his teeth. "Can't last much longer."

"Good. This is torture."

Alec flexed, going deep, wanting to lose himself in the momentum. The motion, her body, felt so incredible. He surged forward just as she clenched her inner muscles, milking his flesh, squeezing as if to hold him in place. As if to capture the moment . . .

But it was like trying to chase quicksilver.

He groaned, tugged back. Then lost it.

Unable to stop, he ground his hips from side to side, bringing them both to a shattering close.

Saturday morning dawned too quickly.

They'd been up most of the night making love. Alec had followed her into the shower, seducing her yet again with soap, warm water, and heated touches.

It was almost as if he couldn't stand for her to be this close without them being physically united.

They made love until Keira wept from his touch. And when she thought she couldn't possibly feel anything again, he wrung the most powerful of all climaxes from her.

Then they slept.

Alec snuggled her on top of him, wedging one of her legs

between his. His arms wrapped around her, holding her in place. It wasn't sexual—it was possessive. Predatory. *Mine.*

The morning light streaming in his windows woke her. She kept still, wanting to sigh, but didn't. After all these years to finally awaken in his arms was bliss.

But her happiness was short-lived. It would pass.

He wouldn't stay.

Checkmate.

She wouldn't leave.

Stalemate.

Acknowledging that was painful.

And while she couldn't go back and change what happened last night, she realized getting physically involved with Alec was a mistake.

She moved to get out of bed, but Alec tightened his grip. She felt the drag of whiskers across her shoulder—felt his lips press kisses there.

And lower, much lower, she felt the prod of his erection.

"Don't leave," he whispered, nuzzling his mouth against her. "We can stay in bed all day."

She winced as his rough chin rasped her skin. "Ouch!"

Alec eased back, examined her reddened skin, then ran a hand along his beard. "Sorry, babe. I'll shave."

She held his arm. "I can't stay."

"Can't? Or won't?"

Shouldn't, she thought.

"The camp out," she said instead. "I'm supposed to meet Franny at noon."

Alec sighed. He had things to do himself. Check on Ian and Beau. Call Ostman. Buy more condoms. Sleeping with Keira was probably wrong, but he knew better than to think he wouldn't do it again.

"Darryl's lending me a tent. It might be late, but I'll be there before dark."

Nodding, she moved to get up, wincing at the soreness between her legs. She caught Alec's sympathetic grin, more pride than pity.

Then her eyes dropped to his thick erection, her mouth watering. No wonder she was sore.

Her nipples contracted as desire rippled down her spine. She wanted him again . . .

She glanced at the clock, looked back at temptation, calculating. She had an hour. And she'd need every second.

Alec's morning erections were killers. It would take at least two, maybe three, orgasms to do it justice. Was she up to it?

She eyed his beard, knew there was no time for him to shave. Which meant *girl on top.*

With a sigh—resignation or anticipation?—she pushed him back against the mattress, flat on his back, as she reached for a condom.

She moved down, crouched between his legs. She tore the foil pack, palmed the rubber. Then she grasped his shaft at the base, amazed at the heat, the strength.

At her touch, Alec jerked. Swore. "Hurry. Or I'll do it."

She knew he referred to the condom. "I think you'll like my way better."

Bending low, she boldly ran her tongue over his flesh, up and down, until her saliva glistened on him. She heard his choked intake of air as she drew back and quickly sheathed him, the moisture from her mouth making it easier to cover his distended penis,

She took a moment to marvel at the miraculous stretch of latex. Then she straddled him.

"I'm driving, okay?" She positioned herself over him, lowered slightly, felt the resistance of her body.

"Fine." Alec grinned, flexing once, pushing deep inside her. He reached up, tweaked her nipple. "I'll just see if I can tune in anything on the radio."

Keira was thirty minutes late picking up Franny. Alec's erection had proved to be a fractious four-banger that they'd finally conquered in the shower.

Franny took one look at her and hugged her. "You did it. How was it?"

Keira felt like she winced with every step, but she'd tried to hide it. Her nipples were sore too. Raw. Felt like they'd been chewed on.

Which they had. While she'd remembered Alec was a breast man, she'd forgotten his obsession for her nipples, his penchant for using his teeth.

"Is it that obvious?"

"It's the razor burns." Franny pointed to the side of Keira's neck. "I'll be right back. I've got something in the shop that will fix that. Unless, of course, you'd like to show off for Scarlet's sake? Whisker burns are like a royal flush—beats anything."

Keira shook her head. While she and Alec were supposed to be acting like they'd renewed their relationship, she didn't want to sport hard proof that they were intimate.

As much as she had enjoyed it, she knew she'd stepped over the line. Making love with Alec could only cause her grief. She couldn't have a physical relationship without involving her heart, which explained why she'd never been interested in any of the men she'd occasionally dated. It also explained why her heart felt tender now.

She loved Alec.

But was there any way to make him love her again . . . enough to stay?

The campground at Culverleaf Park was jammed. Kids swarmed like little termites, on bicycles, skates. Parents followed, pushing strollers or tugging on dog leashes.

Keira and Franny drove slowly through the sites looking for Fred and Mabel's shiny aluminum Airstream. Since Fred participated in the mock battle, they always came up the night before and reserved several adjacent sites.

Mabel waved as they approached.

The self-appointed camp hostess, Mabel, ran the show. "Pitch your tents right over there." She pointed to a shaded, private spot near the woods. "Then grab a hot dog. And hurry. Show starts in an hour."

Both Keira and Franny had new pop-up tents that proved easy to set up. They ate, then followed Mabel to the far side of the park where the *battle* would unfold. Mabel set her lawn chair in front and readied her video camera.

The reenactment of the Battle of Freedom was more fiction than fact, more comedy than drama.

The Native Americans fought valiantly against the white settlers, but couldn't drive them out. Then the chief's son kidnapped one of the settlers' daughters. But the brave fell in love with his captive and eventually set her free.

She returned home, and convinced her father to seek

peace. The enactment ended with a hilarious scene of the settlers passing around jugs of moonshine.

Afterward, most of the crowd drifted to the nearby arts and crafts show. By the time Keira and Franny toured all the booths and returned to the campsite, Darryl was there, which pleased Franny.

Alec had also arrived, but was busy helping Scarlet and Cissy pitch their tents.

"I swear, I just don't know a thing about this outdoor stuff," Scarlet gushed.

Keira scowled, reminding herself she had no real claim on Alec. Nor he on her. Anything between them was supposed to be an act to fool Griggs.

Regret washed over her. Sleeping with Alec changed nothing. Not the past. Not the future.

Sally and Stan arrived with Reggie.

As soon as the tents were pitched, they all drifted down to Culverleaf Lake to swim. Except Scarlet and Alec.

Scarlet had commandeered Alec to help her unload more gear from Cissy's car.

Keira knew exactly what Scarlet was up to: Snagging Alec. Rumors of Keira and Alec renewing their relationship wouldn't stop Scarlet.

The sandy beach was crowded, the water a welcome relief to the afternoon heat.

"Feel like a race?" Reggie swam up beside Keira.

She nodded, pointed to the floating dock anchored about twenty yards out, in the deeper water. The dock, with its twin diving boards, was a favorite spot with the teenagers.

"Last one there loses," Reggie said.

Keira was a strong swimmer, but Reggie won. Swimming back, though, she beat him. And squealed when he dunked her, demanding a rematch.

At dusk, Mabel herded the group to the campsite for supper, then preened while everyone praised her cooking. She'd even baked cookies and brownies for dessert.

Later, the group split, with the women packing up food while the men gathered firewood. By the time it grew dark, a large blaze burned. Mabel tossed around bags of marshmallows, while Fred passed out sticks he'd sharpened.

Alec came over and sat by her. "Where'd your afternoon playmate go?"

Keira shot him a look, wondered how he knew she'd spent time with Reggie. Alec had never shown up at the beach. "Guess I could ask you the same about Scarlet."

Franny leaned forward. "Reggie got a call from some climbing buddies who just made town. Said he might not make it back."

"Good," Alec muttered.

"Ahem!" Sally stood, got everyone's attention. "Time for ghost stories. And I've got a good one."

Scarlet walked up, frowned at Keira, then smiled at Alec. "Can you squeeze in one more?"

Franny scooted closer to Keira, pushed her friend against Alec. "Sorry. No room. You'll have to sit over there." She pointed to the empty lawn chair between Darryl and Fred. "And hush. I want to hear this story."

Sally cleared her throat, again, dramatically. "There was a couple who came into town last year, for the reenactment. They wanted to find a little peace and quiet to, you know—*do it*—in the woods, so they drove to the far side of the park and followed one of the logging roads back to the lake."

"What road?" Cissy interrupted.

"The one near old man Carson's farm," Darryl offered. "Right, Sally?"

Sally nodded. "But when they finally decided to head back, their car wouldn't start. The guy had no choice but to walk back to town for help. Knowing it was pretty far, he told his girlfriend to wait in the car. Now, she's pretty scared. They're in the middle of nowhere, and it's dark. He promises she'll be fine, but just in case, she should lock all the doors and huddle on the floorboard, where no one can see her."

"I would have walked back with him," Scarlet said.

"Shhhh!" Franny hissed.

"Before he leaves, her boyfriend tells her not to get out of the car, for any reason, until he returns." Sally's eyes were wide in the flickering firelight. "Hours pass, and the woman stays hidden. Once she hears this scratching noise, but is too scared to look out."

Cissy interrupted. "What kind of scratching noise?"

"I don't know," Sally snapped. "A regular scratching noise. Then she hears a rapping on the window, and a voice says, 'Ma'am, it's the sheriff's department. Open up.'

"Relieved, the woman unlocks the door, figuring her boyfriend is with him. But the deputy pulls her toward his patrol car, and tells her not to look back."

A log fell on the fire, sending up a shower of sparks.

Sally paused, took a deep breath. "The woman looked back anyway and saw her boyfriend's body hanging from a tree above the car. The scratching noise she'd heard . . . were his toenails dragging against the hood."

Franny grabbed Darryl. "I've heard that story a million times, and it still gives me chills."

"That the dumbest story I've ever heard," Fred said. "Who wants a beer?"

"Wait!" Scarlet stood, hurried to her cooler. "I brought strawberry wine."

Fred did nothing to hide his disappointment as Scarlet handed out plastic cups of wine.

Smiling broadly, Scarlet carried the last two glasses over to where Alec sat, handed him one, then held up her glass. "Here's to Alec's return."

Keira ignored the toast and emptied her glass.

Alec frowned, sniffed the wine. "Strawberry, huh?"

Scarlet nodded. "Yeah. Drink up. I'll go get more."

While Scarlet had her back turned, Fred poured his wine out. When Alec would have followed suit, Keira grabbed his cup and drained it. For all of Scarlet's faults, she did make an excellent strawberry wine, which rivaled moonshine in potency.

When Scarlet returned, she eyed Alec's empty glass. "Ready for more?"

Alec shook his head, held up a can. "I switched to beer."

Sally launched into another ghost story, this one a bastardized version of the Headless Horseman. Fred pronounced it more lame than the first one.

By eleven, everyone started heading toward their tents.

Scarlet latched on to Alec's arm when he stood.

"Would you be a doll and walk Cissy and me to the bath-house? After all those ghost stories, we're scared."

Sally snickered. "Oh man! I forgot to tell the story about the woman found murdered at a campground bathhouse."

Scarlet squealed. Scowling, Alec walked with her and Cissy.

Keira watched them disappear, then followed Franny and Darryl back to their tents. Scarlet was doing every-thing to enlist Alec's help. No doubt trying to get him alone.

Climbing into her tent, Keira stretched out on top of her sleeping bag. She felt restless all of a sudden, knew she wouldn't sleep. The tent was stuffy, which was strange because once the sun went down, the tem-perature had dropped. The heat from the campfire had felt good. Now she was so warm she perspired lightly.

She wondered briefly if she had a fever.

Then she felt a twinge. Low.

Memories of last night replayed in her mind.

She closed her eyes, tried not to think about making love to Alec.

She rolled over, but the brush of the sleeping bag felt coarse on her skin, the air in her tent stifling. In minutes, her clothes were soaked from perspiration.

Easing up, she gathered a towel and change of clothes and slipped from her tent. A cool shower would probably help.

She crept around the side of her tent and started toward the bathhouse. She stopped when she heard voices.

Scarlet.

"Come on, Alec. You know you want it." Muffled sounds.

Keira peeked around the curve and spotted Alec and Scarlet in an embrace.

"Kiss me," Scarlet invited. "Kiss me."

Keira turned away. Yeah, it was obvious Scarlet was coming on to Alec, but it still made her mad. Worse, it reminded her it was all a game.

Going to the bathhouse was no longer an option. There was also no way she was going back to her stuffy little tent.

Her skin pricked with heat.

Retracing her steps, Keira took off for the lake. A swim was exactly what she needed.

Alec grasped Scarlet's hands and loosened her grip on his neck.

"Scarlet. I told you, I'm not interested."

"You will be. Trust me." She hooked her fingers in his belt loops and tugged. "Give that strawberry wine a few more minutes."

Alec saw the gleam in her eye. A few more minutes for what?

He remembered thinking the wine had a faintly familiar smell that he couldn't place earlier. Now he realized the smell was similar to an herbal concoction sold as an aphrodisiac.

"Did you put something in my drink?"

She shrugged. "Why? Are you starting to feel hot? Horny?"

Alec remembered Keira had drunk his wine.

"How much did you use?" he pressed.

"Enough."

"Sorry, Scarlet, but I didn't drink it." He stepped away, no longer able to hide his disgust. "And you better think twice before ever slipping someone a drug, herbal or otherwise."

Ignoring her indignant pleas, Alec turned and hurried back toward the campsite. Keira wouldn't be happy, but she had a right to know.

Her tent was dark. He ducked down, whispered her name, and got no answer.

Unzipping the flap, he poked his head in. Her sleeping bag was flat. *She wasn't there.*

Where the hell was she?

He started back toward his own tent, then stopped. A flash of light in the woods caught his eye. Someone was headed down to the lake. Keira?

He slipped along the path, following.

The beach was deserted. Keira stripped down to her bra and underpants to swim. In the dark they'd pass for a two-piece swimsuit.

She rubbed at her arms, wondering again if she was running a fever. Or had come into contact with poison ivy. Her skin itched. She waded in, then dived into the water, the cool wetness a welcome balm.

She let her eyes adjust to the moonlight, then began swimming toward the floating dock. The itching abated somewhat as she swam, but when she stopped and trod water it started again.

She felt winded by the time she reached the raft. Climbing on top of it, she lay down, alarmed.

Something was definitely wrong. She could hear her

pulse drumming in her ears. Another wave of warmth washed over her.

"Keira."

She started when she heard her name.

She sat up as Alec climbed up the ladder and onto the raft. He was wearing briefs. The wet, clinging fabric stuck to his skin.

She shivered, straining to see the outline of his flesh. "What are you doing here?"

Alec approached cautiously. He'd already noticed her shivering.

"We need to talk."

Keira closed her eyes. Did Alec know she saw him with Scarlet? Did he feel he owed her an explanation?

She suppressed yet another shiver, felt heat rising within her. "I need to get back in the water."

Alec's hands closed over her arms. She looked up at him, nearly drowning as an overwhelming wave of desire washed over her. What was wrong with her? How could she want him like this, knowing he wouldn't stay?

"Scarlet drugged my wine, Keira," Alec said. "With an herbal stimulant. You drank it."

It took a moment for the news to register. "A stimulant? Like speed?"

"Like an aphrodisiac."

Keira almost started laughing. Except the itching . . . Alec's hands on her arms felt good.

She shook her head, fighting it, as something else dawned on her. "Don't tell me you came to offer to—"

Alec cut her off. "I came to make sure you were okay. Those herbs affect everyone differently."

She tried to focus, felt dizzy. "I hate Scarlet."

Alec grasped her wrist, found her pulse mildly accelerated. "You can square up with Scarlet later. Right now I need you to tell me how you feel."

"Hot. Itchy. I thought the water would help."

"It will. Though you shouldn't be out here alone," he chided mildly. He didn't have heart to lay into her. "Exercise will help it clear from your system. Feel like a swim?"

At her nod, he continued. "We'll stay close to shore. Tell me if you feel any cramping or discomfort."

Keira climbed down the ladder first. The water felt delightfully cool. She held on to the rail as Alec followed her in.

"Okay?" he asked.

She shook her head. The trembling she'd felt earlier had started again. Low and steady. And it chanted his name. She wanted Alec. Fiercely.

She moved against him, into his arms, shivering as her skin brushed his. "Make love to me." She closed her mouth over his and pressed her tongue deep.

She wrapped a leg around his hip, rubbed against him. Shock waves of sensation shot through her, quite unlike anything she'd felt before. A physical echo of desire.

Alec kissed her back, tenderly, then brushed the wet strands of hair from her face. "I know you think that's what you want, but it's not. With the dose you got, you won't be able to climax, yet you'll keep trying. You'll literally rub yourself raw."

She struggled to press close again, eager to prove him wrong. It didn't take much. The lightest touch sent searing convulsions across her lower abdomen. Erotic and deeply unsatisfying at the same time. He pulled away yet again.

"Please, Alec." She'd beg if she had to.

Her pleas fell on deaf ears. "You gotta trust me on this one, Keira."

She groaned, lowered her head as tremors of desire wracked her.

"I'll kill Scarlet," she gritted between her teeth, miserable. The temptation to touch herself, to grant herself relief, was strong.

Alec caught her hand. "Don't. Let's swim, see if that helps."

They swam for over an hour, taking frequent breaks. By the time they stopped, Keira was exhausted, but the itching had passed, the tingling lessened.

"How is it?" he asked, as they rested. They were in about five feet of water. Alec held her up.

"Better. Tolerable." The burning had passed, but she still felt . . . on the edge.

Alec checked her pulse, found it to be rapid, but smooth. Exactly what he'd expect after a long swim.

She was over the worst of it. The herb, while intense, wasn't long lasting. He knew there was one lingering effect he could now safely do something about.

"This will help."

Under the water, Alec's hand slipped between her legs, shoving aside the wet fabric of her panties.

Keira drew a sharp breath. The need for release was so sharp, so poignant, it astounded her. It also mortified her that Alec knew. That she couldn't help it. Her body didn't feel like her own. Shame mixed with relief.

Her teeth clenched as she struggled. For control. For his touch.

"Let me," he whispered. "It's okay now. To do this."

He cupped her, fitted her neatly against his palm.

Unable to stop, Keira rubbed. A thousand tiny needles burst against her skin, the sensation exquisite. She repeated the movement, felt fire flash across her abdomen.

"I'm scared," she whispered. This was too intense.

"You're fine. I've got you," he murmured, moving his hand. "You'll have one hell of an orgasm, but you'll feel better afterward."

Keira closed her eyes against the delicious friction. With a slight cry, she surrendered, spreading her legs slightly to allow full access.

Using two fingers, Alec penetrated her. "That's it. Don't fight it, babe."

She moaned in gratitude, tried to move closer.

"Shhhh. Let me control the pressure." With a slow touch that drove her mad, Alec patiently brought her to the brink.

She arched against his fist, undulating her hips. Faster. Harder. And just when she thought she couldn't take any more, Alec lifted her from the water, shoved aside her wet bra, and took her nipple in his mouth. He sucked hard, tugging, teasing. Then gently bit her.

She lost it, flew apart, crying out with the intensity of her release.

Leaving the water, Alec quickly helped her dress, then carried her back to the campsite. At the edge of the path, he set her down.

"You okay?"

Keira looked up at him. "Actually, I'm embarrassed."

She'd lost control. Not the mutual loss of two people. Just her.

He knew exactly what was bothering her. Understood. He cursed Scarlet. Drawing Keira close, he kissed her. "Stay with me?" he whispered. "No sex. I promise."

Keira shook her head, unable to make that same promise. While the uncontrollable effect of the drug had passed, the desire for Alec hadn't. She didn't want to beg again . . .

Better she stay alone and retain some measure of pride. "Good night, Alec. We'll talk in the morning."

Beau Watson hung back, knew better than to risk following any closer. He stared at the jar in his hand, at the bugs he'd been collecting.

He was out of time, thanks to the little show those two had put on. Granted, he hadn't really seen that much. Some titty. He'd heard her squeal when she came though. Griggs would shit when Beau told him what he saw.

And what he'd overheard . . .

Was it still rape if the woman had ingested an aphrodisiac? And what would Griggs pay for that little idea?

Chapter Thirteen

Alec left the camp early. He'd been up most of the night, brooding over Keira's refusal to spend the night in his tent. He wanted to believe he was noble enough to accept a "no" without question.

So why all the self-recrimination? Why had he caught himself heading for her tent twenty times? It wasn't because he was horny. Well, yes, he was horny. Had been horny since first laying eyes on Keira again.

But last night he'd simply wanted to hold her, know she was close. Watch over her.

Not good.

She had definitely gotten under his skin. The problem was knowing what to do about it. His head was at odds with his libido.

And his heart?

He forced his thoughts elsewhere, not wanting to consider his emotions. That would only lead to trouble.

Parking his car, he hurried toward the halfway house. According to their schedules, both Griggs and Beau were confined to the premises all day.

The house was quiet, which irritated Alec.

Ostman had led him to believe Griggs would retrieve the money quickly and leave. But Alec was starting to have doubts. What if Griggs didn't make his move, say, for months?

He immediately rejected the notion. Logically, if Griggs had access to two million, he should be chomping at the bit to get away from the restrictions of parole, from people breathing down his neck.

But what if Griggs really didn't know where the money was?

What if the money's location had indeed died with his brothers? Was Griggs now forced to do the same as others? Search for a hidden fortune?

Or suppose someone had found the money but never reported it? Was living large courtesy of the Griggses?

Either scenario meant Ian Griggs would be around Freedom a very long time. Which presented a whole new range of problems.

Alec had no intention of staying long-term in Freedom. He'd been told the assignment wouldn't last more than a couple weeks.

Why had Ostman seemed so confident Griggs would make a move quickly? Did he know something he wasn't telling? Alec needed to discuss this more in depth with Ostman, see what exactly made the FBI so certain Griggs knew where the money was.

With the holiday weekend over, Alec spent Monday following Beau, who went out to Culverleaf Park. *Again.* Alec watched as Beau parked, then disappeared down a trail.

Alec's gut told him Beau was running errands for Griggs. While Lance Parks and two other reporters sat near the gas station watching Griggs, Beau ran around the countryside, raising no eyebrows.

After Beau returned to the halfway house, Alec went back to Culverleaf and followed the same trail. It was a frustrating dead end that led nowhere. Had Beau gone off the trail at some point? What was he after?

If he was doing something for Griggs, like retrieving the cash, he certainly wasn't coming out carrying satchels of money.

Alec tried calling Ostman but couldn't reach him. He called Keira late in the afternoon, catching her at the office.

"What time do you plan to knock off?"

Keira closed her eyes against the yearning that arose. The deceptively casual question triggered a warning, reminded her not to get too close to a man who wasn't staying. Why couldn't she remember that simple rule?

"I'm leaving in five minutes, but I'm not going home. Tonight's Sally's bachelorette party," she reminded him.

Sally and Stan were getting married the following weekend. Keira and Franny were both bridesmaids. There were wedding-related events scheduled the entire week.

"Call me when you get home," he said.

"I'll pretend you prefaced that with *please*."

"Pretty please. *Babe*." He hung up.

Keira met Franny for supper—Chinese takeout—then they hurried to meet Mabel at McDuff's bar.

McDuff's was a rowdy place on weekends but fairly tame during the week. The bar had a side room, for private parties.

While Keira arranged tables of appetizers, Franny conversed with the bartender. Since the women-only party would undoubtedly attract the interest of the regular bar patrons, the owner posted a bouncer at the door.

Keira, Franny, and Mabel drew straws to select a designated driver. Keira drew the shortest one.

Franny did a little dance. "You'll be sipping root beer while Mabel and I do shots of tequila."

Actually, Keira was just as glad not to drink. She wanted her wits about her later, when she went home.

She'd been vacillating all day, one minute promising herself she wouldn't sleep with Alec, the next minute fantasizing about him until she was on the brink of orgasm. Something had to give. She was tired of the regrets, the second guesses.

Already her heart felt tender. More than once she caught herself thinking *what if.*

What if Alec stuck around?

What if they got back together?

What if she was pregnant?

The last one she dismissed, virtually sure they had missed her fertile window. Since she hadn't been sexually active recently, she didn't keep real close tabs on her periods. But it was typically near the middle-of-the-month payroll.

And except for that first time, Alec had used a condom.

Still, she'd breathe easier when she started. The last thing she needed was an unplanned pregnancy.

She forced her thoughts back to the party as guests streamed in. The room erupted into cheers as Sally arrived, and for the next several hours, the women partied loudly, much to the envy of the men outside in the bar.

At ten, a cop arrived, threatened to arrest Sally for drunken, disorderly conduct. The music died abruptly.

"But I'm at McDuff's," Sally protested. "Everyone here is drunk and disorderly."

A nervous titter ran through the room as the cop snapped a pair of handcuffs on Sally. "For arguing," he said. "Now here's your punishment."

The music struck up again. Loud. Sally's mouth opened as the cop began gyrating his hips in sync to the beat.

Then he started stripping.

He started with his hat, which landed on Sally's head. Then he peeled off his belt, slowly, held it out to her. "Wanna touch my weapon?" He thrust his pelvis forward.

All twenty women started whooping and clapping in approval. The place was in an uproar by the time he got down to his G-string.

"What I wouldn't give to be your age again." Mabel winked at Keira, then tossed back a shot of tequila and started fanning herself.

While the male stripper had been hired to come in and do one number, he ended up staying. At Franny's insistence, he stood at the front of the room and led them through a couple of his favorite moves.

"You ladies feel free to remove your clothes," he yelled.

Keira joined in the fun, which seemed similar to the line-dance classes she and Franny took. Right foot, left foot, right hip, left hip. Pelvic twist. Forward thrust.

At midnight, the party broke up. "This was great," Sally gushed. "You outdid yourselves."

She hugged Keira and Franny, then wove toward the door doing the twist the stripper had taught them. Sally's sister—her designated driver—laughed.

Franny and Mabel headed to Keira's car.

Mabel sat in the backseat, humming. "I bet if I did a few of those moves, Fred might want to jump me tonight."

Franny and Keira exchanged glances. Fred had occasional bouts of impotence, much to Mabel's chagrin, and she was always looking for new ways to stimulate him.

"Some of those moves could give a man a heart attack." Franny grinned. "I can't wait to try them on Darryl."

Keira went to her apartment after dropping off her friends.

First thing, she noticed that Alec's parking spot was empty. Disappointment settled in her stomach. Had she expected him to be waiting for her?

Yes, she had.

They'd made love, and already her heart was making expectations, setting her up for a fall. This is exactly what she didn't want to happen.

She hurried to her door, inserted the key, chastising herself for getting involved again. She knew better, damn it.

She pushed the door open with more force than intended. The door swung wide, bounced off the wall.

Something fell from above, clipping her head before clattering on the floor.

Keira jumped, her hand automatically fumbling for the switch. When the light came on, she saw the note taped to the wall, just above the switch.

GOTCHA BITCH, it read.

The skin at her nape felt crawly.

She shuddered, knowing someone had been in her apartment. But, instinctively, she knew they were already gone.

A red plastic bucket lay on the floor, still listing

slightly from side to side, where it had rolled a few feet from her. A piece of cardboard lay to one side. The bucket had obviously been rigged to fall when the door opened. But why the cardboard? Another note?

As she reached for her phone, a slight movement on her arm caught her attention. Keira glanced down as a large brown spider scurried over her skin.

She screamed, knocking it away.

She abhorred spiders. As a young child, at a school picnic, she'd gotten locked in an old wooden outhouse during a game of hide and seek. The outhouse was infested with daddy longlegs—nonpoisonous, but creepy. She'd been covered with them by the time someone let her out.

Something brushed her forehead. She flicked her hand, saw another spider fall. With a growing sense of dread, she looked down at her shirt. More spiders, large, small, scurried over the fabric.

The crawly feeling at the base of her neck returned, but this time she knew what it was. She was literally crawling with spiders.

The cardboard on top of the bucket had been a lid.

Bending at the waist, she flipped her hair over her head, beat at it, shaking it. Hundreds of spiders were tangled in the long red strands, legs wriggling furiously as they tried to escape.

She screamed as she felt more movement. Beneath her shirt . . .

It was late when Alec returned.

Scarlet had showed up at his apartment, drunk. He'd driven her home, talked with her; but he knew that in her

inebriated state she'd recall little. One thing was clear—
Scarlet was jealous of Keira. He had suspected all along
that was the main reason Scarlet pursued him.

When he pulled into the apartment building, he spotted the sheriff's car parked out front. His eyes swept the
parking lot, confirming that Keira's truck was there.
Swearing, he raced inside.

He found Keira huddled in the hall, head down on her
knees. She had her arms wrapped around her, tightly, as
if she were freezing. The air was heavy with the odor of
insect spray.

He pushed forward, dropping down on one knee. He
grasped her chin and forced her to meet his eyes. "Are
you hurt?"

She shook her head, indicating no.

Alec looked inside her apartment. A uniformed
deputy was in the foyer, talking on the phone.

"What happened?" he asked.

She shuddered. "Somebody left spiders in my apartment."

Spiders. Alec swore under his breath. Everyone who
knew Keira knew her fear of them.

Wrapping an arm around her shoulders, he helped her
to her feet, then moved toward his apartment door, unlocked it, and turned on a light. "Go on in."

Keira hesitated. "Where are you going?"

"To your place. I'll be back in a minute."

Alec went next door, introduced himself to the
deputy, and looked around the apartment. He saw the
note lying on the counter. GOTCHA BITCH.

"Was that on the door?"

The deputy shook his head. "It was *inside* the apartment. Along with this."

Using a pen, the deputy tipped the plastic pail that still held several smaller spiders.

"Poisonous?" Alec asked.

"No. They're common, garden-variety spiders." The deputy picked up a clear plastic evidence bag that held a short wooden shim. He pointed over Alec's head. "The bucket was rigged to fall after the door opened. Keira got showered with them."

Alec felt his temper rise. The trick had been masterminded with no other purpose than to terrorize Keira. He had no doubt who was behind it. The temptation to go over to the halfway house and throttle Ian Griggs was strong.

Except he already knew the drill. Griggs would have an alibi, and he'd accuse Keira of harassment.

"Any clues?" Alec asked.

"Nothing obvious. We'll check for prints, of course."

"How'd they get in?"

"Had to be the fire escape. Keira swears the windows were locked." The deputy shrugged. "They could have been jimmied. Cheap locks."

The locks would be replaced tomorrow. By Alec.

While the deputy went next door to go over his report with Keira, Alec went into her bedroom and gathered up a few of her belongings. Clothes and toothbrush were enough. She'd sleep naked and could use his toothpaste.

"It's late," Alec said when the deputy finally left. "You can have the bathroom first, while I lock up."

"I'll wait." Keira shuddered, her hands going to her

hair as she combed nervously through it. "I've got the heebie-jeebies so bad, I don't want to shower alone."

Alec tugged her close, kissing her until she relaxed against him. "Was that an invitation?"

She nodded.

"Wait right there." He quickly locked up, then picked her up and carried her to the bathroom, resolute. By the time he finished with her, the only memory she'd have of something on her skin would be him.

In the morning, Alec fixed a big breakfast. Omelets, French toast. Keira barely picked at her food.

"I still think you should leave town," he began.

She held up a hand. "If I run, Griggs wins."

"Let him."

His response infuriated her. "I have a business to run, a lot at stake. People depend on me. I've got deadlines to meet, with heavy financial penalties if I miss one. And my competitors wouldn't hesitate to swoop in if I'm not around."

"Then move in here, with me."

She shook her head. "People would talk. And I've worked too hard to get where I am."

"They'll understand."

Keira gave him a look. That was easy for Alec to say. He was leaving. She had to stay and face everyone, people who knew Alec had walked out on her once before. She couldn't do it a second time.

"Willis wouldn't understand. Besides, I've already decided to stay with Franny for a few days while I have my apartment fumigated."

Alec wanted to remind her Griggs wasn't any more

afraid of Franny than he was of her. Instead, he said, "I don't like it."

Beau Watson paced across the small confines of the room he shared with Ian Griggs.

"I'm telling you that hole's been empty a long damn time," Beau said. "You sure you remembered the right coordinates?"

Ian took a drag off his cigarette. The GPS coordinates were correct. Beau had indeed located the right mine shaft.

The shaft Ian's brother selected had a numbered metal plate nailed to a cross support. The same metal plate Beau had photographed.

"Tell me again what you saw."

"Nothing," Beau spat. "I saw nothing! Old leaves, pinecones. Fucking squirrel nests. But no chest containing gold. No aluminum keg with cash."

"And you dug right where I told you?"

"Right here." Beau pointed to a photo. "I bet some fool found it, thinks it's that lost gold everybody around here talks about."

The Lost Confederate Gold. Ian coughed, swallowed. He could remember his father getting drunk and rambling about finding that gold. How it was going to change their lives. How he'd stop beating up on them once things were better.

People in the area had been searching for those nonexistent gold coins for years. How ironic that Ian had found real gold in the armored truck they'd robbed. At the time he'd considered it poetic justice.

"What are we gonna do now?" Beau pressed.

"I'm not sure."

Time was running short. He had a lot riding on that money. Like his life.

Maybe it was time to rethink his plans. Get rid of Keira once and for all, then disappear.

Keira was in Hot Springs early the next morning, to meet with the general contractor to review change orders. She also got word she'd won the bid on the GC's next job, a string of franchise restaurants across the state.

"Congratulations," the man said. "You deserve it."

The news surprised and pleased her. It would be her largest job to date and could mean a host of new opportunities.

After all the turmoil of late, she felt like skipping as she left the construction trailer. Until a familiar-looking Dodge truck pulled up, blocking her path.

The lettering on the truck's door read BARRY BROTH-ERS ELECTRIC.

The window lowered, revealing the smirking face of Eddie Barry. His brother, Frank, was in the passenger seat.

"Heard you got the restaurant bid," Eddie said. "How many blow jobs did you give to get this one?"

Keira's insides quaked. She'd heard it before, from Eddie and others like him. Unfortunately, she knew she'd hear it again. The fact that they were a minority didn't make the insult any less demeaning. Nor made it any easier to ignore.

But she'd learned a long time ago that to explode and show her rage only encouraged them.

She kept walking.

The truck surged forward, tires spinning up dust as it blocked her path again.

"Spreading yourself a mite thin, wouldn't you say?" Eddie taunted. "What with your old boyfriend back in town and all."

That remark hit its target. "Go to hell, Eddie. And take that baboon you call a brother with you."

She turned away, headed straight for her truck, embarrassed to notice several of her employees had witnessed the incident and were headed her way.

Reggie Reeves came up beside her, removed his gloves. "Problems, boss lady?"

"Nothing I can't handle."

Reggie eyed the Dodge as it peeled out onto the street. Eddie Barry yelled an obscenity, flipped up his middle finger.

One of her other employees hurled a broken piece of brick, dinged the back of the Dodge.

"Say the word, and I'll kick both their asses," Reggie said.

She slammed the lid of a toolbox. "Thanks. But I'd like to think I can kick ass myself when needed."

He gave her a doubtful look, then sauntered off with the others.

The incident left Keira feeling cross. She was a strong woman, damn it, and she hated feeling weak. Or dependent. Or self-conscious. She was also private by nature, and it bothered her to think the Barrys knew she was intimate with Alec. Hell, the whole town probably knew. Wasn't that part of Alec's plan?

By evening, she'd convinced herself to get a motel

room and stay in Hot Springs. She had an overnight bag in her truck with stuff she'd planned to take to Franny's.

She worked late and drove through a fast-food place for supper. For the first time in weeks, she felt like she'd exerted some control.

She called Franny—left a message she was staying in Hot Springs, and left her room number in case Franny wanted to call back.

Then she took a long shower and turned on the TV. She must have drifted off to sleep because she awoke around ten, startled.

Someone was knocking furiously on her door. Pounding actually.

And not just anyone.

Alec.

"Open up, Keira."

Fumbling with the tie of her robe, she hurried to the door and opened it a crack.

Alec shouldered his way in. "Jesus, I've been worried."

Keira shoved her hair from her eyes, not quite awake. "Why? What's wrong?" Had something else happened?

"What's wrong? Nobody knew where you were." Alec spoke between clenched teeth. "They said you left the job site at six after having a run-in with the Barrys."

Alec had also been searching for Eddie and Frank Barry, but couldn't find them. "I've been frantic," he continued. "And here you are laid up in a friggin' motel."

His words and tone infuriated her. "Did you think to check with Franny?"

She moved to pass him, but Alec snatched her wrist,

pulled her close. "Franny didn't check her answering machine until late. We've been calling your cell phone. We've *both* been worried."

Keira remembered switching her phone off to recharge it. She jerked her arm free. "Look, Alec—"

He cut her short, eyes glittering. "No. I want to show you something."

Alec had backed her up against the bed. Grasping her shoulders, he pushed her down on the mattress. Before she could react, he tugged her arms over her head, then tied them to the headboard using the sash from her robe.

Shocked, Keira looked from her hands to Alec. She tugged at the bindings but couldn't get free.

Alec stood, paced toward the door.

"Untie me right now," she demanded.

"No."

Keira could have screamed with rage. She looked down, saw that her robe was fully open from her struggles. At least she had on a camisole and panties.

"How dare you!" she hissed, struggling uselessly. "So help me—"

Alec sighed, came over, and sat on the side of the bed. Very gently, he drew her robe closed.

"Now you know how I feel," he said quietly. "I want to help. But you keep tying my hands."

He reached over her head, freed her. Then he stood. "I almost died when I couldn't find you tonight."

The raw tone in his voice tore at Keira. Told her he cared. The thought fanned a small spark of hope.

She softened, grasped his hand, tugged him back down to sit on the bed. "Do you think any of this is easy for me? I'm used to taking action, solving a problem. Not sitting and waiting for something else to happen."

"Then let me help."

She put a finger to his lips. "Can't you see I'm afraid of depending on you too much? Ultimately, you'll leave, and I'll be alone." And the price for attachment was too great.

Alec wanted to deny her words. Couldn't. He and Keira didn't have the impersonal distance of two people doing a job. They had a shared history, emotional baggage.

And no matter how each of them tried to tiptoe around it, they still shared a bond. He'd felt it the first time he'd laid eyes on her. Recognized it had always been there . . . waiting to spring back to life.

And that bond grew stronger each time they made love.

She was right. He would leave. But it wasn't going to be easy. "I don't know what to say to convince you otherwise."

Keira shook her head. "You don't have to say anything. I'm not asking you to commit or make excuses." She reached for the snap of his jeans. "And instead of arguing, let's make love."

She lowered the zipper, tunneled her hand into his jeans, freeing him. His flesh was already erect, grew harder in response to her touch. Her fingers slid over the bulbous head. The sight of him, like this, was more than she could bear.

She wanted to claim this man in a very primal way. Conquer his body if not his heart. And she knew exactly how she wanted to do that.

She fondled him a moment, then stood and unbuttoned his shirt, shoved it off his shoulders. Straightening, she dropped her robe, then slowly, seductively, peeled off her camisole and panties. Standing naked before him, she crooked a finger.

"Stand up, please."

Shrugging off his shirt, Alec stood. Keira quickly tugged his jeans down.

A gasp escaped her as his engorged shaft poked straight out. No matter how many times she saw him naked, the sight of him fully erect stole her breath. His penis swayed, heavy. Bold.

Inviting.

Her eyes drifted up, taking in the sleek rippled muscles of his abdomen, the dark whorls of hair on his chest. She shoved him down to the bed. His hands grasped her waist, pulling her along. She climbed on top of him, her legs spread over his hips.

His hands cupped her buttocks, pressing her close as he ground his erection against her mound.

"Easy," she whispered. "I have plans for you. Lie back."

When he obeyed, Keira sat up. And grabbed his hands, one by one, pulling them over his head.

She had no illusions. Knew he *let* her tug his hands over his head. But she had other strengths.

"What kind of plans?" he asked.

She scooted up, straddling his chest before lowering her breast to his mouth. "Naughty ones."

"My favorite." Alec latched on, drawing her nipple deep into his mouth, then suckling as if he'd devour her.

Keira felt an orgasm build, fought it. She was dripping wet, hot. But focused. She held both his hands in one of hers as she shifted, offered her other breast.

Distracted, Alec didn't realize her game until it was too late.

She tugged the sash that now bound his hands to the headboard.

He frowned. "What's this?"

"Let me show you the only reasons to ever tie someone's hands."

She pressed a kiss to his forehead, then to each eye. She kissed his cheek and gently nibbled at his bottom lip before delving deeply into his mouth. Capturing his tongue, she sucked it. Alec made a low noise of approval.

You haven't seen anything, Keira thought.

Moving lower, she dragged her breasts across his chest, taunting him. The wiry hairs tickled lightly. Her nipples were already sensitized, elongated from Alec sucking them. They drew even tighter with anticipation.

She kissed his neck, nibbled at his collarbone, then took his small flat nipple into her mouth.

When she bit softly, he hissed. When she blew air across the wet surface, he groaned. And when she moved to his other nipple, he begged for more.

His erection pressed along the crease of her bottom. Lifting slightly, she rubbed against it, teasing.

Again, Alec groaned. The bed creaked as he tugged against his restraints. "Careful," she warned. "You'll distract me."

He relaxed his arms. "Wouldn't want to do that."

Moving lower, Keira ran her tongue down his ribs, then bit the tender skin below his navel. She had his erection caged between her breasts, felt the prod of his long shaft.

She looked down at the swollen crown, watched fluid

seep from the tip. She moved, kneading his erection between her breasts.

Alec bucked.

"Can't take it?" she taunted.

"I can take anything you can dish out," he gritted.

Smiling, Keira moved lower. "I'll go easy on you."

"Don't."

Avoiding the obvious, Keira skipped down to the inside of his thigh, running nibbling, biting kisses down to the knee of one leg and back up the other.

When her hand finally closed over his shaft, Alec groaned.

She stroked him firmly, fascinated anew by the length, the width, the heat. This part of him was so unique, so different. So male. The flesh was hard as granite, the skin soft as a whisper, quivering with restraint, straining with need.

She lowered her mouth to the pulsing head, licked the single drop of promise.

A shudder rocked him as her mouth dipped lower, her tongue tracing the crooked vein that ran down one side. She licked at the wide base, teasing, testing, before cupping his sac carefully in her hand, weighing the heavy testicles.

This was power. This was trust.

Alec was bound, at her mercy, vulnerable, as she stroked and caressed this most sensitive area. She felt humbled to realize she'd never hurt this man in a thousand years.

Crooning softly, she moved lower still, mouthing the large glands, squeezing ever so gently, massaging.

Alec started swearing, tugging harder on his bonds.

"Easy," she whispered. "We're just getting started."

Drawing back, Keira took the swollen tip of his penis into her mouth, flicked her tongue yet again along the underside. She gently grazed her teeth along the ridge, then closed her mouth tightly over the head and sucked. Hard.

Alec thrashed from side to side.

Emboldened, Keira took him deeper, then drew back; deeper, then drew back, repeating the motion, taking her time, relaxing her throat, practically swallowing him, until most of his shaft disappeared beneath her hungry lips.

"Christ, babe! Harder!" Alec encouraged.

Keira complied, working her mouth up and down his turgid flesh until she felt his control surge near the breaking point. Then she started sucking. Again.

Alec convulsed. "Stop!"

Keira paused long enough to look up at him, continuing to stroke him with her hand. "You didn't say *please*."

Then she lowered her mouth, resuming the strokes with her lips, her tongue, the pace frantic.

Color burst behind Alec's eyes. He'd never again say *please* if this was the consequence.

He glanced at the straining muscles of his raised arms, felt the fabric digging in at his wrists. Then he looked down at Keira.

Her fiery red hair was spread out gloriously around her, trailing across his chest, his arms. She shifted, flicking her hair aside with one hand, giving him a clear view of her mouth devouring his flesh.

He could have stayed suspended in that moment forever. Watching her mouth exploit his cock, feeling her hot tongue torment him. It was the perfect balance between two worlds: Heaven and Hell. The best of each. The wicked and the sublime.

Alec started shaking. He felt his limbs grow more taut, muscles bunching, a warning. And still Keira kept at it. Sucking harder. Torturing.

Sensation spiraled, winding tighter. The feeling built, sweeter than life. Utopia was within his grasp.

There was a tearing noise as he ripped free of his bonds. Keira felt the bed shift as Alec raised up. His hands dug into her hair, encouraging her, holding, guiding. Praising.

"That's it, Keira. God, that's it."

She flicked her tongue back and forth, just below the head.

He panted as breathing became difficult. A primitive noise tore from his throat, his voice harsh, ragged, as he recognized the warning signs. "If you . . . don't stop . . ."

She paused, glanced up. "You'll what? Lose it?"

Her hand continued to stroke his penis. The shaft was engorged, swollen to a painful shade of deep purple. His skin felt stretched to bursting.

Locking her eyes on his, she slowly, deliberately lowered her mouth, ran her tongue over the crown, licking him. *In control.*

He hissed, tried to speak.

"Give it up, Alec. You're mine," she whispered.

Her mouth closed over him for what she knew would be the final time. She'd give him no choice but to surrender.

Taking his shaft willingly, deep in her throat, her hands groped lower, closing over his testicles. She clutched softly but firmly, then rubbed her thumb along the circle of flesh just behind his sac.

She felt him jerk, struggle for restraint. She pressed, squeezed, denying him that option.

Alec bucked once, twice, knew he was lost, and reveled in her selfless gift. He felt himself start to come, the hot ejaculate seeming to sear his insides as he exploded into her mouth with a raw shout.

She didn't let up, drawing him even deeper as he went over the edge, shouting her name.

Chapter Fourteen

Alec rose before dawn, to resume his watch on Griggs.

But he couldn't leave without making love to Keira one more time. His cock surged, greedy. He nuzzled her neck, barely bringing her up from sleep before driving into her with a strength and fullness that surprised him.

The room smelled of sex and sweat, with a faint overlay of honeysuckle. They'd made love countless times during the night. That he could even get a hard-on after Keira went down on him was a miracle. He'd never experienced an orgasm that deep, that powerful. That draining.

She stirred beneath him now, all soft, all feminine. So tight. So hot. He pumped his hips, fast and furious. She came quickly. Alec, too, the intensity all the sharper for the brevity. He held her close, felt a sharp yearning for time to stop. A wish it could be this way always. It wouldn't.

"Go back to sleep, babe," he whispered before leaving.

He stopped at a diner outside of town and grabbed coffee to go. He debated briefly about taking a cup back to the motel for Keira. She was probably still in bed . . .

A Dodge truck pulled into the diner's parking lot. Eddie Barry climbed out, sauntered over to where Alec stood.

"Heard you were looking for me yesterday." Eric scratched his beard. "Got a problem?"

Alec had a problem with anyone who harassed Keira. Especially the Barrys' particular brand of harassment. "No. You do. Stay the hell away from Keira Morgan."

Eddie smiled. "If she can't take the heat, she needs to find a different line of work."

"Maybe it's you and your brother that need to find a different line of work. I hear she's practically run you out of business."

The other man's smirk disappeared. "We can't compete with somebody who spreads her legs to get business. And everybody knows that's how she steals our jobs."

Alec moved closer, felt his temper flare. "She gets bids because she gets the job done right. Without trying to extort kickbacks."

"Why you—" Eric took a swing, caught Alec's jaw. "'Course, maybe I'd feel the same way if I was fucking her."

Alec retaliated with a punch to Eddie's stomach. Eddie swung again, missed.

Alec caught him with a solid uppercut. "You're not fit to say her name."

Eddie fell back, hit the ground, and rolled away.

A hand grabbed Alec's shoulder. He turned quickly, fists drawn, and found two of Keira's employees standing behind him. The men had obviously stopped for breakfast on their way to the job site.

Jake, Keira's senior crew chief, looked at Eddie. "If I were you, I'd stay down."

At first Eddie didn't move. He swiped a hand

across his mouth, saw the blood. "If my brother had been here . . ."

Alec shrugged. "Your brother knows where to find me."

The other man, who had arrived with Jake, cracked his knuckles. "He knows where to find me, too. We'll settle it once and for all."

Swearing, Eddie pushed to his feet, making his way to his truck on unsteady feet.

"Keira won't like it when she hears," Jake said. "She doesn't want anyone fighting her battles."

"Guess she'll have to fire me," Alec replied.

He talked with the men a few more minutes, then headed back to Freedom.

Decking Eddie Barry had felt damn good. And while he doubted the man would change completely, he'd bet Eddie would think twice before harassing Keira again while Alec was in town.

But would he remember the lesson once Alec was gone?

Back at the motel, Keira tried to go back to sleep but couldn't. Her mind wandered down dark tunnels, even as her body ached with a desire that seemed only to grow with each encounter. As if she gave a little part of herself to Alec each time they made love.

Last night, he had again urged her to move in with him. It was tempting, but she held back.

Moving in with him seemed too . . . permanent. Too much like a long-term commitment. And it was fraught with potential for heartache. It was too easy to form attachments, to surrender her independence.

To be shattered when he left again.
Restless, she rose, showered, and headed to work.

With Sally's wedding looming, Keira only stayed one night in Hot Springs. She saw little of Alec, though they talked frequently on the phone.

She knew his frustration over the assignment mirrored her own. The sheriff's department had found no clues from the spider incident the other night. Griggs seemed indeed the model parolee.

She'd heard about the brawl between Alec and Eddie Barry. Normally, the news would have infuriated her. Instead, it made her feel soft, which she resisted.

Soft meant vulnerable. A no-no where Alec was concerned. And even though Alec didn't really work for her, she made a point to chew him out in front of a few other employees. She wouldn't tolerate her authority being undermined.

Thursday evening the bridesmaids treated the bride to dinner, and Friday was the rehearsal. Keira spent both nights with Franny.

While she still felt uneasy about being in her apartment, she'd forced herself to spend a little time there each day.

It angered her to think that someone had shattered the sense of safety she'd always felt at home. Still, she had a sophisticated alarm system installed. And found herself more frequently checking the gun Alec had given her.

Saturday morning dawned with the promise of beautiful weather. A perfect day for a wedding. Even the un-

relenting heat took a vacation, leaving the air comfortable and pleasant for a change.

The bride and her attendants descended early on
Franny's shop, which was closed to the public.

The other salon hairdressers manicured, pedicured,
washed, and rolled the females of the bridal party, then
glitzed and glammed them till they sparkled like jewels.

Mabel limited them to two glasses of champagne
each. "Don't want anyone stumbling up the aisle," she
said firmly. "And there'll be plenty of time to party afterward, at the reception."

Sally looked radiant, with her dark glossy hair and
huge brown eyes. Her gown was a delicate, strapless cre-
ation of lace, pearls, and crystals, with a long, fan-shaped
train.

The six bridesmaids' dresses mirrored the bride's
summery strapless look, but in pale green silk. Pearls and
baby's breath were woven into the bridesmaids' hair,
completing the simple but elegant look.

At three-thirty, two limos arrived for the ladies, transferred them to the church.

A string quartet played at the front, near the altar, as
guests were escorted in. Finally, the groom and his party
entered with the preacher.

A hush fell over the crowd as the organist began playing. All eyes turned as, one by one, the bridesmaids
started up the aisle.

Keira found herself looking for Alec, knew he was
there. She'd spent two restless nights dreaming of him,
of making love to him. Her thoughts as she glided up the
aisle were definitely not suited to a church.

When the wedding march started, a collective *"oh"* went up from the crowd as they pushed to their feet.

Sally's father accompanied his daughter up the aisle in a motorized wheelchair. When they reached the altar, her father suddenly stopped the chair and stood, walking the last few steps to proudly announce that "her mother and I give our daughter, in love."

There wasn't a dry eye in the place.

Keira watched the ceremony with a lump in her throat. The candlelight service, traditional and reverent, was lovely beyond words. Boisterous, energetic Sally could scarcely repeat her vows.

I, Keira, take thee Alec . . .

How many times had she practiced those words? Then banned them from memory.

It was times like these, when the beauty of a moment threatened to overwhelm her, that she realized how embittered she'd grown after Alec's betrayal. She really hadn't gotten over him. She'd put away her feelings, learned to soldier on. Had even built a satisfying life.

But she'd never contemplated marriage with anyone else.

The guests erupted in applause, and Keira realized the preacher had just announced them man and wife.

She dabbed at the corner of her eye, thankful once again for Mabel, who'd handed each bridesmaid an embroidered handkerchief just before the service started.

The bridal party remained at the church with the photographer. The next thirty minutes were a haze of flashing lights and commands to smile.

At last, they were free to join the reception at the adjacent social hall.

Alec approached Keira as soon as she entered, pressed a drink in her hand. His eyes flicked over the pile of curls pinned atop her head. He'd have fun undoing it later.

He bent forward and pressed a kiss to her forehead. He glanced down, admiring the soft swell of bosom visible above her gown.

"You look gorgeous," he murmured. "And sexy. I hate when you're dressed like this around other men."

Keira found his remark titillating. "All the bridesmaids are wearing the same dress."

She accepted the drink, a champagne cocktail, letting her eyes drift approvingly over Alec. He looked exceptionally sharp in a dark Armani suit and tie.

She noticed several women eyeing him with interest Until he took her hand and kissed it. There was no doubt about the possessiveness of that action. She'd just been claimed. A shiver coursed up her arm.

Darryl and Franny joined them. Darryl nodded at Alec's glass. "You'll need several to catch up to them. I know a case of champagne was delivered to the salon this morning."

Franny giggled. "There were a lot of us there. Besides, Mabel cut us off, made us promise not to get drunk until after the *I-do's*. All bets are off now, though."

Alec looked at Keira and lifted his glass in a mock salute. "The ceremony's over: Time to celebrate. And I'm *your* designated driver. Have at it."

The wedding coordinator appeared and herded Keira and Franny off toward a front table.

Dinner was a sumptuous, nontraditional Hawaiian luau. The best man and maid of honor narrated a brief slide show featuring the most embarrassing childhood pictures of the bride and groom. Afterward, toasts were made and the cake was cut.

"Party time," Sally announced loudly. She raised her glass to Keira and Franny. "To girlfriends."

"To girlfriends." Keira drained her glass.

By the time the music started playing, Keira was feeling no pain, but neither was anyone else. It felt good to be in a safe place, surrounded by friends, raising the roof for a happy occasion.

After the required first dances for the bride and groom, and parents, the DJ announced a dance just for the bridal party. Alec pulled Keira to her feet and onto the floor.

"You're not part of the bridal party," she pointed out.

Alec shrugged. "So?" He swept her softly to the music. "I'm tired of sharing you. For the rest of the evening, you're mine."

His words, the tone, made her feel wistful, made her want to melt. She tried to keep distance between them, but Alec wouldn't cooperate.

He tugged her close, pressed his mouth against her ear. "Did you ever think about us having a big wedding like this?"

Keira misstepped, but Alec covered, leading her right back into sync. A sharp, familiar spasm washed over her.

Regret.

An emotion she was tired of feeling. And the only way to banish the emotion was to face it.

"I think every female entertains the idea at some point," she began cautiously, avoiding his eyes. "Franny and I probably planned our weddings a hundred different times."

"To a hundred different men?"

She faltered. Franny had planned to marry several rock stars. But Keira had only ever wanted to marry one person.

"Dozens," she hedged.

"You probably hated that I asked you to elope. To give up a big church wedding."

The song ended, and Keira had no choice but to meet Alec's eyes. It was tempting to lie. To simply agree. But that had never been her style.

"I hated you for not coming back," she whispered finally. "The lack of a fancy ceremony never entered into it. Being together was all that mattered."

Alec's grip tightened, holding her in place. "If you could do it all over again," he began.

Keira cut him off. "I wouldn't. Had I known it would hurt so badly, I would have chosen to *never* meet you, Alec."

Having said more than she meant, she turned and headed back to her table. Franny intercepted, dragging her off toward the bathroom.

Franny checked to make certain they were alone. "You look upset. What's wrong?"

Keira shook her head. "It's— I don't know. Weddings. Always a bridesmaid—"

"Is it Alec?"

Keira nodded. "I shouldn't have gotten involved again. I don't want to be hurt when he leaves."

Franny shook her head. "Maybe if you gave him some encouragement, he'd stay."

Keira looked away. If only it were that simple. *Encourage him.*

With what?

He'd left once because Freedom—her love—wasn't enough. She couldn't bear the thought he might grow bored . . . and leave again. Alec had another life, away from Freedom. A life of dangerous undercover assignments.

She recalled the scars on the backs of his legs. He'd been injured at least once. And still he went back to it. Did playing secret agent satisfy the thrill seeker in him?

Other guests drifted into the bathroom.

"Let's get out of here," Franny whispered. "And think about what I said. If Alec is what you want, then go for it. Life's ugliest regrets aren't the opportunities that never come. It's the ones we let slip by."

Go for it. Simple words, but did she have the courage to try again?

Alec was waiting just inside the reception hall, keeping his eye on the door in case Keira tried to slip out.

Her words had cut. Deep. *She wished she'd never met him.* How the hell could he overcome that? And why was it so important that he did?

When she reappeared, he moved to her side, offered his arm. When she took it, he exhaled, led her toward the bar.

"Can we pretend our last conversation didn't happen?" he asked. "And start over?"

At her nod, he ordered two drinks. He clinked his glass against hers.

"Here's to the future." He kept his voice low and drained his glass.

"The future." Keira emptied her glass and found herself swept back onto the dance floor.

The rest of the evening was a sparkling blur of dancing. Of champagne cocktails. Sally had both a live band

and a DJ. Between the two of them, they kept the party hopping.

When it came time for the bride to toss the bouquet, Franny dragged Keira to the center of the floor. Keira stepped back into the crowd, hoping Franny would catch it. She watched as Sally drew back, did a fake throw before tossing it high in the air.

Straight into Keira's hands.

She stared at the bouquet, dumbfounded, as everyone clapped. Then Alec was there, kissing her, laughing, pressing another drink into her hand.

The party started breaking up around two, after the happy couple took off for their honeymoon.

Darryl and Franny walked outside with Alec and Keira.

Franny and Keira sang a duet about strong women and straight whiskey. Keira shimmied while Franny did a pelvic twist. Both women giggled.

Darryl shook his head, slapped Alec's shoulder. "You're driving, right?"

Alec nodded. He'd purposely had soft drinks all evening, while making sure Keira had plenty of champagne. He was determined to woo her back into his bed through fair means or foul.

He knew the main reason she'd stayed at Franny's the past few nights was to avoid him, to avoid the growing intimacy between them. Or at least that was what he wanted to believe.

He'd given up trying to define his feelings for her. Nothing fit. There had always been something extraordinary between Keira and him.

Soul mates? Scary shit.

They definitely had a kinship that went beyond the physical. He had run from it ten years ago. Was maybe only now coming to realize what he'd run from.

At twenty, he hadn't been ready to embrace an all-encompassing love. Was he now?

He didn't know.

But he could no more deny his attraction to her than he could stop the blood from flowing through his veins. He wanted Keira with a need that felt overwhelming. A need to have her, hold her, at any cost. *Very scary shit.*

The night was starry and clear. Keira sang as they made their way to Alec's Jeep. He laughed at her exaggerated sway, then helped her in. He buckled her seat belt and earned a kiss.

Still smiling, he started the car. Before putting it in gear, he reached over and trailed his fingers along her bare shoulder. To put clothes on skin this soft and pretty was a sin.

"Nice night. Feel like taking a ride?"

Keira shrugged, opening the moon roof. She leaned back slightly in her seat. "Sure. Where are we going?"

Alec put on a CD. "You'll see."

Keira recognized the spot immediately. The old fire tower.

The first place they'd made love.

"Feel like a climb?" Alec asked.

She looked at her gown. His suit. "We're not exactly dressed for it."

"Never stopped us before. Hold on."

He climbed out and came around to her side. When he opened her door, she saw he had grabbed a flashlight.

"You carry the light, I'll carry you."

Before she could protest, Alec had her in his arms and was heading down the trail.

"I'm supposed to believe this is spontaneous?" she asked, then hiccuped. Champagne bubbles outnumbered oxygen molecules two to one in her veins.

"Nope. I admit, I planned it. This used to be a great place to watch stars."

And to make love beneath them, Keira recalled. The fire tower was a big open loft nearly sixty feet in the air. Private. Romantic.

Choruses of baby tree frogs chirped, the air alive with night sounds.

Alec set her at the foot of the ladder, then shone the flashlight straight up. "Just like I remembered." He looked down at her heels. "Can you climb in those?"

She hiked her gown up. "Actually the dress is more of a challenge."

Alec watched her climb a few rungs, admiring her taut butt. He started right behind her, careful to keep his arms outside of hers in case she slipped.

Her agility amazed him. So, too, her spirit for adventure. She was the only woman he knew who would tackle a climb like this in high heels and a gown. And would look like a perfect lady when she reached the top.

The ladder ended at the trapdoor in the floor of the tower. Alec boosted Keira through the opening, then climbed up.

He quickly surveyed their surroundings. The platform was about twelve feet square, with waist-high side rails and no roof. Beer cans and cigarette butts littered the floor.

"Guess things haven't changed," he observed.

Keira stood at the rail, felt the breeze ruffle the loose tendrils of her hair.

Things had changed tremendously over the past ten years, she thought. But here, in this little space of forest, things were the same. The fire tower was still a clandestine meeting place for lovers.

"The park service threatens to tear this down every year, but the locals have fought them," Keira said. "A lot of native sons and daughters were conceived up here."

Alec chuckled. He came up behind Keira, placed his hands on either side of the railing, neatly boxing her in. He liked the thought that she was trapped in his arms, with nowhere to turn but to him.

He stared over her head, off to the east, toward Fire Mountain. While he couldn't make out the shape, he knew the lone light high above the horizon was Willis's cabin. "Your grandpa still leaves the light on."

"He and Motel 6." Keira smiled. In the tradition of scores of Morgans before him, Willis kept a light burning in the uppermost window of the house.

"To light your way home," she whispered.

Alec lowered his lips to her shoulder, nibbled the bare skin. "Remember the first time we made love?"

Keira shivered. From the memory. From the feel of his lips, the way his teeth rasped her skin.

"A girl never forgets her first time."

"And you think the guy who gets to be her first does?" He kissed the little spot below her ear. "We'd gone to the drive-in. Watched *Gone with the Wind* for the millionth time."

Alec pressed another kiss, lower, to her nape, inhaled the delicate scent of female. Perfume.

"You were wearing a yellow halter top and white shorts," he continued. "I took one look at your nipples poking through the fabric and nearly shot my wad on the spot. Drove me nuts to know you were braless. Especially when you had to walk back to the concession stand to use the bathroom. Knowing other guys would see you. See *them*."

Keira felt his hands brush down her shoulder blades, felt the zipper of her dress being lowered. Cool night air kissed her skin, reminding her she was braless tonight, too. "I don't remember you complaining about what I wore. Or didn't wear."

"Hell no. I liked the way I could reach in from the back," he continued. "And feel your breasts."

His hands crept inside her dress, worked around to the front. Unhurried, yet willful. Purposely tormenting her.

She gasped as her dress fell forward, and Alec's hands cupped her breasts. Her nipples peaked. Ached. And he didn't disappoint. He caught the tips, plumping them between thumbs and index fingers, tugging, coaxing. They tightened, sensitized, electricity running on invisible lines from her womb to her breast.

Alec's touch drove her wild. Those slow hands. Gifted fingers. It made her crazy for more.

She leaned back against his chest, deliberately raised her arms up, over her head, looping them back around his neck. The movement thrust her breasts forward, allowing him full access as he kept up the divine play with her nipples.

"We left the movie early," Alec continued. "And came here."

Keira remembered. She'd picked *Gone with the Wind* because she'd seen it so many times. She and Alec went to the drive-in to make out. To pet. To do everything but make love.

"I remember you said you had an early birthday present for me." Alec's hands tightened again. "You told me to close my eyes."

She drew a sharp breath, recalling the night, her intention. It had been an incredibly selfish gift, as much for her benefit as Alec's.

"I closed my eyes and felt your hand go to my belt." Alec turned her around to face him. He caught her chin, raised it, forcing her to meet his eyes. "You unzipped my pants, reached in to fondle me . . . and started crying."

Keira felt a tear roll down her cheek. That Alec remembered all this overwhelmed her.

At sixteen she'd thought she'd known it all. She hadn't.

"I was so embarrassed, Alec. I wanted to be suave and sophisticated. I wanted to make love to you. And—"

"You were scared to death." He kissed her cheek, caught the tear with his fingertip. "So was I."

She blinked in disbelief. "You? But you were so—"

"Macho? Swaggering? It was an act." He laughed. "I was worried I'd disappoint you. Afraid I'd come in your hand before even touching you. At eighteen that's a huge concern."

"I remember wishing I'd done it before," she admitted. "Wished I knew what to do."

He growled. "I was glad you didn't know what to do. I liked being your first. Your only."

He lowered his mouth and kissed her, his tongue sweeping into her mouth.

For a moment, Keira was sixteen again.

They'd left the drive-in and come here. She'd been a nervous wreck until Alec kissed her. And the fire that had always been between them flared, swept her over the edge of reason.

They had a blanket, one condom, and less than an hour. They were out of their clothes in no time. That first touch of bare skin on bare skin had been shocking. The feel of Alec's erection, frightening. It was so big. So hard.

But he'd kissed her and touched her until she'd gone mad for more. Melted. Then slowly he pressed in, past the precious offering of her hymen.

"You're so tight," Alec murmured.

Keira was lost. Her dress was hiked up, bunched around her waist as Alec's hand moved between her legs. He had shoved her panties down and worked a finger inside her.

"So wet," he murmured.

She groaned, shimmied, as her panties fell around her ankles. Lifting her legs, careful not to dislodge his fingers, she stepped free of her underwear. Her greedy hands tugged at Alec's pants, unzipped them. She reached in, grasped his swollen shaft.

"I was so afraid it would hurt worse than it did that first time," she murmured, her hands stroking his length.

Alec had been the first male she'd ever seen nude. His fully erect penis had frightened and fascinated her at the same time.

With surprising patience, he'd taken her hand in his and let her touch him, feel him, his hand over hers, rubbing, stroking. Encouraging. She watched wide-eyed as he grew longer and harder in her hand.

Then, their hands still entwined, he'd explored her center, touching her clitoris, kneading it, finding what she liked, while whispering in her ear how he couldn't wait to have his cock, there, inside her.

"I was afraid of disappointing you, hurting you." He inserted another finger inside her, slid his thumb up between the wet folds, rubbing. "It's a miracle we managed it."

But manage it they did. Alec had sheathed himself, then moved on top of her, entering slowly, slowly. It burned, a sweet, painful fire that baptized her in bliss even as it robbed her of breath.

She had been so determined not to, yet in those first, aching seconds, she'd wept. And Alec had wanted to stop right then. *I can't bear to hurt you, babe.*

"Don't stop," she cried, knowing that if they didn't push forward, she'd never have the courage to try again.

And then he'd moved against her fast, pushing all the way into her. The pain disappeared, replaced by a feeling so sublime she thought she'd die from pleasure.

Like now. "Alec, please." His touch drove her crazy.

"Easy," he soothed.

She felt his hands leave her, felt him fumble with a

condom. Then he lifted her straight up, grasping her waist as he lowered her slowly, pressing in.

The sensation was to die for. The fullness. The stark shock of invasion. Of hot flesh being parted. Split.

She wrapped her legs around Alec's waist, held on to his shoulders as he controlled the movement, supported her weight. Impaling her. Her sheath clasped him.

His hands shifted, gripping her tightly at her hips. He ground full into her, sliding her down, then up, on his hardness. There was no other feeling in the world like this. Of being in her. Only her.

"God, I won't last long," he choked.

"Good." Keira sank her teeth into his neck, then laved the injury with her tongue. "Come with me, Alec."

Alec slammed into her hard, fast, frenzied. He snarled, pumping, pumping—felt her womb tighten over him.

Keira let out a small scream and climaxed in his arms. Alec felt her drenching release and held her tightly, as his own body burst forth with a violent, satisfying eruption.

"I—" she began, overcome with emotion.

"Shhhh. Just let me hold you," he said, rocking her slightly.

How long they stood there joined, she didn't know. Didn't care.

Then she felt the sharp drag of latex-covered steel as he withdrew. She winced at the slight hindrance as her body clung to his, resisting the inevitable separation.

He whispered comforting sounds as she moved to readjust her clothes. Only now did she realize they were both still dressed.

Alec straightened his own clothes, then turned to zip her gown.

"Let's go home. And I'll prove I can be a gentleman."

She raised up, kissed his chin. "It's more fun when you're *not* a gentleman."

He ran a finger along her cheek. "I'll love you all night long if you'll let me."

Keira looked at him, at the stars over his head. She knew he meant *making love*. But what about the other? He had loved her once, could she make him love her again?

"Let's go for it," she whispered.

When they reached the apartment parking lot, Keira leaned across the seat, wriggled into Alec's arms. She felt replete. Well loved. A little drunk.

Happy.

"Mmm. Where are we?"

A seductive smile spread across Alec's face. "Home," he murmured, leaning in to trail kisses down the side of her neck. "You look good enough to eat." He ran his lips across the swell of her cleavage.

Keira shuddered as his tongue delved between her breasts. Her nipples peaked, throbbed. Begging for more.

"Let's make love here," she said, her hands going to the knot of his necktie. Suddenly she didn't care they were in a parking lot. She didn't want to wait, she didn't want to debate. She wanted him.

Alec stayed her hand. "Making love in a car is severely overrated. Especially when we're less than thirty seconds from a comfortable bed." And especially when he planned for it to be a prolonged session.

Keira's shoulders dropped. "I guess you're right."

He laughed out loud at the disappointment in her voice. "If you didn't get enough of the great outdoors at the fire tower"—he wagged his eyebrows—"we could climb out on the fire escape. Naked."

At her soft intake of air, he tightened his grip, pulling her closer. "I'll go down on *you* this time, while you see if you can keep from screaming out loud when I make you come. Over," he kissed her. "And over." Another kiss. "And over."

Keira met his lips this time. "Promise?"

He nodded. Shifting her only slightly, he climbed out of the car, then leaned back in to scoop her into his arms.

He looked at her dirt-smudged satin shoes. "I think they're ruined, babe."

"Doesn't matter. They were dyed to match this dress, and it's getting burned."

"Burned?"

They were in the lobby. Keira pressed the elevator call button. "It's bad luck to keep old bridesmaids' dresses."

"I don't follow the logic," he said. "Why burn a perfectly good dress?"

Because hanging in her closet they were tangible reminders of what she'd never have. *Always a bridesmaid, never a bride.*

And this one in particular would remind her of making love to Alec.

"It's a girl-thing." She struggled for levity. "And I'd much rather talk about what we're going to do on the fire escape."

They were in the elevator now. She loosened Alec's tie and was working to unbutton his shirt. "More specifically, let's talk about what I'm going to do to *you* on the fire escape."

Grinning, Alec retaliated, shifting her enough to grasp the zipper. With luck, they'd make it inside his apartment while they were still decent.

Then all bets were off. He might have to have her in the foyer, him standing up, her braced against the wall. Then there was the kitchen . . .

He tugged the zipper down on her dress. She shimmied. Her bodice dropped, freeing her breasts.

He growled. She did that on purpose just to provoke him, knowing his hands were busy as he carried her.

"You'll pay for that," he promised.

"God, I hope so." She ripped the last button from his shirt.

He stepped out of the elevator and headed toward his door, kissing Keira as he walked.

A movement in the landing caught his eye.

Scarlet Chambeau rounded the corner. She drew a sharp breath, then gave Keira a harsh look.

Keira quickly folded her arms to cover herself as she tried to tug her top back in place.

"Alec," Scarlet said. "We need to talk."

"We have nothing to discuss," he began.

"We do!" she scoffed. "And we have to talk now!"

Alec shifted Keira closer against his chest, kept his voice even.

He knew Scarlet had been drinking. He recognized the slurred tone of her voice, the way she swayed. The other night when she'd showed up drunk at his apartment, he'd talked with her, drove her home—put her to bed.

Tonight he'd call a cab.

"You need to leave, Scarlet. This isn't the time or place."

"That's not what you said the other night when you took me home. You said I was beautiful, desirable. That a man would be a fool not to want me."

Scarlet's words hit Keira with the force of a physical blow.

She looked from Alec to Scarlet, waiting for a denial. Alec looked disgusted, Scarlet triumphant.

"Put me down. Now." Keira struggled to be free.

Instead, Alec tightened his grip, then turned and walked to her door. Still holding her, he unlocked her door, reached in to enter the disarm code on her alarm, then set her down. Slowly.

Keira struggled with her dress.

"Let me talk to Scarlet, and I'll be back," he said quietly.

But Keira had heard enough. "Don't bother, Alec. I never want to see you again."

Chapter Fifteen

*A*lec had been with Scarlet.

Keira slammed her apartment door, locked it. Damn him to hell.

And damn her for being a fool.

Loving Alec had cost her a broken heart once. How could she have been so stupid, to let it happen again? A lump formed in her throat.

He had given no indication he was interested in anything beyond sex. Yet she'd foolishly plunged headlong into a full-fledged affair—thinking his heart would come around.

She'd forgotten the basic tenet: Alec was only in Freedom because of his job. His *involvement* with Keira had been part of his cover. She'd known that going in. And still she'd crossed the line.

She headed straight for the shower. She wanted to wash his touch, his scent, from her body. From her memory.

She looked at her rumpled dress, saw the torn edge, recalled how she and Alec had made love in the fire tower—had practically made love in the parking lot. That she'd planned to make love to him all night long. Dumb, dumb, dumb.

Stripping off her dress, she caught sight of her body in the bathroom mirror. Signs of his physical possession abounded. Her mouth was red from kisses, her nipples swollen. And lower, her nether lips were tender, engorged, still unused to the invasion of Alec's member.

She turned away, climbing into the shower. She stayed under the spray until the hot water was gone.

Tugging on a T-shirt, she climbed into bed. A few minutes later she heard the angry rapping at the window.

Alec's muffled voice came through the glass.

"I know you can hear me, Keira. Let me in."

She flew out of bed, threw the drapes apart. "Go away," she yelled. "You're the last person I want to see right now."

"We need to talk."

"No, Alec. You need to stay away from me. For good."

"Scarlet's lying."

"You didn't say those things?"

Yeah, he'd said those words and more. He'd meant that Scarlet needed to leave him alone because Alec was only interested in Keira.

"She took them out of context. She was drunk—"

Keira cut him off. "That seems to be your MO. I'm drunk. Did you sleep with her too, Alec?"

As soon as the words were out of her mouth, she regretted them.

"I haven't slept with anyone but you since I've been here."

Since he'd been here. The words were a cold reminder Alec had a life away from here. That Keira was nothing more than a temporary diversion. She didn't matter in the big picture. Neither did Scarlet.

Suddenly it hurt to breathe. She looked at him, shook her head. "Just leave me alone, Alec. Please."

He swore. This wasn't how he'd imagined the evening unfolding.

Aside from making love to her all night, he had hoped to talk her into going to Seattle, to stay in his town house until Griggs left.

Hell, he even hoped she'd want to stay beyond then.

He wanted a chance to test those ties that bound her heart to Freedom. To at least stretch them, see if she couldn't imagine a life outside of Freedom, away from Fire Mountain.

It was wrong to get involved with her again.

And he could have no more kept his distance from her than he could have cut off his own arm.

"We have to talk. But later. Go to bed," he said finally.

And with that, Alec moved away.

Keira awoke with a sore heart, red eyes, and a new determination. She'd also started.

The realization that she *wasn't* pregnant should have elated her. Instead, it added to her sense of loss.

Well, she'd gotten over Alec Dempsey once, she'd do it again. And be stronger for it.

His denial echoed in her ears. "Scarlet's lying." Was he telling the truth, that he'd only been intimate with Keira?

What did it matter? She and Alec had no future.

It was also time to face the hard, ugly facts about Ian Griggs.

So far, it seemed Ian had no intention of leaving Freedom. But did he honestly think he could continue to harass her without getting caught?

The cat-and-mouse games had to end.

How, she didn't know. But she firmly believed solutions came only after one was clear on the problem.

The phone rang.

"Are you okay?" Franny asked when she picked up.

Keira closed her eyes. She knew by Franny's tone exactly what she referred to. "How did you hear?"

"Cissy claims you and Alec broke up last night and that he went home with Scarlet."

Keira knew the latter was untrue—or was it? Alec had been on her fire escape, then left. Had he indeed gone to Scarlet's? "It doesn't matter."

Franny hesitated. "You sure?"

"Yes. No." Keira sighed. "I don't know what to think. I've behaved poorly since Alec hit town. I should have kept my distance."

Franny clucked. "I have the perfect cure for hindsight. *Shopping.* I'll pick you up in thirty minutes."

No sooner had Keira set the phone down than it rang again. It was Alec.

"Don't hang up."

She frowned. Hanging up was childish. No matter how good it might feel in the moment.

"I'm in a hurry, Alec. What do you want?"

It was on the tip of his tongue to apologize.

Except he'd done nothing wrong. Scarlet was simply out to make trouble for Keira. Unfortunately, Scarlet had no idea what was at stake, that Keira was an integral part of Alec's cover. That his alleged "romance" with Keira wasn't even real.

So, if it wasn't real, why did it bother him so?

He scowled, recalling his new pact to keep a platonic distance.

"I'm spending the day on surveillance. I wanted to see what your plans were."

For a moment, she was tempted to say, "None of your business." Instead, she answered honestly. Alec was only doing a job. "I'm going shopping with Franny."

"Call me when you get back. *Please*," he amended quickly. "And be careful."

Franny and Keira spent the day in Hot Springs, literally shopping till they dropped. It was late by the time they returned to Franny's.

It took several trips, but finally they had all their booty upstairs. Franny surveyed the shopping bags covering most of her living room floor. "Tell me these aren't all mine."

"Ninety-seven percent are," Keira said. "I bought face cream, a CD, and two romances, though God only knows where they are."

Franny grinned. "Why don't you spend the night and help me sort through this mess? We can order pizza, make margaritas, and watch something with Brad Pitt."

"What about Darryl?" This was normally his day off.

"Working. He traded days to attend Sally's wedding." Franny tossed Keira the telephone. "I want everything but black olives. And you might as well call Alec and let him know where you are. He'll call here if you don't."

Keira frowned. Alec had called twice that afternoon. *Just to check on them.*

She got angry the second time, until Franny reminded her of their car wreck and all the little incidents since. "He cares," she insisted.

Knowing he would indeed call if she didn't report in, Keira left a message on his answering machine that she was staying overnight at Franny's.

Then she ordered pizza.

Franny made margaritas while they waited for pizza to be delivered. After they ate, they methodically sorted through the shopping bags.

"Gee, I guess I did buy a lot," Franny said, when they finished.

"I knew you were in trouble when you started saying, 'This is too cute to leave in the store.'"

Franny shrugged. "So pour me a glass of liquid painkiller and load Brad into the DVD player."

When the movie finished, it was late. Franny yawned. "I'm hitting the sack. Spending all that money took a lot out of me."

Keira carried their glasses to the kitchen. Halfway there she stopped.

"Do you smell smoke?"

Franny sniffed the air, then backed up, and sniffed again. "Yeah. Faintly."

"Is something burning?" Keira started looking around the apartment. "Did you light a candle earlier?"

"No."

The electricity suddenly went out, plunging them into darkness. Franny shrieked.

"Walk toward my voice," Keira said. "I'm right here."

"The smell is getting worse."

Keira's eyes slowly adjusted to the dark. "We better call the fire department."

Franny grabbed for the wall phone. "It's dead." Her voice was tinged with panic now. "Where's my cell? My purse?"

"Here."

Franny quickly retrieved her cell phone and called Darryl. "They're on their way. Darryl said to get out fast."

The apartment's smoke detectors went off.

"Come on." They were closest to the door leading downstairs to the salon, but as soon as Keira cracked it open, smoke roiled in. She saw a flicker of orange flames just before shoving the door closed.

"The shop is on fire!"

"My salon! No!" Franny grabbed for the doorknob.

Keira stopped her. "You can't go that way. We'll go out the back and check from the front."

They hurried toward the stairwell leading down to the back door. But when they reached the bottom landing, the heavy metal door wouldn't open.

"Shit!" Franny kicked at the door.

"Let me try." Keira shoved her shoulder against the door. It wouldn't budge.

"Open, damn you!" Franny cursed the door as she tried the knob again, then turned away. "Now what?"

"We can climb out the windows."

They raced back upstairs to the living room. The smoke was thicker now. Choking.

"Stay low," Keira instructed, her heart slamming in her throat.

Both women were coughing when they reached the double windows. Keira raised a pane. A small ledge was just below the casing, which led to the main part of the roof. "Follow me."

They climbed out, holding hands.

"I'm scared." Franny wept, then screamed, as below

them, at the front of the house, flames burst through a
window, the glass exploding. "No!"

She surged forward, but Keira held her arm.

Sirens pierced the night.

"We've got to move," Keira tugged her friend away.
"Toward the back of the roof."

When the first fire truck pulled up, Darryl jumped
from the cab. The women screamed in unison at him.

"Stay right there!" he yelled.

Within seconds, a truck backed onto the lawn. A hy-
draulic ladder lifted to the roof. Darryl climbed up, tucking Franny beneath an arm.

"Is either of you hurt?" he barked.

Keira shook her head.

"My house," Franny wailed, collapsing.

"I'm going to carry her down," Darryl said. "Can you
make it?"

Feeling helpless, Keira climbed onto the ladder. Another fireman was there, ready to help.

Seconds later, Darryl cleared the ladder, carrying
Franny. He set her down, yelled for an EMT. "Tell me
you're okay."

Franny nodded, unable to speak.

"I've got to go help. Stay right here." Darryl dashed
away, shouting orders into a handheld radio. "Let's get
another truck in here! Now!"

Firemen charged around, their hoses crisscrossing the
lawn. Darryl directed some men to the opposite side of
the building.

With growing horror, Keira realized that if the fire
spread, the entire downtown could be destroyed.

Alec raced up, followed by Fred and Mabel.

"We were at the bowling alley," Fred said, panting. "They announced over the loudspeaker your place was on fire."

Alec moved in beside Keira as a paramedic checked her pulse. The smell of charred wood was thick in the night air, the sound of sirens interspersed with the *whoosh* of spraying water and shouts by firemen.

"They're okay?" Alec asked the EMT.

The paramedic nodded. "Shock."

Alec helped the man spread a blanket over each woman's shoulders. He drew Keira's blanket tight around her, hugging her briefly before moving to help Franny.

"Darryl," Franny whispered.

"Shhhh. He's doing his job."

Within minutes the flames had disappeared. The smoke, while still pouring out of the building, was not as thick.

Darryl sauntered up, tugged his helmet free, and crouched in front of Franny. "It's under control. Can you tell me what happened?"

"I don't know. We . . . we smelled smoke." Franny wiped her cheek on the blanket. "The fire blocked the salon steps, and the back door wouldn't open. Thank God, Keira was there. I totally lost it."

She leaned forward, into his embrace, sobbing.

Alec and Darryl exchanged glances. "What do you mean the back door wouldn't open?" Darryl asked. "Was it locked?"

"It's always locked," Franny said after a moment. "But the inside is a latch, so I don't need a key to get out."

Keira nodded. "The knob wouldn't turn."

Darryl shifted Franny into Alec's arms. "I'll be right back."

When Darryl returned a few minutes later, his face was grim. "Looks like the lock's been tampered with. Jammed. I'm sealing the area till the fire marshal can investigate in the morning."

Keira listened to the exchange, uneasy. "You mean this was done on purpose?" The thought that someone intended to trap them inside made her ill.

Darryl shrugged, but without conviction. "It's too soon to tell."

Alec knew Darryl had to take into consideration all probable causes. The salon had a lot of electrical appliances, many of them heat generators. A wire could have shorted and started the fire.

But it wouldn't have jammed a door lock.

A small crowd had gathered. Darryl motioned to the closest deputy. "Clear them out and secure the area."

"Can I go inside?" Franny's voice was tight. "I want to see—"

"Not tonight." Darryl soothed. "My men will be here a while longer. For now you're going home with me."

"But Keira was spending the night—" Franny started.

"I'm going to my apartment," Keira said.

Alec nodded. "I'll stay with her. Don't worry."

When they reached Keira's, Alec paced to the kitchen and helped himself to a beer. Wished it could be something stronger.

Keira sat on the couch, dazed. He knew by her silence she was still in shock, wondered how she'd react if he took her into his arms. Not for the first time, he wished the issues between them were resolved.

"What are you thinking about?" he asked finally.

She shook her head. "What if Franny and I had fallen asleep? We—"

"You hadn't."

Keira turned, her eyes bright with unshed tears. Angry. "How can you be so calm? If the fire was set on purpose, it was probably targeted toward *me*. Whoever set it endangered my best friend, destroyed her home and business."

"I've urged you to leave."

"Do you honestly think it's as simple as that?" Her voice raised, cracked. "Even if I left, I can't stay gone forever. What if Griggs *never* gets the money? Never leaves? Do you really expect me to live my life in his shadow?"

Alec set his beer down, hard. The thought of Griggs being a permanent resident of Freedom was disconcerting.

"Arguing over what Griggs might or might not do is a losing proposition. Let's wait and see what Darryl comes up with on the fire. If Griggs is behind the fire, maybe he left a clue." Sooner or later, he'd slip up. What scared Alec was the thought of what could happen in the meantime.

He ran a hand through his hair. "It seems like all we've done the past two days is tiptoe around each other. Or argue."

"Thanks to Scarlet." Keira instantly regretted the words. "Look—"

"No. I take it back, Alec."

Alec reached out to touch her cheek, caught himself. *Platonic*, remember?

"You look exhausted."

Keira nodded. She was tired. And the last thing she wanted to do was argue with him. Now. Or later.

"I'm staying here tonight," he said. "On the couch. Okay?"

Not okay. She would have preferred him in bed, with her, but knew the couch was safer.

"Do you need to use the bathroom?" she asked. The apartment's only bath was in the bedroom.

He shook his head.

Moving mechanically, she retrieved a pillow and blanket, set them on the couch, then bid him good night, and closed her bedroom door.

But even after a hot shower, sleep eluded her. The fire. Ian. *Alec.* Her thoughts hopscotched from one to the other.

Around three, she heard a light tap on her door. She sat up, alert. Need clawed at her. Did Alec miss her as much as she did him?

"Yes?"

Alec poked his head in. "Sorry. Now I need to use the bathroom."

Grateful the dark hid her disappointment, Keira lay back down. She listened as Alec padded across the room, closed the bathroom door. There was a long stretch of silence. Then she heard the toilet flush, heard the faucet.

She held her breath as he opened the door. She knew he paused in the doorway—probably letting his eyes adjust before navigating back through her room.

She kept her eyes tightly closed as he padded around her bed, then once again stopped.

"Good night, babe," he whispered.

And without waiting for a response, he shut the door.

Keira was up early and in a foul mood because she hadn't slept well.

Alec offered coffee. "Why don't you take the day off?" he suggested. "You've got two crew chiefs who can handle anything that comes up."

She nodded. "I need to go by Franny's. See if I can do anything. And see how the shop looks."

"I'll check with Darryl to see if they've found any clues."

Keira took a sip of coffee. "If they find proof Griggs was behind this, I may shoot him."

"You'll have to stand in line. Look, I've got a meeting in Hot Springs first thing this morning." He was meeting Miles Ostman. "But I'll keep it short. And I'll call when I'm on my way back."

Ian Griggs had been upset to learn Keira had escaped, uninjured, from the fire. Beau was a worthless arsonist. A worthless partner.

Now, however, he was glad she'd escaped. Looked like he still had a need for her.

He stared at the ivory-colored paper in his hand.

The Legend of the Lost Confederate Gold.

He'd just lifted it from a kid. The family—up camping for the weekend—had stopped for gas. The kid had come in to buy a soda and showed Ian the map.

At first, Ian wished the kid would shut up and leave. Then the brat mentioned a gold coin necklace worn by a woman at the Lucky Nugget.

A woman with long red hair and a tool belt.

Ian almost smiled.

He questioned the kid, learned the woman had claimed her grandfather gave the necklace to her. And that the owner of the Lucky Nugget swore the coin was part of the Confederate treasure.

The kid's father interrupted, told his son to go back to the car. Dropping a handful of change to the floor, Ian distracted them long enough to hide the map, then shrugged as the kid started crying over misplacing his map.

What a baby.

When the family finally left, Ian withdrew the purloined paper, examined it closely.

It showed the entire area, including Culverleaf Park. Key historical points were starred, with the biggest star denoting the Lucky Nugget Mining Company.

Lacy Hicks owned the Lucky Nugget. He was also close friends with Willis Morgan.

And the Morgan family had been searching for the Lost Confederate Gold longer than anyone else in these parts.

Had that old coot Willis found Ian's money and gold? The necklace . . .

Ian needed to see it to know for sure. And soon.

Joseph Ciccone was breathing down his neck, demanding Ian fulfill his end of the bargain immediately, claimed the FBI was growing suspicious.

Ian had been given twenty-four hours to produce the gold and the money. Or else.

Which meant Ian had to locate it, secure it, and get the hell out of town.

With or without his revenge.

He crumpled the map.

Chapter Sixteen

A small crowd was gathered across the street from Franny's salon, their faces somber. Keira recognized several shop owners from downtown, knew more would come as word spread.

Yellow tape fluttered in the morning breeze, keeping back the curious and framing the desolate scene.

The once-beautiful Victorian looked awful in the bright light of day, her pristine exterior blackened with soot, the majority of the first-floor windows broken.

The thought that someone set the fire deliberately had troubled Keira most of the night. Seeing the damage, the true horror of what *might* have happened hit her, causing her stomach to cramp.

Two firemen stood on the porch, surveying the damage.

She caught sight of Franny near Darryl's car and hurried over. The two women embraced.

"It makes me sick," Keira began.

"Me too." Franny wept for a few minutes, then waved a hand toward the building that was her home and business. "Honestly, it looks better than I'd hoped. I had nightmares the roof collapsed during the night. I was afraid I'd come here and find a pile of rubble."

"How bad is the inside?"

"Bad." Franny shrugged, feigning nonchalance and failing. Her voice cracked. "The fire marshal said the downstairs will have to be gutted, but the flames were contained quickly, so structural damage is minimal."

"What about the upstairs?"

"Smoke damage mostly. Darryl said the sentimental items could be salvaged and restored. Furniture, clothes . . . It will all have to be replaced."

Keira bit her lip, choking back her own tears, hurting for her friend. And feeling guilty. "Do they have any idea what caused it?"

"They're checking now. You know Darryl won't rest until he's found the cause. And speaking of Darryl." Franny held her hand up. A diamond the size of Rhode Island sparkled on her finger as new tears welled in her eyes. "He proposed."

Keira gasped. "Oh my God! He did it."

"It was supposed to be my birthday present, but he gave it to me last night."

Keira hugged her friend. "Did you set a date?"

"Not yet, but it'll be at least a year from now. You know me. It has to be the biggest bash this town has ever seen, and that will take a while to plan."

"You can stay with me," Keira said in a rush of words. "Until we get this place fixed. I'll redo all the wiring myself, and—"

"Actually, Darryl and I decided to buy a house right away," Franny interrupted. "You know how we joked about buying the mayor's house, up on the hill? Well, we've got an appointment to see it this afternoon. It's vacant, so I can move in right away and live there till the wedding. Which means I can finally expand the shop."

For months, Franny had talked about moving out and converting her apartment into a day spa with a full cosmetics boutique and tanning salon. She had even considered renting the apartment next to Keira—the one Alec currently occupied.

"It's a great idea," Keira encouraged. "We'll have you back in business in no time."

Darryl walked up, accepted Keira's congratulatory hug, asked how she felt. "Good thing you're here. The fire marshal needs to speak with both of you."

It was early afternoon by the time Keira left Franny's. While the fire marshal emphasized he wasn't finished with his investigation, it was clear he believed the fire had been purposely set.

Keira's gut instinct was that Griggs was behind it. Darryl explained the story to the marshal.

When the insurance adjuster arrived, Keira left. She climbed in her truck, eyeing the building one last time.

If Griggs was behind the fire, that meant he'd tried to harm someone dear to Keira after all. Franny was like family. Had that been part of Griggs's plan all along?

For a moment, she was tempted to go down to the gas station where Ian worked and confront him. Except what was the worst she could do? Tell him off? Call him names? Throw something at him?

She thought about the gun she had stowed behind her seat, recalled how it felt in her hand. She totally understood her grandfather's motivation now.

Frustration built. Too restless to go back to her apartment, she decided to head up to her cabin, to work off her nervous energy. Maybe she'd visit Willis later, too.

She went by the office to pick up tools. Reggie called while she was there.

"Heard about the fire," he said. "Sounds like you were lucky."

"We were."

"I thought you were taking the day off?"

"I am. Just stopped by on my way to the cabin."

"Need help? I'm on my way back from Hot Springs. I'll be there in about thirty minutes."

The thought of having company, someone to talk to, was appealing.

"Sounds good, Reggie. Meet me there."

As soon as Keira hit the trigger of the nail gun, it blew the breaker.

She sighed. For some reason, the air compressor was being temperamental. She'd looked at it twice already, couldn't find the problem.

She'd have to finish mounting the braces for the cabinets the old-fashioned way: With a hammer and elbow grease.

She checked her watch. She'd been there over two hours. And no Reggie. He must have changed his mind about coming. She wiped the sweat from her brow, debating whether to call it quits.

She heard gravel crunch in the drive. *Reggie.* Maybe she'd get a few cabinets installed after all.

Grabbing the hammer once more, she concentrated on nailing a brace. She heard the front door open, heard footsteps echo in the living room.

"I'm back here," she called out. "Come on in."

Keira pounded one last nail, then backed down the ladder. "I was beginning to think you'd had a better offer," she said, turning.

But it wasn't Reggie who stood in the doorway. It was Beau Watson. Ian Griggs's roommate.

"A better offer?" Beau's eye gleamed. He flexed his arms forward, cracked his knuckles. "What was the first one?"

He was shirtless, his jeans riding low on bony hips. Dark blue tattoos covered his entire torso, gory pictures of skulls and knives. A nude woman, crucified.

Twin silver hoops pierced his nipples.

She didn't bother to hide her revulsion.

"What are you doing here?" she demanded. "This is private property. You're trespassing."

Beau grinned, held up her truck keys. "We need to talk."

Then he grabbed her cell phone from the sawhorse. Dropping it on the floor, he crushed it beneath his heel.

Alec had lunch with Miles Ostman, in Hot Springs.

"I want Keira Morgan out of Freedom. By force, if necessary."

"You've got no proof Griggs had anything to do with the fire," Ostman said.

"Yet," Alec shot back. "I don't need proof to know she's in danger."

"From what I understand, there are other people in town with axes to grind. I can't control what they do."

The only other people Alec knew of that disliked Keira for any reason were the Barry brothers. And Scarlet.

Scarlet had done her damage by insinuating Alec was interested in her. And as much as he despised the way the Barrys disrespected Keira, Alec didn't believe they were behind the fire. They might vandalize a job site. They would certainly call names and launch a verbal assault.

But they were idiots, not psychos. And only a real psychopath would lock two women in a burning building.

Alec glanced at Ostman, wondered briefly if the man actually knew that much about the inner workings of Freedom or was simply grasping for excuses. He'd bet it was the latter.

"Keeping Keira safe is my primary concern."

"Your primary concern is recovering the money."

Alec leaned forward. "I think if we remove Keira from the equation, Griggs will go ahead and make his move. Right now she's a distraction."

"To you or Griggs?"

"If you don't get her out, I will."

Ostman swore. "If you cost me this investigation, I'll—"

"You'll what? Pull me off the case?" Alec checked the time. He needed to get back. "I doubt that. It's too late to establish another cover."

In the end, Ostman promised to check on a nearby safe house. "Just don't do anything with the Morgan woman until I get back to you."

When Alec returned to Freedom, he drove by the halfway house. Beau's car was already gone. Was he at Culverleaf Park again?

Next, Alec went by the gas station. Griggs was inside the office, talking on the phone. Before starting the assignment, Alec had asked Ostman about phone taps. Not enough probable cause, Ostman claimed.

Still, Alec wished he knew to whom Griggs talked and what he said. If it was dark, he'd slip up next to the building and eavesdrop.

Pulling into the busy laundromat across from the station, Alec opened his laptop computer and activated the homing device on Beau's car.

While the system booted up, a truck pulled into the gas station. Alec recognized the driver. Reggie Reeves.

Reggie looked around, then went straight into the office. Without pumping gas.

Curious, Alec sat forward . . . until Reggie grabbed a bottle of motor oil off the rack, set it on the counter.

Alec checked the computer screen. CHECKING COORDI-NATES, the dialogue box read. He sighed, impatient, and tried Keira's cell phone. When he got no answer, he called her office.

Tina knew exactly where she was. "At the cabin, but she's not answering her phone."

Alec felt his temper flash. "Did she go alone?"

"Reggie was supposed to meet her there, but he called and said he's running late."

Alec watched Reggie pay for the oil.

At that moment the homing device on Beau Watson's car pinged, giving its location.

Beau was on the private road heading up to Fire Mountain.

"Keep trying to reach her," Alec barked. "And tell her I'm on my way."

Beau backed Keira into a corner, slowly, menacingly.

She felt the edge of the unfinished kitchen counter bite into her back. She stepped sideways, angling for the door. The last thing she wanted was to be trapped.

"We have nothing to talk about. Get out," she repeated.

"I want to see the necklace your grandpa gave you. The one with the gold coin."

His request surprised her. There was only one reason Beau could be interested in the coin she wore. "Those stories about the Lost Confederate Gold aren't true. It doesn't exist."

"Why don't you let me be the judge of that. Give me the necklace."

When Keira shook her head, Beau took a step closer, grinned. "I was hoping you'd fight me over it."

Grabbing a nearby hammer, he charged.

Keira dashed sideways but wasn't quick enough. Beau caught the back of her shirt, spun her around. The neck of her shirt split, buttons flying.

"That wasn't so hard, was it?" Holding the hammer up menacingly, Beau reached forward and yanked the necklace, breaking the golden chain.

While he examined the necklace, Keira reached around behind her, feeling around the counter for a weapon. Her fingers closed over a two-by-four.

Swinging it as hard as she could, she caught Beau across the midsection.

He went down, screamed.

She dashed through the door, into the yard, and sprinted across the clearing, heading straight for the woods.

If she ran down the road, she'd be out in the open. Beau could easily run her down in his car. At least in the woods, she could hide.

"Stop, you little bitch!"

Keira heard a gun fire and ducked, rolling through the brush. Diving into a thicket, she paused, listening.

Long seconds ticked by. The only sound she heard was her own heavy breathing. Where was Beau? Would he come after her or give up and leave?

She tried to purposely slow her respiration.

She had the advantage, knew these woods better than Beau. All she had to do was stay hidden till nightfall, then she could make her way to her grandfather's cabin.

The woods remained quiet, and for a moment, she thought she'd lost him. Then she heard a branch crackle.

Another shot rang out, this one close enough it split the leaves over her head.

"You won't get away," Beau shouted.

Keira darted forward, heading for the densest part of the forest.

She leapt, clearing a fallen tree. Dropping low, she ran, zigzagging to make as difficult a target as she could. The ground inclined sharply as the terrain grew rockier.

She headed toward a large outcropping of rock, cut around it, and started running as fast as she could.

Without warning, the ground gave way beneath her.

Keira fell into a long, dark pit.

She hit bottom with a painful jolt. Sand and rocks rained down on her from above. Then all grew silent.

She moved gingerly, not wanting to trigger an avalanche of dirt. She'd fallen into an old mine shaft or cave. The area was honeycombed with them.

From above, she heard Beau call her name. "I know you're here!"

She leaned back, ignoring the pain as she hugged the wall of the shaft. If Beau spotted the hole, he might look in.

Or worse . . . if he didn't watch where he was going, he'd fall in with her.

As soon as he arrived at the cabin, Alec knew something was wrong. Keira's truck was there . . . and so was Beau's beat-up Toyota.

The site was eerily quiet.

Alec drew his gun, thumbed off the safety. He called out her name.

The element of surprise was gone, and if Beau had Keira trapped, Alec wanted her to know he was there. Wanted Beau to know, too.

Alec slipped in the front door, cautious, carefully looking around. His gut told him the place was deserted, but still he checked every room. He found the smashed remnants of her cell phone in the kitchen. Right beside a bloodstained two-by-four.

Keira.

He stepped onto the back deck, scanned the tree line.

Then he heard the sound of gunfire. A single deadly shot.

He turned in the direction he thought it came from— his left—aware sound echoed, especially near water. He could only hope he'd pinpointed the direction correctly.

A second shot sounded.

Cursing, Alec raced toward the trees.

A steady stream of dirt and rock trickled into the hole. Loosened by her fall, the opening slowly eroded. If it continued, the sides would cave in, burying her.

Keira heard someone call her name and grew quiet, even holding her breath. She was scared, she was injured; but facing Beau was still her worst fear.

Overhead, footsteps sounded, growing closer. But this time when she heard her name called, she recognized the voice.

"Alec! Help me!"

"Where are you?"

She called out again.

Alec spotted the hole she'd fallen into, approached carefully.

"Are you hurt?"

"A little. Look out!" She coughed as a fresh spew of sand fell. "Beau has a gun! Be careful!"

Alec flattened himself against the ground and eased forward on his belly until he reached the edge. She'd fallen into an old mine shaft and was at least thirty feet down. That she hadn't broken her neck in the fall amazed him.

He eyed the exposed timber supports. They looked rotten.

"I'll need a rope to get you out," he called. "I'll be right back."

Alec raced to the cabin, all the while watching for Beau. But when he reached the cabin site, Beau's car was gone.

Going to Keira's truck, he grabbed a heavy coil of rope and quickly made his way back to where she was trapped, grateful the sides hadn't collapsed while he was gone.

Tying a loop in one end, Alec tossed it over the edge.

"Tie this around your waist, and I'll pull you up."

Keira secured the rope. "If you hold it steady, I can scale the wall," she yelled. "It'll be quicker."

Alec wound the rope around the closest tree, knotted it. Then he held it taut, shouting encouragement.

As soon as Keira cleared the top, he grabbed her, tugged her away from the edge. The sides of the shaft gave way, sending up a billow of dust.

She fell to her knees, winded.

"Easy." Alec loosened the rope, then gently grasped her chin. Blood trickled from a cut in her scalp. She was pale, her shirt torn and muddy. Long scratches marred her neck.

He pressed two fingers to her wrist, found her pulse erratic. "Do you think you broke anything in the fall?"

She shook her head. "Did you find Beau?"

"He was gone by the time I got back to the cabin."

Keira accepted his help getting to her feet, then swayed unsteadily.

Alec caught her. "You're going straight to the hospital. We'll call the sheriff on the way."

En route to the hospital, Keira told Alec about Beau showing up at the cabin site.

Alec frowned. Why was Beau so interested in her necklace? Had he taken the tales of the Lost Confederate Gold seriously? "Do you know where your grandfather found that coin?"

She shook her head. "I'm not so sure he actually found it, Alec. The one time I questioned him on it, he grew real defensive. I suspect he bought the necklace and just made up the tale."

"I want to talk to Willis," Alec said, as they reached the emergency room.

The cut on Keira's scalp required several stitches, but she did not have a concussion. Her ribs were bruised, too.

"You'll be sore for several days," the doctor warned.

When they returned to Freedom, Deputy Carl Winters met them at Alec's apartment.

"Did you find Beau?" Alec asked. It was a long shot, he knew. Beau had gotten a pretty good head start while Alec freed Keira. The man was probably in another state by now.

"You won't believe this," Carl began. "He's at work, swears he's been there since early afternoon, in the back stockroom. Showed me his time card."

"Anybody can punch a time card and leave," Alec pointed out.

"Or get someone else to punch the card for you. I know. But there's two people at the store corroborating his story."

Keira, who'd been quiet until then, swore. "What's it going to take to nail this guy?"

"A bloody two-by-four ought to do it," Carl said. "Tire tracks. Fingerprints. I'm on my way out to your cabin to gather evidence now. Don't worry, we'll get him this time."

After Carl left, Alec insisted that Keira lie down and take one of the painkillers the doctor had prescribed.

"I need to run out for a few minutes," he said. "Carl's got a unit parked out front, so you'll be safe."

"You're going to see Beau, aren't you?"

"Yes."

She closed her eyes, her head throbbing. "Be careful. He scares me."

Alec went straight to the grocery store. Beau's Toyota was in the parking lot.

Hurrying inside, he looked around, then ducked through the stock doors in the produce department. He found Beau in the back, near the loading docks, sweeping.

Beau looked nervous when Alec approached. "You're not supposed to be back here."

Alec grabbed the other man's collar. "Oh yeah? What are you going to do about it?"

Beau flinched.

"What's the matter?" Alec asked. "Catch a two-by-four in the ribs?"

"Fuck off."

Alec shook him again. "What do you want with Keira Morgan?"

"Hey, I just talked to the cops. She's got nothing on me."

"The hell she doesn't. For starters, there's a chunk of board with your blood on it. A deputy is getting finger-prints as we speak. And unless you start giving me some straight answers, I'll swear out an affidavit that I saw you there myself. With a gun. I'll have your parole re-voked. *Today.*"

That got Beau's attention. He swallowed. "What kind of answers you looking for?"

"Is Griggs behind this?"

Beau didn't respond at first. Then, "He says it's her fault his brothers are dead."

"You've been helping him, haven't you? The night her car got run off the road. The doll. The dead animal. The spiders. Bet you even set the fire."

Guilt flashed in Beau's eyes, but just that quickly it was gone. He rallied, grew cocky.

"Griggs has people lined up fighting to help him. People that will do most anything. Everyone thinks they'll get a cut of his money."

Alec tightened his grip. "Including you? You've spent an awful lot of time at Culverleaf. Something tells me the money's hidden there. Maybe I need to organize a search party to comb the park. Claim that reward myself."

"Griggs doesn't know where the money's at," Beau said finally. "It ain't where he said. Are you happy now?"

"Not quite. Why the interest in Keira's necklace?"

"Griggs knows it's from her grandfather, and he wanted to take away something with sentimental value."

Alec recognized the lie. "Bullshit. You're going to jail."

Beau held up a hand, nervous, eyes shifting from side to side. "Look man, I'm working for the cops. You get me busted, they'll be pissed."

The cops?

Or the FBI?

"Who's your contact?" Alec pressed.

Beau hesitated.

"Who?"

"A guy named Phelps," Beau spat.

Horace Phelps.

Beau was reporting in to Phelps, which explained where Ostman got his information on what happened in Freedom. Alec was being used. And he didn't like it.

He loosened his grip, but only slightly. "If you go near Keira Morgan again, I'll kill you."

"What's going on in here?" Another store employee had walked in, took one look at Alec, and backed away.

Alec released Beau, patted his collar back in place. "Nothing going on. Just checking on an old friend."

Chapter Seventeen

On his way back to his apartment, Alec tried calling Miles Ostman, but couldn't reach him. Or Phelps. He left urgent messages for both men.

It infuriated Alec to learn that Beau worked for Ostman. Why the hell hadn't Ostman clued him in? Maybe Alec could have gotten direct information as to how Griggs was harassing Keira. Clues that might have led to his arrest.

Except Ostman didn't want Griggs arrested.

Alec had known from the beginning Ostman was after Joseph Ciccone. What he hadn't realized was how low Ostman would sink to get him. Would Ostman jeopardize Keira's safety for a mob bust? *Yes.*

And if Ostman kept Beau's recruitment secret, what else had he not told Alec?

Next, he called Willis Morgan, told him about Beau's assault on Keira. "And before you go taking matters into your own hands, I wanted to tell you I'm getting Keira out of town. Against her will, if necessary."

"Whatever it takes," Willis agreed. "We should have made her leave as soon as Griggs arrived. Probably would've had to hog-tie her, though. Still might."

Alec hoped it wouldn't come to that, but he hadn't

eliminated it either. "I trust you'll help me convince her to leave."

"Count on it."

"There's one more thing," Alec began. "The necklace you gave Keira. Where did you find that gold coin?"

Willis grew quiet. Then gruff. "Who wants to know?"

Alec explained Beau stole the necklace. "I'm trying to figure out why he wanted it so bad. Something doesn't add up."

"Yeah, well, maybe I need to go visit this Beau person myself."

Immediately, Alec regretted mentioning it. "No, Willis. I'll handle it. Carl Winters is involved, too. I'll call tomorrow and let you know where I'm taking Keira. In the meantime, you stay put."

Keira was asleep when Alec got to his apartment. He heated leftovers for supper, mentally reviewing his plan, wanting to have an answer for every conceivable excuse she'd offer. Keeping her safe was all that mattered.

When she woke up a short time later, he had food ready.

As they ate, he brought up the subject of her leaving Freedom. "I've got a place in Seattle. And friends who'll watch you."

Keira pushed her plate aside, then looked him straight in the eye. "Do you really think Griggs will make his move if I'm gone?"

"Yes." Alec honestly didn't know what to expect. But one thing was certain. Keira would be safer out of town, out of Griggs's reach. If what Beau said was true, and Griggs had others helping him . . .

"I need a day to meet with Tina at the office and talk with my grandfather."

Her capitulation surprised Alec. "You mean you'll leave?"

She nodded. "Tomorrow. But I want my grandfather to go, too. Maybe you can help me convince him."

"We'll go see him first thing in the morning," Alec promised.

They fell asleep on Alec's sofa.

Around midnight, Alec awoke and carried her to his bed, then headed back to the living room.

Only half-awake, she caught at his shirt, struggled to sit. "I should go to my own apartment."

"I want you here."

"Then I'll sleep on the couch. I won't run you out of your own bed."

Unable to resist touching her, he brushed the hair from her eyes. "If you went back to your apartment, I'd be sleeping on the couch there, so it doesn't matter."

She scooted to the far side of the bed. "This is a king-size mattress. Take half."

Too tired to argue, Alec stretched out, intent on moving back to the sofa as soon as she was asleep. Being in bed with her and not holding her was hell.

Being in bed with her and not making love was a thousand times worse.

He didn't realize he'd fallen asleep until a hard knocking on the front door woke them. He knew by the light coming in the windows that it was close to dawn.

They were snuggled, side by side, both of them naked.

Sometime during the night, she'd climbed on top of him. Touched him. He'd lost it, entered her, content not to move—just to be entwined. They had made love, excruciatingly slowly, then fallen back asleep.

The knocking at the door sounded again.

Keira moved to get up.

"Stay put," he whispered, grabbing his jeans. "I'll get it."

Tossing on a shirt, Alec checked the door. It was Carl Winters. The deputy's face was grim.

As soon as Keira joined them, she knew something was wrong.

"Beau Watson was found dead this morning," Alec told her.

Keira closed her eyes, then opened them. It was hard to feel pity for the man. "What happened?"

"Gunshot," Carl explained. "In the back of the head. Found his body in his car, out near Culverleaf."

"And there's witnesses who heard me threaten Beau yesterday," Alec finished.

"But you were here with me, all night," Keira protested.

"I know he didn't do it," Carl said. "But I've still got to take him downtown. For questioning. Get a statement."

Alec had briefly explained to Carl he was undercover, promising to tell him the full story when they reached the station.

"Look." Alec turned to her. "I'll have this straightened out shortly. Be ready to leave when I return."

"But—"

"No buts, Keira. A man has been murdered. It's more important than ever that you leave."

Carl's radio crackled. He was needed downtown. "We have to go."

Alec kissed her, then moved away. "Don't worry. I'll be back before you're finished packing."

Keira tried calling her grandfather, but didn't get an answer. He could be in the bathroom, she rationalized. Or outside in his garden, where he couldn't hear the phone.

She would have to drive up to Fire Mountain.

She'd made up her mind that she wouldn't leave Freedom without him. If necessary, she'd play on his sympathies, tell him she needed him to protect her.

Mind made up, she called the sheriff's department, wanting to tell Alec she was going to see Willis. She had started to leave a note, but wanted to hear his voice.

Carl Winters answered. "Alec just left. He told me the whole story, Keira. In fact, his supervisor from ATF is on his way here with some backup officers."

"ATF?" Keira interrupted. "You mean FBI."

"Actually, it's a joint venture. Alec works for ATF but is on loan to the FBI. It's confusing."

Confusing? Try deceitful . . . Had anything Alec told her been honest? Ever?

Stunned, Keira hung up.

ATF. Alcohol, Tobacco and Firearms. Alec was a revenue agent . . . who had grown up in the heart of moonshine country.

A joint venture. ATF and FBI. She knew what the FBI wanted. What about ATF?

A sick feeling started in her stomach. Had Alec been passing along information on Willis and his buddies while watching Griggs? She didn't want to believe it, but for Willis's sake, she had to at least consider it.

She tried calling her grandfather again. When he didn't answer, she grabbed her keys, recalling what Carl said about backup officers. *ATF officers?*

While Keira had never made moonshine, she had centuries of Morgan blood flowing in her veins. When a revenue agent came around, usually as part of a raid, all stills within a hundred-mile radius were destroyed. If she couldn't reach Willis to warn him, she'd go up and destroy his still herself.

She quickly called Lacy Hicks, using the old friend-of-a-friend routine. While she felt betrayed anew by Alec's deception, she couldn't bring herself to expose him as an ATF agent. Lacy didn't stop to question how she knew, he simply thanked her and hung up, eager to spread the word.

Keira hurried to her truck and cranked the engine. Putting it in reverse, she turned to look over her shoulder.

A hand came over the seat, from behind the extended cab, and grabbed her neck, jamming it against the headrest. She saw the glint of metal as a gun was raised, then paused beside her right eye.

The same gun Alec had given her for protection.

"Going somewhere?" Ian Griggs laughed. He was directly behind her, his left hand resting across her throat, his other one holding the gun. "Better go nice and easy, now. Wouldn't want my finger to slip. Shoot out your eye."

Keira gripped the steering wheel, fought to control the trembling in her arms. "What are you doing here?"

Griggs tightened his grip on her neck. "Thought we'd take a little ride out to visit your grandfather."

Her heart skipped. "This is between you and me, Ian. Leave my grandfather out of it."

"He's already involved. But you do exactly as I say, and we'll see if we can't figure a way to get him out alive. Now go."

Griggs slid the gun toward the back of her head as he hunkered down, hiding.

"Why don't you just get your money and leave?" she asked. "Isn't that the real reason you came back here?"

"Everybody thinks it's that fucking easy. Get the money and run." Griggs snorted. "Even Beau, the little bastard. He planned to double-cross me all along."

"You killed him, didn't you?"

"He had it coming. He planned to get the gold from your grandpa and run."

Keira glanced in the rearview mirror, trying to make sense of Griggs's words. *The gold from her grandfather?* Was that why Beau had been so eager to get her necklace? Had Beau thought Willis had found the gold?

"If you think my grandfather's found the old treasure—"

Griggs started laughing. "It's not that stupid Confederate gold, Keira. I found a chest of coins on the armored truck. My brothers didn't want to take it at first, thought the cash would be enough. Till I calculated its value. Problem is, not only is my gold missing, the money's gone, too. Once I saw the necklace, I realized Willis probably has both."

"You're crazy."

"Am I? Beau saw him out at the mine shaft twice, trying to cover his tracks. Now we're almost even.

Willis has something of mine." Ian nudged her head
with the gun. "And I've got something of his. Think
he'll trade?"

Keira's mind raced as she sorted through her options.
There was little she could do now. They were heading
up the single curving road that ended at the top of
Fire Mountain.

"What if Willis isn't home?" She prayed her grandfather was indeed gone.

"We'll wait."

When they arrived at her grandfather's cabin, Ian
made her lie flat on the seat. He held the gun to her head
while he got out. Then he ordered her to get up. "Stay in
front of me. And don't do anything stupid."

She walked to the door, called Willis's name. The fact
he hadn't already opened the door was a good sign.

When no one answered, Griggs indicated she should
open the door.

The interior of the cabin was as cold and quiet as the
stone walls. Griggs followed her from room to room, as-
suring himself each was empty.

"Let's check out back." He shoved her toward the rear
door.

Outside, Keira checked her grandfather's workshop
and garden, found both deserted.

"He's not here." She tried to keep the relief from
her voice.

Griggs pressed up close behind her, the gun biting
into her spine. "Guess we'll go inside and help ourselves
to a bit of whiskey. Old Willis is a master when it comes
to 'shine."

To her horror, Griggs stuck out his tongue and licked

her neck. "Besides, we got a little catching up to do. Remember?"

His foul breath told her he'd already been drinking. She had a flashback to five years earlier, when he'd attacked her. He'd been drinking then. And this time he had a gun.

Inside, Griggs sat at the kitchen table, the gun still trained on her. "Pour me a glass from that jug." He nodded toward the counter.

Keira did as he asked, pouring two fingers into a glass. Her hands shook.

"I'll say when," he said.

She tipped the jug, filled the glass.

"When. Now bring it here."

Keira set the glass on the table.

Griggs took a gulp, drew back his lips. "The devil's own brew." He took another swig, then raised the gun, leveled it at her. "Now, let's talk. Beau told me about your little show at the lake. How about you take off your clothes for me, Keira. Nice and slow."

The thought of what he had in mind made Keira ill. She took an involuntary step backward, shook her head. She'd never willingly comply.

Griggs slammed the glass down, sloshing whiskey across the table.

"Maybe this will make you reconsider." He cocked the gun.

Keira closed her eyes and screamed as the gun discharged, the sound loud in the confines of the cabin. She braced, expecting pain.

She opened her eyes quickly as she realized she had not been hit. Had he fired a warning shot?

To her horror, she saw Griggs facedown on the

table, the back of his head blown to a bloody mess. The gun slipped from his grip, clattered onto the floor. Her stomach lurched, heaved.

"Keira."

She recognized the voice, turned toward it. "Reggie!"

Reggie Reeves stepped past Ian Griggs, kicked the gun to the far side of the room. "Don't worry. He's dead."

Dead. Shaken, Keira nodded. The urge to be sick grew. "We need to . . . to . . . call—"

Reggie was beside her. He placed a hand on her shoulder, drew her close. "Shhhhh. You're okay. And Griggs will never harm another person."

Keira went willingly into his embrace, desperately needing comfort. Horror mingled with confusion.

Reggie's fingers wove through her hair, gentle.

But only for a moment. His hand closed, taking a handful of her hair and twisting painfully as he pressed the metal barrel of his gun to her temple.

"Where's your grandfather, Keira?"

Alec's supervisor not only vouched for his presence in Freedom, he promised to launch an investigation into Miles Ostman's handling of the case. "As soon as I can get ahold of the bastard, that is."

Neither Ostman nor Phelps had returned Alec's phone calls, so Alec doubted his supervisor would have much luck.

As soon as he left the sheriff's department, Alec returned to Keira's apartment. She had left a note saying she'd gone to her grandfather's. Actually, the note appeared to be unfinished. Had she been interrupted while writing it?

His cell phone rang.

"It's Horace Phelps."

"Where the hell are you? And Ostman?" Alec demanded. "Beau Watson is dead, and I want some straight answers."

Phelps was silent. "Ostman's disappeared. I think Ciccone got wind of what he was doing and had him offed. Beau warned us Ciccone had his own man planted in town. Said it was an electrician. Ostman laughed because he thought they meant you."

Alec's mind flew back to the scene yesterday of Reggie buying oil at the gas station. From Ian Griggs. "I know who Ciccone's man is." *Reggie Reeves.*

"Then I better tell you the rest of the story." Phelps quickly explained about the gold coins and Ostman's dreams of glory. "He was obsessed with nailing Ciccone."

Alec started cursing as the confusing pieces fell into place. Stolen gold coins. The Lost Confederate Gold. Keira's necklace. Did Ian Griggs think Willis Morgan had found his stolen gold?

"Call this in. To your supervisor and mine."

No sooner had Alec hung up than Carl Winters called. "Wanted to warn you and Keira. Ian Griggs is AWOL. I went over to the halfway house to interview the staff. Turns out Griggs had promised one guy money in exchange for favors. The guy admitted fudging attendance logs. He's not happy to be left holding the bag."

Alec quickly filled Carl in on his conversation with Horace Phelps. "You go find Reggie Reeves. I'm going up to Fire Mountain to get Keira and her grandfather."

*   *   *

Reggie forced Keira into the middle of the living room before releasing her.

"This is the last time I'm asking. Where's your grandfather?"

"I don't know." She looked at him, at the gun he held. "What do you want with Willis?"

Reggie reached in his pocket and dug out her necklace. He tossed it at her feet.

"That armored truck Griggs robbed belonged to my boss. And he had a very old, very rare gold coin collection on it. That's one of the coins. If your grandfather found the coins, I bet he found the money. Griggs swore they were hidden in the same place. I'm just here to collect my boss's property."

The news stunned Keira even as she tried to sort out the stories.

With awful clarity, she understood why everyone was so interested in finding Willis. Her grandfather hunted for the Lost Confederate Gold regularly. Or at least he had up until a few months ago . . .

Come to think of it, he hadn't been searching for the gold in a while. Claimed he was too busy helping Lacy. What had Willis gotten himself into?

"Am I supposed to believe you're just wanting to take the coins and leave? Providing my grandfather even has them, of course?"

The awful silence was an answer.

Reggie shook his head. "I really did like you, you know. You're a strong woman. I'd hoped to pull this off behind your back, then quit. So we could date. Dempsey is a loser. From what I heard, he was never good enough for you."

Keira's mind raced. "You and I can still—"

"It's too late. I know he's working for the FBI."

Reggie tossed her his cell phone. "No more talking. We need to figure out where your grandfather is. *Now*."

Alec stopped before reaching Willis's driveway. A truck was parked in the woods, half-hidden in the trees. He recognized the vehicle. *Reggie's*.

Abandoning his Jeep, Alec approached Willis's cabin from behind, hiding in the dense trees lining one side. Keira's truck was in the yard.

Staying low, he peered in a window, saw Reggie with a gun trained on Keira.

He cursed his own blindness. Alec hadn't liked Reggie from the beginning but had blamed it on his own jealousy. He hadn't suspected the other man of anything except wanting to get in Keira's bed. Obviously, he'd been after more.

Alec knew he couldn't storm the cabin and risk Keira's getting hurt. He also didn't want to leave her alone while he went for help.

Tucking his gun in at his back, he walked straight up to the door and knocked.

No one answered.

"I know you're in there, Keira! It's Alec." He hoped to make it sound like he was simply looking for her. Not that it mattered at this point.

He heard a slight sound, like a scuffle. Then Keira said, "Come in. Door's unlocked."

Alec pushed the door wide, then stepped through.

Keira sat in a straight-backed chair in the middle of the living room. Reggie stood behind her, a gun held casually to her head.

"Don't move, Dempsey," Reggie ordered. "Now put your gun on the floor."

Alec lowered his hands. From the corner of his eye, he saw Ian Griggs's lifeless body in the kitchen.

Reggie moved closer to Keira. "Don't try anything stupid."

Moving slowly, Alec tugged his gun free and set it on the floor.

"Kick it over here." Reggie said. "Do the same with your other one. I know you've got a backup piece."

Alec shook his head, doubting Reggie would check. "I came straight from jail."

Reggie shrugged. "I don't believe you."

Keira saw Reggie swing his gun toward Alec. She screamed as he fired, the roar deafening so close to her ear.

Alec jerked, then fell forward.

Moving without thought, Keira swung her legs, kicked Reggie, then dived for Alec's gun, retrieving it as she rolled across the floor, her only thought to get to Alec.

When she sat up, she saw Reggie had his gun trained on her. "You lose. Drop it."

"Go ahead and shoot." Keira steadied the pistol. "But I swear, I'll take you with me."

Reggie smiled. Then moved his gun sideways toward Alec. "I'll shoot him, then. Again. He's still breathing, you know. Maybe he's got a chance."

Keira heard a metallic *click* as a gun cocked.

Not hers. Not Reggie's.

She glanced off to the side. Willis Morgan was crouched half-in, half-out of a trapdoor near the fireplace, a rifle aimed at Reggie. The trapdoor led to a small tunnel that exited south of the cabin, an escape route first used during Indian attacks and later during moonshine raids.

"Drop it," Willis ordered.

Reggie swung his pistol toward Willis.

Keira fired, but her shot went high.

Reggie, however, dropped to his knees, clutching his bloody hand. The gun had been shot right out of his grip.

Bewildered, Keira looked at her grandfather. She knew her shot had missed Reggie.

Willis nodded toward the door. Carl Winters was crouched in the door, revolver in hand.

"I got him." Carl cautiously approached. "Check Alec."

Keira was already at Alec's side. He hadn't moved. Gingerly, she checked for a pulse. *Please be alive,* she prayed. *Please.*

Blood was everywhere.

Willis moved up beside her. "Help me turn him."

"Should we move him?"

"Gotta see how bad it is, gal. Stop the bleeding."

Alec groaned when they turned him over. Keira saw the wound in his abdomen. Her heart stopped.

Willis pressed a towel against it to stem the bleeding. Alec tried to speak.

"Don't talk, boy," Willis said. "Save your strength."

Keira heard Carl, behind her, on his radio, shouting for backup. She bent low, pressed her lips to Alec's temple. "Help is on the way. You're going to be fine."

Alec looked up, saw the pain in her eyes. He'd hurt her yet again, and this time there wouldn't be a second chance.

He'd seen men shot before, knew his injury was severe. And they were miles from a hospital. Already he felt cold, recognized that he'd pass out soon. But there was one thing he had to tell her.

"If I could do it all over, I'd grant your wish," he whispered. "I'd have never come into your life."

Keira's cheeks were wet. "No! I was wrong, Alec. If I could do it again, I'd have still loved you. *Only you.* Then and now."

He coughed, felt the strangling. Time was short. "I'll hold you to that. I—"

The sound of sirens cut off his last words. Carl Winters tugged her back as others surged in. Paramedics. Deputies. Alec was hoisted onto a gurney.

"They're landing a chopper at the base of the mountain," Carl told her. "We've got to get him out of here as fast as we can."

Keira followed to the door, then stopped as the ambulance sped away.

Once again, Alec was leaving Fire Mountain. *With her heart.*

"I love you," she whispered through tears. "I'll always love you."

And as long as he lived . . . nothing else mattered.

Epilogue

Alec Dempsey pulled into the cabin site but didn't get out of his car.

Completely finished, the cabin looked perfect. Wisps of applewood smoke drifted from the chimney, scenting the air. Curtains hung at the windows.

Keira had built a home.

The thing he'd always looked for but never found.

Until now.

Was it too late?

He climbed out, pausing to look around yet again, before grabbing the cane. He had intended to stay away until he didn't need it anymore. He had promised himself he wouldn't come back until he was one hundred percent whole.

But he couldn't stay away. He had learned he wouldn't recover without her. She had his heart . . . He'd left it with her over ten years before, and never even realized it.

God, he'd been a dumb ass.

And like scores of dumb asses before him, he prayed he wasn't too late, that he hadn't totally screwed it up. That Keira would give him the barest of chances.

Right after the shooting, she had stayed by his side, night and day, while he clung to life in intensive care in Little Rock.

He'd had complications. Infections. A severe reaction to a medication. He'd been unconscious most of the time, so had only a few scattered memories of Keira being there when he called out in the night. His angel of mercy.

Once he stabilized, he'd been transferred to a Chicago hospital, where an orthopedic wizard knit his lower spine back together. Then he'd endured months of grueling physical therapy. Alone. He hadn't wanted her to see him crawl.

Dumb ass. Dumb ass. Dumb ass.

He hadn't seen her since leaving Little Rock. Wondered how she'd take seeing him now.

He was back for good. He had accepted a position with the sheriff's department—as soon as his doctor released him, that is. Would that please her? Or would she care?

He understood she'd been upset to learn he was ATF. That he'd deceived her.

He also understood he couldn't go back and change the past. Any of it. Life could only be lived facing forward.

He went up to the porch, rapped on the door.

"Door's unlocked," Keira called out. "I'm in the kitchen."

Alec entered, followed the short hall. His eyes took in the warm luster of log walls. Antique woodworking tools decorated the foyer.

He found her standing at the kitchen sink, her back to him. His eyes devoured the long tumble of red curls.

"Hello, babe. I guess you're expecting someone else," he said.

He watched her spine stiffen, her shoulders

straighten. She twisted, her gaze sweeping up and down, missing nothing.

She turned away briefly, reached for a hand towel.

"Hello, Alec. I was expecting Franny." She kept drying her hands. "You look good."

"So do you." She looked fabulous. The yearning to touch her, hold her, rose up hard and fast. His carefully planned speech flew out the window.

"The place looks great." He motioned toward the stove, the pots and pans she had set out. "Expecting a crowd for Thanksgiving?"

"Franny and Darryl."

"Willis?"

She shook her head. "He took all his buddies on a cruise with part of his reward money. Old coot's never left the state in his life, and he picks a holiday to start."

Alec grinned. As it turned out, Willis had indeed found the stolen gold, though from what he'd heard, the FBI had a hell of a time convincing him it wasn't the Lost Confederate Gold.

When Willis finally relented and took investigators to the mine shaft where he'd found the coins, they discovered that the money was still there, but buried even deeper, beneath a landslide from a previous collapse.

Willis had promptly claimed the reward.

"I—" Alec began.

"I—" They both spoke at the same time.

"You first," Alec said.

Keira took a breath, recalling the vow she'd made months ago: If Alec recovered, she'd never ask for another favor from life. As much as she wanted to see him, she'd stayed away.

If you love something, set it free . . .

"I'm surprised to see you back here. I know this place doesn't have a lot of good memories for you."

Alec took a step closer. "On the contrary. It's got some of my best. Might be a good place to build more."

Keira felt her heart rate accelerate. "What does that mean?"

"I finally figured out what I was looking for, Keira. A home. *You.* If you'll have me, that is."

She felt light-headed, dizzy. "But, but you didn't like Freedom. You left me."

"I didn't like myself." He shifted his weight. "And I left because years ago I had nothing to offer you. It never dawned on me we could build whatever we wanted together. Right here. *Right now.*"

At her silence, he took a step closer, held out his hand. "I came back to ask you to give me another chance. To give *us* another chance."

Keira stared at his hand, at the distance separating them. Did she dare close the gap?

She closed her eyes. Felt the doubt. Felt the love. She moved forward.

Alec met her halfway. He drew her fingers to his mouth, kissed them one by one. "I love you, Keira. I always have. Always will. I'm sorry it took me ten years to realize that."

"I—"

"Let me finish. Will you marry me?"

Tears overflowed in her eyes. She nodded, unable to speak.

Alec released the breath he'd been holding. "I'd like to get married today, but I'm sure you want to wait until Willis returns."

Keira laughed, recovered her voice. "Actually, we should do it while he's gone. Willis won't be keen on having a revenuer in the family, but he might think twice about shooting my husband."

Dear Reader,

While Freedom, Arkansas, is a fictional town, with a fictional buried treasure, the story of lost Confederate gold isn't new.

According to various accounts, in 1865 the last of the Confederate treasury disappeared, along with money from other southern banks. There's a story that it was buried on the grounds of the old Chennault Plantation in Georgia, and that after heavy rains, gold coins have been found in the dirt near the plantation. Other reports say the gold and silver were divided and sent off to England and Florida.

Willis O. Morgan, my fictional character, prefers to believe some of that gold is still buried in the Ozarks.

Best wishes,
Lauren Bach

About the Author

Lauren Bach loves to write almost as much as she loves to read. A member of Romance Writers of America and Heart of Carolina Romance Writers, Lauren writes contemporary romantic fiction with a definite sensual slant. Her official motto is: Life Is Short—Read More Romance.

Lauren's love of writing can be traced back to her childhood. One of seven children, she was born in Iowa but raised in Florida. She currently resides in North Carolina and is busy working on her next book. Visit her Web site at www.laurenbach.com.